The Glorification of Al Toolum

Robert Alan Aurthur

The Glorification
of Al Toolum

RINEHART & COMPANY, INC.

NEW YORK   TORONTO

To the Family

The Glorification of Al Toolum

One

It was the Sunday just before April Fools' Day, and, when Alfred Toolum opened his eyes to see the sun shining brightly through the half-open window in promise of a warm day, he groaned a little sadly to himself, closed his eyes again and wondered briefly why his prayers for rain hadn't been answered. Why, he demanded fiercely to himself, can't a man who works hard all week have just *one* day when he can sleep and relax?

There was no answer, and as the sounds from the kitchen below penetrated his unwilling consciousness, he wearily swung his legs out of bed, yawned, stretched; and then, sighing, he got to his feet.

Leaning at a slight angle, one hand holding the drawstring of his pajamas, Al made his way toward the bathroom. Once there he peered at his image in the mirror, debating the need for a shave. Like most men, Al Toolum ignored the total image: the disheveled hair, the slightly sagging pouches under his eyes, the fact that, at forty, he could easily afford to take fifteen pounds off the midsection, and the most discouraging fact that in a crowd Alfred Toolum would blend, with not one distinguishing feature, into the herd familiarly known as The Common Man.

"I'll shave," he said aloud, reaching toward the medicine chest.

"No, I won't," he said, arresting the movement; and then, "Oh, the hell with it, I'd better. . . ."

Down in the kitchen, surrounded by a growing mound of sandwiches, Emily Toolum prepared for the First Picnic of the Season. Also surrounding her was a mob of boys that, when broken down, proved to be just three individuals: Herman, twelve; Sherman, just nine; and Little Louie, five and a half. Two years younger than her husband, Emily Toolum was a slender woman in whom traces of prettiness, not completely wiped away by fifteen years of marriage, still remained. Up since seven in the morning, she was dressed in a flowered print dress, and her hair, showing the slightest streaks of gray, was tied in a neat bun. Only her hands, worn and reddened with chipped, colorless nails, showed that Emily Toolum carried on her shoulders the massive job of homemaker for four males.

"Little Louie," she said, "take your hand out of the peanut butter and call your father."

Scrambling down from his perch at the kitchen table, Little Louie darted from the room. The youngest Toolum was a sturdy little boy who looked as though he still hadn't rid himself of all his baby fat. There was also the air of the bedraggled angel about Little Louie, an air that was somehow belied by the glint in his large, dark eyes. His hair went in different directions, his high brown shoes were always scuffed and dirty, and his trousers, passed down through two brothers, were a patched, faded blue. On his head, despite parental disapproval Number 77B that dealt with wearing hats in the house, was a Roy Rogers cowboy hat that was the only thing he was proud enough to call his own.

When the door had closed behind Little Louie, Sherman, fair-haired and slightly built, stole a look at his older brother who was wrapping sandwiches in wax paper.

"Hey, Mama," Sherman said, "Herman's taking his bathing suit today. He said he's going swimming."

"Herman can take fourteen bathing suits," Emily said calmly, "but he's not going into any water. It's much too cold."

Herman stared icily at his brother. As the athletic member of the Toolum family, he had a reputation to uphold; nevertheless, he welcomed his mother's ruling. He'd had no intention of going swimming.

"Well, I *ain't* gonna sit around writing po'try like Ferdinand," he said.

A past mistress of the art of allegiance-shifting, Emily said, "I think you're right about that. On such a nice day I want to see Sherman and you playing ball."

"Ah-h-h," Sherman, the poet, said.

"Although it would help if you got marks in school like Sherman did," Emily said, once more on Sherman's side.

"Ah-h-h," Herman, the athlete, said.

The voice of Little Louie, filled with the disappointment of not being able to rout his father out of bed, floated down the stair well with the information that Papa wasn't in the bedroom.

"Then he's in the bathroom," Emily called. "Tell him to hurry, because we want to get an early start."

"I heard her," Al said, when Little Louie opened the bathroom door. "Early start," he muttered. "You have to get up at the crack of dawn, break your neck——"

"It's nine o'clock," Little Louie said. He'd seated himself on the edge of the bathtub and was watching his father shave. The only sound then was the scrape of the razor against stubble. "Say, Papa," Little Louie said, "when am I gonna get my motorcycle?" He meant a real one.

"I *told* you when you'll get your motorcycle. When you've saved up the money yourself, and when your legs are long enough to reach the zoomer."

Little Louie examined his stubby legs that dangled down the side of the bathtub. "I want it now. You could advance me the money."

"The one you want costs five hundred and ninety-eight dollars."

"So? I want it now."

How did I ever get myself mixed up in such a stupid fantasy? Al Toolum asked himself. Aloud, he said, "What's the hurry?" He paused, and then stared at his youngest son. "You're not on that business again about not reaching the age of six, are you?"

"Well . . ." Little Louie pursed his lips stubbornly.

Al put down his razor and sat down slowly next to Little Louie. He put his arm around the boy's shoulder, and gave careful consideration as to what he would say.

This was a problem he was willing to admit had him licked. Imagine a kid who was just past five years old and said he didn't think he'd live until his sixth birthday! It had him and Emily floored—and they had thought they'd seen and heard everything that had to do with small boys. Wolves and ogres they'd dealt with; angry teachers, irate neighbors, complaining police authorities had been handled with reasonable diplomacy; problems of every sort and nature had been met and solved with a minimum of wear and tear—but this!

"Tell me," he said, "what is going on with you, Little Louie? Your mama and I are pretty worried about you. You don't eat any more, you wake up hollering in the night . . . Has anybody been doing anything to you?"

Little Louie shrugged. Personally, he didn't think there was anything the matter with him. He was just convinced that he wasn't long for this world.

"Come on," Al said, urging Little Louie to his feet, "let's get downstairs and get ready for the picnic. We'll have a nice day, and if you forget all about this baloney you're worried about you can go over to Ben's tonight and watch the television."

The promise of this special treat brought Little Louie to attention, and together they left the bathroom.

"Al," Emily said, when, fully dressed, her husband had entered the kitchen, "you can begin loading the car."

"How about breakfast?" he said, pecking her cheek.

"There's cold cereal and hot coffee ready. Now, hurry, because we don't want to get tied up in that miserable Sunday traffic."

"You sure it isn't going to rain?" he asked hopefully.

"No, it isn't. Now let's get going."

With the aid of Herman and Sherman, Al packed the trunk of his battered 1947 model sedan. As usual there was enough food for a dozen people, a fact which he would carefully bring to his wife's attention and which she would indignantly deny until it was time to come home and the leftovers would have to be repacked. Then she would say, "I can't understand why nobody ate," and would try to stuff more sandwiches into an already bloated family rather than admit she had miscalculated.

He forced down the door to the trunk just as a window in the Carroway house next door opened with a bang. Ben Carroway, rubbing his eyes, thrust his pajama-clad shoulders into the opening.

"What's the racket?" he demanded. Then, sizing up the situation, he looked pityingly at his neighbor. "Oh, a picnic."

"Yeah."

"Too bad it can't be winter all year 'round," Ben said.

Al nodded.

"Well, back to bed." Ben Carroway withdrew, and Al glanced toward the bedroom a little longingly and then went back into his house.

"You forgot the jug," Emily said.

"I'm not opening that trunk again. Not for anything."

Emily took a last quick look around the kitchen. "Well, then, let's go. The boys can hold the jug in the back."

They trooped outside where the car was standing in the driveway. The car always stood in the driveway even though a garage went with the house. But the space ordinarily allocated for a car had years ago been cluttered with screens or storm windows (depending on the season), old worn-out tires that Al "was going to do something with someday" and other sundry articles. To clean the garage was something else he was going to do "someday."

When they were all seated comfortably in the car, Al inserted the key in the ignition and was just about to press the starter when Sherman said quietly, "Papa, you said before you wouldn't open the trunk for anything—remember?"

"Can't you even hold a jug?" Al demanded irately.

"It's not the jug," Sherman said. "We've got a flat."

Slumping in his seat resignedly, Al withdrew the key and slowly opened the door.

"Hey, Papa," Herman said, as they all surveyed the flattened rear tire, "why don't you just turn the tire over. It's only flat on one side."

The boys roared with laughter as their father seemed to give this suggestion some consideration. Actually, Al was concentrating on holding his temper in accord with a promise he'd made Emily the night before. His wife regarded him sympathetically.

"I'll take the stuff out of the trunk, Al," she said.

When the car had fallen off the bumper jack for the fourth time, Emily asked, "What's the matter, Al, won't it go up?"

He stared at her grimly, opened his mouth to say something, and then closed it again as he bent to try for the fifth time.

On the seventh try the car finally stayed up. Then he attacked the lugs with the lug wrench, sweating and grunting as the lugs, rusted solid, refused to budge.

When five minutes had passed, Emily asked, "What's the matter, Al, won't they turn?"

He straightened up, hefting the wrench and gazing coldly at the line-up of family. "Go away," he said to them. "Go away and don't bother me."

"I only wanted to help," Emily said indignantly.

"Go away!" he shouted, and, sniffing angrily, Emily said, "Come, boys, your father is in a state again."

"State," he muttered to himself as they disappeared around the front of the house. "Who wouldn't be in a state? Lousy, stinkin' car!" He kicked at the wheel furiously.

"Al." He looked up to see Ben once again at the window. "What's the matter, Al, got a flat?"

He closed his eyes. Ben said, "Hold it till I get some pants on. I'll give you a hand."

In twenty minutes the tire was changed, and, feeling contrite, Al called cheerily to his family that they were ready to leave. They marched stiffly toward the car, their attitudes indicating that they weren't that easily ready to forgive. Silently, the car was repacked, and then they drove out onto Bigelow Street and down through the Main Street of Fernvale, quiet but for the few early churchgoers whose cars lined the curb in front of the First Methodist.

The town of Fernvale, twenty-five miles from New York City on the south shore of Long Island, had once been a peaceful com-

munity with a population around ten thousand, its isolation aided
by the peculiar habits of the Long Island Railroad. But even this
deterrent to enjoying the proximity of the city had been ignored by
the hordes of former city dwellers who, since the war, had poured
out onto Long Island in unbelievable numbers to seek a home of
their own or haven from the atom bomb. The woods that had surrounded the original Fernvale had been torn up and replaced by
thousands of "ranch houses"; the population had quadrupled.

Al and Emily Toolum were unusual inhabitants of Fernvale
in two respects: they had both lived in Fernvale all their lives
(although Emily's parents had moved there from Brooklyn when
she was a year old), and Al was one of the very, very few Fernvale-
ites who did not commute to the city to a job. For sixteen years he
had been employed by the Acme Tool & Die works, Fernvale's only
native industry.

It was Emily, in a forgiving tone, who voiced the statement
that one of them never failed to make as they rode through the town.
"The old place certainly has changed," she said.

Al's breath had returned to normal. Safely away from the
house, he could relax. "It sure has," he said.

Little Louie's voice came from the back seat. "Papa, can you
turn around?" he said. "I gotta go . . ."

The best time on a picnic, as far as Al was concerned, was
when he and Emily could sit quietly and relax once all the work
was done. In the fall they'd look at the trees and talk about how
beautiful the colors of the leaves were and what a shame it was
that soon they'd all be gone; in the spring they'd look at the trees
and say how pretty the buds were and how nice it was that summer
would soon be here. Once they had exhausted that subject, they
usually went on to the boys and discussed the various problems that
arose with the care and feeding of three growing children. But today
Emily had something else on her mind. She waited until Al had
returned from the water faucet where he rinsed their eating equipment, and when he had sunk down next to her on the soft grass
with a deep sigh of contentment, she said:

"Al, I've been thinking . . ." His eyes had started to close, and she poked him gently in the stomach. "I said 'I've been thinking,' Al."

"Don't think," he said. "It usually leads to trouble."

She pursed her lips in brief anger at his lack of response, and then the feeling passed. It was awfully hard to get mad at Al. This was a man she'd known most of her life. She had known him so long that she didn't remember the first time they'd ever seen each other. She could recall a chubby, rather shy boy in high school whose clothes never seemed to fit him, a completely undistinguished boy, really, but when you remembered Al in those days you always recalled his smile and his desire to be helpful. And because they lived in the same neighborhood, he would sometimes walk home with her, and once in a moment of real depression, occasioned by the fact that he'd been cut from the football squad on the first day of practice, he had told her the thing he wanted most in the world was to earn a varsity letter. He never did, although he tried in every sport. To Emily, at the time, Al was important only because of his exalted position of being a senior when she was just a sophomore, and she had felt sorry for him, feeling that she had just seen deep into something terribly personal. That moment of confidence had extended into an invitation to the Christmas dance. She didn't know that Al had mentally rejected every girl he really wanted to take, feeling that he would be turned down and wanting to spare himself the tortured embarrassment, and to her the invitation to her first formal was the most exciting thing that had ever happened. So exciting that she easily forgave him the lack of corsage (which he couldn't afford) and the fact that he was one of three boys at the dance who didn't have a tuxedo.

That had just been an interlude, and it could have been all there was to the story if, five years later, they hadn't met again. In those five years Al's father had died; for two years Al had been a runner on Wall Street for twelve dollars a week; and for two more years he had just been another blank-faced, depression-defeated boy who, with his friends, would stand most of the day in front of the "Vets" candy store passing cigarette butts among themselves and talking in dragging monotones about girls and job possibilities. Sometimes, on her way home from the bank where she worked a computing machine, Emily would see him, and she would nod, not only to Al but to all the boys, and hurry by, conscious of the stares that followed her down the street and slightly embittered that no one did anything about it. . . .

And when again they met at the home of one of their mutual friends who was having a baby shower, it was as adults and with the vague realization that all that had gone before was somehow completely removed from the present. Later they also admitted to themselves that both had wanted desperately to leave Fernvale and become part of a more exciting life. But the acceptance of Fernvale was also an indication of their being adult, even though the longing for something more had never left Emily. But Al wasn't chubby any more; nor was he so shy, and from the party they had drifted into an alliance that soon both admitted was love. And a year after Al had got his job at Acme they had been married. . . .

Funny, she thought now, looking at Al and then at Little Louie and knowing that this is what Little Louie will look like thirty-five years from now.

Her long silence caused Al to open his eyes and struggle up on his elbows. "All right," he said, "so you've been thinking. So what?"

She drew her finger through the grass. "Nothing."

"Oh, please, don't give me that nothing routine. What's on your mind, Em?"

That could fill a book, Emily thought ruefully. She looked around the picnic area that was dotted with a hundred other families.

"I was thinking last night," she said, "what a terrible rut we're in."

He looked surprised, and she hastily added, "I mean, why do we have to go on picnics just because it's the first nice Sunday and get mixed up in all that traffic, and——"

"*What* have I been saying for five years?" he demanded.

"Oh, I know." She shrugged. "But what else is there to do?"

He leaned back again. "What would you like to do?" he asked.

"I don't know. Just—something."

"You've either been talking to your mother—or reading those ladies' magazines again. You want me to be named Gregory and take you to fancy night clubs. Well, we can't afford night clubs, and if my folks had named me Gregory I'd've punched them in the nose."

"I gave up reading those magazines," she said.

"No more helpful hints from *Family Friend?*"

"I take that for recipes."

"Hey, that reminds me," he said, getting to his elbows again, "what's with Sherman and all those questions he was asking me a couple of weeks ago? It had *something* to do with *Family Friend* magazine."

"I think it's another contest he's entered."

"Oh. Well, *that's* nothing to worry about. He hasn't won anything yet." He glanced toward the ball field where Herman and Sherman had become part of a baseball game. "That Sherman asked more questions than the FBI when we started war work at the plant."

"Sherman's all right," she said. "It's Little Louie who has me going around in circles."

Directing a baleful look toward Little Louie who was digging in a sand pit, he said, "That kid's got me nuts too. He was on that silly business about his sixth birthday again this morning." When he looked back at Emily, he felt a rather familiar feeling of guilt that recurred whenever the subject of Little Louie came up. Emily had never had a chance to get over having Little Louie. These days she always looked tired.

"What are we going to do about him, Em?" he asked uneasily.

"Maybe it's just what the books call a phase," she said. "Maybe he'll grow out of it soon. Most of the time he's okay. It's just that sometimes . . ."

"Yeah," he said. "Listen, it's getting chilly. How about getting everything together, and we take off."

"All right," she said. "You round up the boys."

He stood up, and as she reached for the big basket that had contained the sandwiches and which still was half full, she said, "I can't understand why nobody ate . . ."

Two

On Wednesday afternoon the telegram arrived, but up until the moment of its arrival life went on as usual in the Toolum household. The fact that, at the instant Sherman entered the kitchen for his after-school chore of taking Little Louie to the park, destiny was reaching out with an offer of startling glory never caused a ripple in the minds of either Sherman or his mother, who was busy making chocolate pudding. Had Sherman, the perpetrator of the entire affair, known what he had done, he might have begun running for his life.

Emily turned from the stove. "You're late," she said.

" 'Rithmetic," Sherman muttered.

"What was that?"

He picked up a spoon and carefully licked it. " 'Rithmetic. I missed a couple of problems and had to stay after school." He regarded his mother balefully. "Mama, what d'ya have to study that junk for?"

Emily shook her head doubtfully. Although she had once earned her living working computing machines, she still had to use her fingers when counting additions over ten. Nevertheless, it was necessary not to foster a defeatist attitude. "It's necessary," she said firmly.

Sherman had heard that answer too many times in the past, so he changed the subject. "Where is he?" he asked, with an expression of distaste.

"In the living room."

Walking to the door that led to the inner part of the house, Sherman shouted, "Hey, c'mon, you," and strode to the outside door as Little Louie slowly entered the kitchen.

"Mama, can't I just listen to the radio?" Little Louie asked.

"Yeah," Sherman said hopefully.

"You're going out," Emily said. "And don't forget your cap." She pushed her youngest son toward the door. "If you see your father, tell him dinner's at six."

The door closed on Sherman's voice. "When was it ever any other time?"

Emily sighed and resumed her stirring activities. Hopefully, however, she kept her eye out the back window. On Wednesday Al had half a day off, and although he'd called to say he was staying an extra hour or two there was always the chance that any moment he'd come whistling up the walk. Somehow, recently he'd got out of the habit of coming home Wednesday afternoons, preferring to stop at Ed Warren's barbershop for a pinochle game, but she had hoped that he'd take the hint when she'd voiced her complaint about being in such a rut.

If only something would happen, she thought longingly—but of course, nothing ever did.

Walking to the park, with Little Louie tagging closely at his heels, Sherman was in a different world, that of the creative artist. Under the athletic shadow of Herman, Sherman had recently decided that his only chance to shine lay in the field of letters. Since then he had devoted almost his full efforts to writing verse for profit by entering contests. But, although he had added innumerable last lines to limericks and had described dozens of commercial products in twenty-five words or less, he had not yet won anything; but with a realistic attitude worthy of a poet many times his age

Sherman attributed his lack of success to the crass demands of the commercial market.

Just last week, almost at the point of complete despair, he had seen "The Life of Lord Byron" on television, and with renewed faith he immediately entered his father in the Yankee Doodle contest. Also, with the vision of the pale bard burned in his mind, he spent several hours behind locked doors practicing the slouched, drawn look of an esthete and wondering how he might develop just a slight case of tuberculosis. Sherman envisioned for himself a miserably happy life as a brilliant poet.

Right now he was bothered about his slogan for Bink's Bubble Gum. He had firmly decided on "Bink's Bubble Gum—It Bounces Back," but just today in school he had seen a word, used to describe a sailboat, that fascinated him. A perfect word for bubble gum, but he had to choose between: "Bink's—It's Billowy"; or "Bink's— The Billowing Bubble Gum." He liked the first for brevity, but the second had a more musical quality. Perhaps the solution was to send in all three.

The loud sound of boys' voices brought Sherman back to the world of reality. He and Little Louie were approaching the baseball diamond, and there was Herman kneeling, a bat between his legs, in the coach's box at the first-base line. Herman waved wildly as a boy scampered from first to second.

"Hullo." Sherman knelt beside his brother and plucked some grass from the ground.

Herman, stocky and dark, his face round and smooth, said, "Hi." Then, to the new batsman, "C'mon, Eddie, smack it a mile."

"Who's winnin'?"

"We are. Wanna play?"

Sherman jerked his head toward the rear. "Can't. I got Little Louie."

With no solution to this insurmountable problem, Sherman sadly regained his feet and walked back to his small brother. "Want to have me swing you?" he asked, having decided to accept his fate.

Little Louie shrugged, and Sherman persisted, "So what do

you wanna do? We could figure out a game, or maybe you want to go into the sand pit."

"I ain't got any toys."

"Swipe 'em from some smaller kid."

"You play with me, huh?" Little Louie pleaded.

"I'll watch," Sherman said. He had been graduated from the sand pit two years ago.

Little Louie stood hesitantly on the steps leading to the sand pit. Critically he surveyed the other children, his mind weighing the chances of participating in their games. One small girl who sat quietly in a corner was out of the question. She was too well-dressed, and even though her toys looked like fun Little Louie knew that the hard-faced nurse standing guard would prevent any conquest. Another boy dug sullenly in the sand with a large shovel. From past experience Little Louie knew that this shovel could easily be turned into a defensive weapon. Fleetingly he considered sneaking up and wrenching the shovel away from the boy, but the move was loaded with danger of failure. The other two boys playing in the pit were too old to allow him to play with them.

Thoughtfully he swung around to the parapet that walled the sand pit and began gnawing on the iron railing, relishing the chilled bitter taste. Maybe he should ask Sherman to swing him after all, but Sherman, sitting on a bench a few feet away, was staring at the sky in a funny way that Little Louie had noticed him doing quite often lately. Sometimes you would call to Sherman three or four times before he heard you.

Then Little Louie saw his father hurrying down the walk that bisected the playground. "Hey, Sherman. *Sherman!*"

"Wha'?"

"There's Papa over there."

Following Little Louie's pointing finger, Sherman waved wildly, "Hey, Papa, Papa," and when his father looked up, he shouted, "Mama says don't forget dinner's at six."

Al Toolum nodded quickly and waved back, but instead of stopping to talk to his sons, he increased his pace. Boys playing in parks meant bruises, and at forty Al was beginning to wonder whether he was getting too old for bruises. Lately it seemed that he ached all over for no reason at all, much less going around asking for it.

When he heard a shout rising from the baseball diamond, he glanced over to see Herman speeding around second base as another boy chased the skipping ball deep in the outfield. Al felt a thrill of pride, and he wished that Ben Carroway were with him so he could say, "Look at that kid of mine, Ben." It wouldn't be long until Herman was ready for high school sports, and then he'd sit in the grandstands and cheer. Boy!

He felt so good that he almost turned toward the diamond to offer his services as umpire, but the last time he'd done that the game had ended in something resembling a riot. It hadn't been *too* long ago when he might have even participated in the game—well, five or six years, anyway—but at forty . . .

He was out of the park now and walking more slowly down Main Street. Okay, he argued with himself, what's so bad about being forty?

Not so bad, he answered himself; hell, everybody gets to be forty if he lives that long, but such a fuss is raised about it. You'd almost think I'm an old man, he said angrily to himself. Take Henry Muller; he says to me, "Take it easy, Al, don't strain yourself. Let the kids do it."

Sixteen years he'd been working for Henry Muller. And in that time the world and everyone in it had suddenly grown younger, except for Al Toolum. Other people did the playing, the fighting, the loving. No more challenge to a job that had become tiresome.

And Em, he said to himself with growing indignation, with that put-up job on my birthday. Bringing in a cake with only one candle and saying, "Boys, when you reach forty you quit counting," and the kids had thought that was so funny.

At the corner of Third and Main he waved to Ed Willnick standing in the doorway of his bar and grill, and as he drew abreast of Warren's barbershop, he slowed down. Up until this moment he had had every intention of going home. Maybe he and Em would sit around the kitchen for a couple of peaceful hours just talking the way they used to do. Or maybe there was time to take a little walk.

"But maybe she'll say we're getting too old to go walking," he told himself.

He stared into the barbershop where a pinochle game was in progress.

"Or she'll try to ruin my afternoon off by making me take down the storm windows," he said half aloud in tones of deep self-righteousness.

Abruptly he turned and strode into the barbershop.

At the precise instant that Al Toolum walked into Warren's barbershop, something was occurring some twenty-five miles away that was to affect Al Toolum's entire life. It was happening in an office he had never seen, through an organization he had never heard of, and involving people he had never met. The finger of Fate was pointing to Alfred Toolum and beckoning seductively, while, unaware of the great thing that was happening to him, Alfred Toolum was bidding three ninety on a hand that hadn't a chance and was praying that somehow the ace of hearts would be one of the three hidden cards. . . .

Three

Standing in his position halfway down the long council table, John Bell had an excellent view of Paul Welton, and part of his mind was devoted to judging whether Welton showed pleasure or displeasure at what he was saying.

". . . this plan," he heard himself saying, "has everything. In the title alone we get the whole feeling of America. The many thousands of entries show us that the public takes to the idea whole-heartedly——"

Am I overselling? John asked himself anxiously. Is this too much hokum? But no; Paul Welton was nodding, and there was even a slight smile on his face. Funny, John thought, how much like a church this room looks. The soft, artificial lighting, the misty, dust-laden beams of light shafting down through the ceiling-high windows, the dark, heavy furniture—even the soft drone of his voice.

And soft he kept his voice, because men did speak softly in the presence of Paul Welton. Purely out of deference to his genius, they said. His was the fabulous name that had once led the firm of Welton, Walton & Weil to a position in the advertising business where it handled more billing for a longer period of time than any other agency in history; the history of the world, that is. Empires of finance had tottered when Paul Welton, claiming boredom and a too active ulcer, had retired—but only for a short time—to his Connecticut farm.

". . . actually," John was aware of himself saying, "this is the simplest idea, yet in its simplicity it has its greatest strength. I hate to admit"—here he allowed himself a short chuckle—"that I dreamed this whole thing up one morning while shaving—"

That will appeal to Welton, John thought, because Welton appreciated simple beginnings. Hadn't he thought of the idea for the American Advertising Consultants, the superthought agency, while fooling around on his farm?

"It was while I was clipping an azalea bush that I dreamed up the AAC," John had heard Welton say. "Yes, gentlemen, right off the top of my head—while clipping an azalea bush."

And his listeners would shake their heads in wonderment, knowing deep down inside that there was something very special about Paul Welton. Most of them, after all, spent a great deal of time clipping azalea bushes, but not one had come up with anything like the AAC.

Occupying just a quarter of a floor in the Madison Avenue skyscraper, the AAC had none of the bustle or feeling of a boisterous big business of the ordinary agency. There were no booths where buyers met billers, no photo murals or maps on the walls to show extended power, and *nowhere* was there a single commercial product displayed. For the AAC dealt only in ideas, and these were locked in the minds of the men who made up the American Advertising Consultants.

A bitter joke told along Madison Avenue, sponsored by former clients of the 3W agency whose sales had tumbled with Paul Welton's retirement, told how without the backing of the AAC the United States could declare no wars, arrange no peace or elect even the most popular candidate for the presidency. One particularly malevolent enemy of AAC started the vicious rumor that subversive elements had infiltrated Welton's new organization who were going to establish a campaign for the abolishment of Mother's Day.

Other than to redound to the credit of AAC, these stories had no effect. Many a time, when appearing before congressional committees for one reason or other, Welton was able to insert into the record the fine work of his organization, and now the American people, though not really knowing its function, sensed that AAC stood only for good and important work.

"Public Service," Paul Welton always said. "We have raised Public Service to a point where we are dedicated to the enlargement of the great American tradition—and in so doing we have created a greater market for our clients by the generation of trust in the great American public."

Welton also had something to say on the vacuum left in the public mind by the failure of the opinion polls in the '48 elections. "People *want* something to believe in, *demand* some institution that will give them security. We of the American Advertising Consultants fill that need. People believe us."

Only once had the AAC shown that it too had human frailties, and after this single mistake Paul Welton had installed the Machine, thus doing away with any possibility of future failure.

Even now, men shuddered when thinking of that one mistake, and *no one,* on the pain of dismissal, breathed the words Miss One World, the subject of the failure.

Actually, and Paul Welton never said otherwise, Miss One World had been a sensational idea, the brain child of Jess Baker, now a hardware salesman in the Arizona–New Mexico territory. Hired after the incident had been closed, John Bell had never known Baker, but secretly he admired the mind that had dreamed up the world-wide search for the girl in whose veins flowed the blood of the greatest number of the fifty-odd member nations of the UN. After many months of checking and screening, she had been pronounced to be Miss Toy Hollingshead, an American, of Guthrie, Oklahoma. Accompanying the crowing of the American press, a sudden news black-out of the contest had occurred in Russia, and it was rumored that two members of the Politburo had been purged.

It was only after Miss One World had been living in her duplex on East Fiftieth Street for three months where she entertained UN delegates and, presumably, fostered better relations between everyone, that she was unmasked by a suspiciously left-wing newspaper as a phony. Miss Hollingshead, it seemed, had last worked as a kooch dancer in downtown Los Angeles, and, despite forged birth certificates and other documents, was one-sixteenth Cherokee Indian and the rest Scotch-Irish. The publicity man who had engineered the whole affair was still in Leavenworth. . . .

Careful, John told himself, looking at Paul Welton who, though he appeared to be dozing, was actually paying strict attention. His interest told John that Welton had a lot of faith in his latest employee.

John tried to picture himself now as Paul Welton might see him: a tall young man dressed in the tweeds that identified him as belonging to Creative rather than the serge of Sales, his hair closely clipped, and his brown eyes flashing with just the right amount of enthusiasm. Here was the embryo genius, Welton's latest discovery who would, John fervently prayed, make his mark. It was Welton who had searched out the real author of the slogan that had sold more automobiles for Haggard Motors than any other campaign in history. It was Welton who had found the junior copywriter and hired him for AAC at a fabulous salary.

You'll Never Be A Laggard
Riding In A Haggard

. . . had been the slogan, and John had been the first to admit that he had been tremendously surprised when it had got a big saturation play in magazines, newspapers and billboards all over the country. And he had been even more surprised when he was awarded the Buyers and Sellers Club's special BS award of the year.

Now, perhaps, he was about to fulfill Paul Welton's trust by creating something that would be discussed for years to come.

"I have here," John said, giving the speech all his attention, and waving a fistful of perforated cards, "names of twenty people who have been chosen from the thousands of entries on the basis of the forms submitted. Our next step is to contact these people and have them take the final test, an exhaustive questionnaire worked out by our experts under the guidance of Mr. Gordon." He nodded in the direction of Arthur Gordon, a stocky sandy-haired man at his right. Gordon was officially in charge of the Machine.

Taking advantage of the pause, Paul Welton cleared his throat. "And how do you propose to administer this questionnaire? I assume these men are scattered all over the country."

The other members of the board nodded sagely. Good point. They directed querying glances at John Bell.

John smiled respectfully. "Naturally, I had taken that into consideration. The questionnaires are already in stamped envelopes, and at your go-ahead they'll be air-mailed to our branches in the cities nearest the candidates. Full instructions will be enclosed. At the same time I have telegrams ready to go to the candidates themselves instructing them when and where the test will be given. The cost, as opposed to any other system, will be negligible. The finished tests, sealed, will be returned by air mail and processed through the Machine."

Paul Welton nodded again. "Seems sound enough," he said,

"and every point appears covered. When can we be ready to announce the winner?"

John stared briefly at the high, beamed ceiling. "According to schedule, a week from this Friday. We can hold it for Sunday afternoon release to get the Monday-morning newspaper breaks."

A general murmur of assent rose in the room, and, encouraged, John continued, "Then, just for the record, I'd like to read the names and addresses of the twenty candidates." He paused. "Ready, Barbie?"

Barbara McClain, sitting at Mr. Welton's left, nodded, and John began, "Henry T. Applegate, forty-seven Morse Drive, Duluth, Minnesota."

Toward the end of the list Barbie interrupted, "How is that last spelt?"

"Toolum," John Bell repeated. "T-O-O-L-U-M, nine hundred and thirty-three Bigelow Street, Fernvale, New York."

Paul Welton's trim form came to attention. "Isn't that a little close to the city, Bell?"

John Bell flushed. "Well, sir, I know it's against established policy for anyone around or in New York to win a contest. In most cases New Yorkers' entries are automatically discarded, but I didn't think we should—I mean"—he helplessly indicated the perforated cards—"the Machine."

"Hmmm, yes—the Machine. All right, continue."

The meeting adjourned ten minutes later, and John hurriedly caught up to Barbie as she reached her desk.

"You'll get those wires right out, won't you, Barbie?"

Coolly, "Certainly, John."

Starting away, he paused, and returned to the desk. "Look, I—did I do anything last night to make you sore?"

"Of course not. I enjoyed every moment of those four hours that we—or, rather, you—talked about your Mr. Yankee Doodle. I can think of nothing I'd prefer to do unless it be to curl up with some hot novel like *Pilgrim's Progress*."

"Oh. I mean, oh . . ." He scratched his cheek thoughtfully.

"I guess I was pretty much of a bore, but you *know* how important this is to me."

"So you've told me, but it still makes a grim conversation piece."

Before he could answer, she had walked quickly out of the office. Why did she have to be so condescending to his ideas all the time? She'd even got to the point the night before where she had told him she admired his mind, and this was the most cutting thing she'd ever said to him. Although Barbie had a first-rate mind herself, it was the last thing John admired in her.

These damn physical attractions, he told himself. They have no place in the office, and, more, they don't give a man a chance to weigh and select with any degree of coolness. Try to look past Barbie's gray eyes to see what lay behind them, and you were stopped by the little greenish flecks that sparkled when she was happy and glinted like polished granite when she was mad. Try to find out how good a dancer she was, and before you could make a fair estimate you were practically transported to some Shangri-La by the softness of her long blonde hair that tickled your nostrils and the mind-whirling aroma of some exotic perfume. Try to look at her objectively to decide whether she would make a good strong wife and mother, and you found your pulse leaping and your skin getting tingly at the vision of the way she moved, so smooth and catlike. Try——

Oh, the hell with it, he told himself. She could type, take shorthand, and—and make the damn'dest shashlik he'd ever tasted.

He stamped into the office that he shared with Arthur Gordon. Tucking the perforated cards carefully into a file, he succeeded in dismissing Barbara McClain from his mind, and he even smiled quietly to himself. This was the biggest thing he had ever done or ever had a chance to do.

Closing the drawer to the file he found himself wishing that he could be in every house when the fateful telegrams arrived. What joy would reign, what excitement. And for the final lucky man— immortality!

Well, he said lamely to himself, a kind of immortality.

Approaching 933 Bigelow Street at fifteen minutes to six, Herman and Sherman, talking busily, were oblivious to Little Louie who, trailing them at a distance of a half-dozen yards, was bawling at the top of his voice. But a few feet from the house, a two-story clapboard of prewar design and construction, the two boys stopped and waited for their brother to catch up to them.

"Why'd'ya kick him?" Herman asked Sherman.

"I felt like it," Sherman answered laconically.

Herman nodded. He, too, often felt like kicking Little Louie, but as the oldest, he rarely gave way to the impulse. "He'll tell Papa," he said, "and you'll get a licking."

When Little Louie appeared anxious to plunge past his brothers, Sherman held out a restraining arm.

"Don't yell so loud," he said in a kindly voice, "or you're liable to get a Charley horse in your tonsils. Remember what Papa said about your voice turning into a frog's if you yell like that?"

Little Louie's chubby face was a mass of tear-stained wrinkles as he bellowed all the louder. Shaking his head sadly, Sherman reached into his pocket and drew forth a well-chewed glob of Bink's bubble gum. As he popped it into his brother's mouth the noise ceased immediately. Little Louie was plugged up.

"You can chew it until dinnertime," Sherman said.

"Glub-glub," Little Louie said.

"Not a minute more."

"Glub-glub-*glub*."

"Dirty blackmailer," Sherman muttered. "Okay, then, till your bedtime. But not in your bath. The last time it got soapy."

At the sound of a whistle from behind them, the three boys turned to see their father approaching briskly.

"Now remember," Sherman said in a low voice to Little Louie, "not one word about me kicking you, or . . ." He made a threatening fist.

Little Louie nodded manfully.

"Hi, Papa," Herman said, as Al drew up to them. "Did you have a good pinochle game?"

"Yeah, fine. There was one hand I held— Hey, what's the matter with Little Louie's face?"

"It's just gum," Sherman said.

"Oh, for a minute I thought he had the mumps."

Herman laughed. "He's already had 'em. You can't have mumps twice."

"Where Little Louie is concerned I wouldn't place any bets."

Familiar kitchen smells drew them through the back door, and they found Emily setting the table. Stripping off his jacket, Al said, "Anything I can do, Em?"

"Yes. Go read the paper for five minutes."

He paused as the boys skidded through into the living room. "What's the matter? You sore about anything?"

"I thought you were coming home after work."

"Oh. Well, I was. Then I got to Warren's, and I figured— Hey, you should've seen one hand I had. I bid three-ninety, and I need the ace of hearts for a hundred aces and a flush. Em, you're not listening."

"I heard you. You need the ace of hearts."

Stepping over to her, he planted a warm kiss on her cheek. "I'm sorry, Em. Listen, next Wednesday I'll come home real early, and we'll do something. Maybe we'll go into the city—you know, the whole afternoon and evening. Dinner and go to a movie."

"That would be nice," she said.

He walked toward the door. "I got that ace of hearts," he said. She smiled after him as the door closed.

There were two copies of the evening paper delivered to the Toolum house, a necessary extravagance that precluded any struggle for the paper. One was for Al, and one was for the boys. The boys had already spread the funnies out on the floor when he settled down for a glance at the headlines.

Nothing distinguished this living room from any other along Bigelow Street, except perhaps the absence of a television set. The furniture suite, its worn plush hidden by neat, faded slipcovers, dated back to Al and Emily's prewedding buying spree. The walls, newly painted last year, were dotted with scenes carefully clipped from calendars and enclosed in homemade frames. Over the fire-place was everyone's favorite, a large David Low reproduction that Emily had got with a five-year subscription to *Family Friend* maga-zine. A cheerful picture of the interior of an English tavern of the eighteenth century, it was known in the Toolum family as the Jolly-Good-Fellow picture, because obviously that was the song being sung by the mug-waving merrymakers.

In one corner, half hidden by Al's favorite chair, was the radio-phonograph console that was his pet and which he had purchased with his mustering-out pay from the army. No one but Al was per-mitted to touch its controls, and for ordinary listening there was a small, plastic table radio in another corner. Just recently Al had installed a three-speed motor in the console, his final acceptance of long-playing records having arrived after a deliberate wait to see whether there would be a fourth, or maybe even fifth speed, and the grudging admission that long-playing records were here to stay. It was his sons' cry that their father waited much too long in his acceptance of progress, and Al, while a little ashamed of his apparent reactionary instincts, secretly held to the theory that some-how the world had started along the unhappy road to destruction the day the Wright brothers had proved that a heavier-than-air ma-chine could fly. Al didn't know why he blamed the Wright brothers particularly, except that for him the airplane was the symbol of all that was wrong with the world. He wouldn't ride in one.

He had just finished what he called his "evening shudders" (reading the world news) when Little Louie, cupping his bubble gum in his hand, said:

"Hey, Papa, look back and tell me who won the fourth at Jamaica, will you?"

Emily opened the door as Al stared at Little Louie. "Why? You betting on the horses?"

"Nah, but I was in Mr. Willnick's when Officer O'Malley put two bucks down. I wanta see if he won."

Turning back to the racing results, he said, "I thought I told you to stay out of that horse room."

"I just stood in the doorway. He was givin' me some candy.

Anyway, you said I can go to work for him—if I ever get to be six."

Emily sniffed. "If you want candy you should go to a candy store and not a bar. And besides, your father was just joking."

"Mr. Willnick gives it to me free," Little Louie said to his mother. Then, almost tearfully, he turned to Al. "You weren't fooling, were you, Papa?"

Al turned haughtily to Emily. "I was simply following directions from that latest book you made me read that said, and I quote, let children follow their natural desires even if it goes somewhat against the parents' beliefs. I suppose"—he shrugged—"that includes if Little Louie wants to deliver horse slips for a living." When there was no reaction from Emily, he peered back at the paper. "It says here a horse named Lover's Dream won the fourth race."

"Ha," Little Louie said. "Officer O'Malley had one named Brutal Sergeant he was betting on a hunch."

"No one better get in Officer O'Malley's way tomorrow," Sherman said.

"I thought they closed up those betting rooms," Emily said.

"They just have to pay off the cops more," Little Louie explained. "Mr. Willnick was telling me what with high taxes——"

A further expansion of Ed Willnick's financial difficulties was interrupted as the front doorbell rang.

"Now who could that be?" Al said, getting to his feet.

"Whoever it is," Emily said, turning back toward the kitchen, "cut it short, because dinner's ready."

But her progress was interrupted at the words "Western Union" that came from the front door.

"What is it, Al, a telegram?" she cried.

He handed the boy a quarter, and then closed the door.

"A telegram," he said, weighing the yellow envelope, and looking at Emily. "Nobody in the family ready for a baby, nobody was sick——"

"Open it," she said, and looked at the front of the envelope. "For goodness' sakes, Al," she said, "it's addressed to Sherman."

"Sherman!" He peered at the address. "It is! But I signed——"

"Me? Oh, boy." Sherman leaped up from the floor.

"I should have figured it," Al said, chagrined. "Nobody ever sends me a telegram. Not since four years ago when Aunt Sally had her baby."

"That was addressed to me," Emily said. "It was *my* sister."

Al glared at her. "It was addressed to both of us."

Emily didn't say anything, but her lips moved, forming the words, "No, it wasn't."

Turning to Sherman, Al demanded angrily, "Who are you to be getting telegrams?"

Taking the envelope from his father's hand Sherman quickly opened it. Herman crowded his shoulder while Al looked the other way, the expression on his face showing that he didn't care what the telegram said.

It took a long while for Sherman to read the message, and Al laughed nervously, looking at Emily. "They probably want him in Hollywood to take Hopalong's job." Another deep pause followed, and then Al shouted, "Well, what does it say?"

Sherman's face mirrored wonderment as he looked up. "Papa," he whispered, "we won a contest."

"Contest?" Al's face immediately cleared. "You mean money?"

Sherman shook his head.

"A refrigerator?" Emily asked.

"No," Sherman said. "Yankee Doodle."

"Well, isn't that fine," Emily said. "A year's supply of Yankee Doodle."

Al was disappointed. "A breakfast cereal—or is it a soap?"

"It's—it's not any of those things. It's a person. It's *you.*"

"Me? Yankee Doodle?"

Herman interrupted rudely, "You didn't win anything. It only says Papa's in the finals." Snatching the telegram from Sherman's fingers, he read, "Please be advised that your father Alfred Toolum has been selected for the final screening of Yankee Doodle fifty-two Stop Please report with him to the offices of the American Advertising Consultants four hundred and sixty-two Madison Avenue Tuesday April fifteen three-thirty PM Stop If circumstances prevent his appearance please repeat please call Meridian seven five-thousand Stop John Bell."

Al looked dazed as Emily said, "My, what an expensive telegram. They said please four times." She started toward the kitchen. "Now let's have dinner."

"Wait—wait a minute." Al fell limply into his chair. "What is this crazy business?"

"It's perfectly plain," Emily said. "They want you to go there next Tuesday."

"They're gonna put Papa through a sieve," Little Louie said.

Al gripped Sherman by the arm until the boy winced with pain. "Sherman," he demanded threateningly, "what is this all about?"

"Lemme go, Papa." Released, Sherman ran to an end table and dug out a copy of *Family Friend*. Turning to the inside back cover, he said, "Here, Papa, see? It's the Yankee Doodle Fifty-two contest."

Al glanced at the big, black type and rubbed his eyes.

BOYS!!! GIRLS!! the heading screamed, IS YOUR DAD THE AVERAGE AMERICAN FAMILY HEAD??? ENTER HIM NOW IN THE GREAT YANKEE DOODLE '52 CONTEST.

Al's eyes lifted from the page and met those of his eager son. "Is this what you were asking all those crazy questions for?"

"Sure. Wait a minute, I'll show you." Sherman ran toward the stairs as Al peered back at the advertisement.

"Somewhere in the United States," he read, "there is a man who, more than anyone else, represents the ideals, dreams and down-to-earth way of life of the average American. By entering YOUR father NOW you may win for him FAME and the opportunity to be the spokesman for his fellow Americans." At this point Al swallowed hard. The rest of the advertisement told how entry blanks could be obtained at any store that sold one or more of the participating products, a list of which followed.

Al looked up at Herman. "Did you know about this?"

"Nah. He's always entering things like that and never wins. Who pays attention?"

"Looks like he's done it now," Al muttered.

Racing down the stairs Sherman held a sheaf of papers. "See, here's copies of the things I had to send in." He thrust a letter at his father, and Al stared at it.

Dear Sir: I wish to submit my papa Alfred Toolum as a candidate for Yankee Doodle '52 as seen per your Advertizement in the Family Freind magazine. Instead of telling you why I think he is average in 25 wds or less I have wrote a poem which I hope will be OK.

MISTER ALFRED TOOLUM

Mama says he's sure the best and that is really true.
He's the man to pass the test for Yankee Doodle '52.
I inclose our pikture and the filled-out entry blank and five wrappers from Bink's Bubble Gum.

Sinsirely yours,
Sherman Toolum (9)

"Where'd you get the picture?" Al demanded, when the document had been digested.

"From the album. It's the one Uncle Ben took at Jones Beach last summer."

"My stomach sticks out," Al said.

"So what? Ain't that a good poem, though, Papa?"

"It rhymes," Al admitted. Then he returned to reality. "I ought to smack you, Sherman."

Little Louie leaned forward with anticipation.

Sherman expressed hurt surprise. "But, Papa, I thought . . . Look, it says you'll be famous."

"Do you think I'd be crazy enough to go through with anything like this?"

Tears sprung into Sherman's eyes. "Aw, Papa . . ."

"Please, everybody," Emily pleaded, "let's have dinner."

Sherman ran to her, crying, "Mama, Papa isn't going to go on Tuesday." The door swung shut behind Herman and Little Louie as they followed their brother into the kitchen.

Comic books! Al cursed, his appetite suddenly gone. It had to be the comic books that made kids do what they did these days. Imagine Sherman entering me into a stupid—and *winning!* Or almost winning. Not that I could, he told himself. It's just a trick to get me into something that costs dough.

He thought back to the week when Sherman had badgered him with countless questions. At the time he'd figured it had something to do with school. How old was he? Where was he born? Where did his parents come from? How much money did he make?

He had balked at the last question. "It's enough I have to tell the income tax man how much I make without broadcasting it," he had said to Sherman.

Emily had been sitting sewing. "Your father makes ninety-three dollars and forty-two cents take-home pay a week," she had said calmly as Sherman wrote the figure down. "And he hasn't had a raise since almost a year ago, and with the way prices are going up . . ."

"The union's working on the new wage formula now," Al had said angrily.

"And by the time those smart alecks get through figuring prices will be up again."

"I *told* you, Emily, it's an escalator clause. If prices go up, wages go up with them."

"How can they if wages are frozen?" Emily asked triumphantly.

"So are prices."

"Ha," Emily cried. "Big joke."

In the ensuing argument he had forgotten to be mad about her telling Sherman how much money he made.

There had been other questions: What were his hobbies? Had he been in the service? His favorite color, movie star?—so many questions, that when Sherman was through he asked, "Do you want me to sign the loyalty oath now?"

"No, it doesn't ask that," Sherman answered, studying the paper. "But it does ask what political party you belong to. You're a Democrat, aren't you, Papa?"

"Sometimes," he said.

"What do you mean, sometimes?"

"Well, it depends on how much I'm offered. Some years the Republicans pay more, so I vote for them." He met Sherman's shocked look with a straight face.

Sherman said, "Mama . . ."

"He's a Democrat," Emily had said firmly, "and you don't get paid for your vote. You should be ashamed to say such things, Al."

He had tried his best to look ashamed.

If he had only known what Sherman was up to, he sighed to himself now, he would have hit him with the dining-room table.

Emily, standing in the doorway, interrupted his reverie. "Aren't you hungry, Al?"

"I guess so." He entered the kitchen, and sat down.

Emily passed him his plate. "I don't suppose you'll have any trouble getting off Tuesday," she said quietly. "Just tell Henry why you want to go to the city."

Buttering a piece of bread, he said, "I'm not going. Sherman can just call them up."

"He's never won a contest before," Emily said. "It would be awful if the first time he won he couldn't collect what was coming to him."

He looked at his wife and saw a particularly stubborn look on her face that usually spelled trouble. Fifteen years of moods and countermoods had given each of them a fair insight into the other and good judgment on how to act under certain circumstances. This stubborn look he saw now was one he had long ago decided was never worth fighting. But now he was determined! There was, in Al's German ancestry, a streak of stubbornness too.

"*He* isn't collecting," Al said. "I am, and I don't want any part of it."

"Sherman says the child who sends in the winning father gets a lot of prizes," Emily said, even more quietly.

"A bicycle," Sherman said.

"And boxing gloves," Herman said.

"And a sandbox for the back yard," Little Louie said.

Al studied the array of faces. "Do you want me to be the joke of the neighborhood, the prize schmo of the year?"

"And there's a two-week trip, all expenses paid," Emily said, ignoring his question, "for the mother and father to any place of their choice in the United States. We could visit California, Al."

"Who would mind the kids?"

"Mom could come."

"No!" He smacked his hand on the table.

"But . . ."

"*No!*" He stood up. "I won't do it. Absolutely, positively *no!* I'll drop dead before I do anything like that." He glared around the table, slowly lowering himself back into his chair. "Now, everybody eat . . ."

Four

The façade to the imposing building at 462 Madison Avenue was decorated with relief figures of naked cherubs winging their way about the carved head of a Greek goddess haloed by the words TRUTH *ADVERTISING* HONOR. Crowds of people poured in and out of the revolving door and the two swinging doors that flanked it.

Sherman tugged at the reluctant figure of his father. "C'mon, Papa, we've only got five minutes."

Al swatted futilely at the fist that clenched his coat sleeve. "Let go, you're ruining the crease."

"Come *on*."

Al stood firmly in his tracks. "How about if I buy you an ice cream soda?"

"We just had a milk shake. That's why we're late."

"We could go to a movie. Radio City, maybe. You're always saying Herman's been there, and you haven't."

"Papa . . ." Sherman paused. "Remember what Mama said?"

These last words started them in motion, for Al certainly did remember what Emily had said. This past weekend would go down in his memory as one of the blackest in his career. Never, he had decided, had one man been so badgered. All he had said was that he didn't want his friends to think him a damn fool, and he wasn't going to any blanking (this last statement was made in the privacy of their bedroom) Advertising Consultants on this or any other blinking Tuesday, and before he knew it he had been called every kind of criminal from wife-beater to child-murderer. There had been several moments during the weekend when he had seriously considered both extremes.

The American Advertising Consultants, a large directory board told them, was on the twenty-third floor, and an imperious man in uniform directed them to an express elevator. A series of clicks from some instrument in the starter's hand sent the elevator hurtling skyward, leaving Al's stomach somewhere in the lower region.

Stepping directly out into a large, quiet room, they found themselves in the anteroom of the AAC. Across the carpeted floor was a curved desk monitored by a red-haired receptionist. The main feature of the room was a huge monogram made of gleaming wood that jutted out from the paneled wall behind the desk. Spelling out the letters AAC, it had been adapted by Paul Welton from an Arp sculpture. To Al it looked like three fish locked in mortal combat.

Miss Breen, the receptionist, regarded the man and small boy suspiciously.

"May I help you?" She was sure she couldn't. It was inconceivable that anyone could help a man wearing a lavender shirt.

Al cleared his throat. "I was supposed to be here at three thirty."

"You *were?*"

"I'm—I'm Alfred Toolum."

Aware of the chilly atmosphere, Al was now pleasantly surprised to see that the mention of his name caused an instantaneously favorable reaction.

"Oh, *yes,* Mr. Toolum, we've been expecting you." Al searched her face for a hint of laughter, but the girl seemed perfectly serious. "Just a moment, and I'll call Mr. Bell."

Backing slowly away from the desk, his hand tight around Sherman's, Al felt a wave of terrible resignation. A moment ago he could still have run, as he had wanted to, but now it was too late. He ran a free finger under the tight collar and had difficulty breathing. Darn Emily anyway for insisting he wear a new shirt, the one she had got him for Christmas.

They had barely been seated on one of the couches lining the wall when a large door swung open, and a pretty, blonde girl came toward them with her hand outstretched and a warm smile of greeting. Al scrambled to his feet.

"Mr. Toolum, I'm Miss McClain, John Bell's secretary."

"Yes, ma'am." There was something disconcerting about Miss McClain's perfume.

"And this, I suppose, is the young man who sent in the winning entry."

"That's Sherman all right." Elbowing the openmouthed boy, "Say hello."

Sherman gulped. "Hello."

"If you'll come inside," Miss McClain said, "Mr. Bell is waiting for you." She correctly interpreted his helpless glance at Sherman. "Oh, Sherman can come too. We have a surprise for him."

During the next ten minutes Al suffered a confusing period in which he met Mr. Bell, a tall, serious-looking young man; a Mr. Gordon, who looked brisk and scientific in a gray smock; and a Mr. Welton, tall and sedate, who appeared briefly, and, during a respectful silence from the others, bade him welcome and wished him luck in a soft, trained voice that reminded Al of a famous minister's he'd once heard and admired on the radio. Then Sherman was led out, rather willingly it seemed to Al, by Miss McClain, and he was alone with John Bell and Mr. Gordon.

John offered him a cigarette. "Don't be nervous, Mr. Toolum. We're here to help you as much as we can."

"Dinner's at six," Al muttered. It was the only thing he could think of to say. He shifted uncomfortably in the ultramodern chair that fitted in with the rest of this office's decor. There was no place to rest the back of his head, and somewhere at the base of his spine was an empty space. It all felt so insecure.

"This won't take more than an hour or so," John assured him.

Al opened his mouth to say something, but John, holding up a sheaf of papers, spoke first. "Mr. Toolum, all over the country at this very moment other men are preparing to take this same test . . ."

Briefly, Al wondered why no one asked him whether he *wanted* to take a test, but he was afraid to interrupt.

". . . and one man out of the twenty involved will be chosen as Yankee Doodle Fifty-two."

Al winced. "Wait a minute," he said. "I don't know whether I'm quite sure I know what this is all about."

"That's what we're here to explain to you," Mr. Gordon said patiently.

"No, you don't know what I mean. I'm not sure I want to go through with this thing," he started bravely, but his protest crumbled at the sight of the shocked expressions that passed over the faces of the two other men. "What I mean," he said lamely, "I never was much good at tests."

"This is more than just a test," John Bell said. He drew a deep breath, hoping he could sound convincing. "It's an affirmation of what *you* represent, Mr. Toolum."

"America," Arthur Gordon said.

John fired him a sharp glance, and Gordon shrugged slightly. "What Mr. Gordon means," John said, "is that the name Yankee Doodle, originally a term of derision used by the British, has come to mean everything wonderful about the average American—his openness, his friendly nature, readiness to accept new ideas, his rugged individualism. We're at a time now," John said thoughtfully, "when there is a need to reaffirm these things."

Al shifted in his chair. It all sounded very good the way Mr. Bell said it, but there was one thing bothering him. "Tell me something," he said. "Does it cost me any money?"

John blinked, and then he laughed. "You see, that's what I mean, Mr. Toolum. In every average American is that strain of Yankee shrewdness and suspicion."

"No one will ever sell *him* the Brooklyn Bridge," Arthur Gordon said.

Al leaned back, feeling better. "I guess not," he said.

"Now," John said, "for the test. Uh—you were in the army, weren't you, Mr. Toolum?"

Al sighed. "Three-and-a-half years."

"Then you won't be unfamiliar with this type of test. It's on the same style as the army classification tests."

"Only much more scientific," Arthur Gordon interjected sharply.

"It better be," Al said. "I'm a machinist—have been for sixteen years. So I spent eighteen months on Guam as a base artillery gunner."

John nodded understandingly. "I was in the army too."

"But it wasn't so bad," Al said. "Kind of peaceful. Never shot a gun once." He looked up at John Bell. "Mister, one more thing I want to get straight: Is this a gag?"

John appeared overcome by the question. "A gag?"

Waving his hand, Al said, "All this, what for? How did you

get to me? Okay, so my kid sent in some stuff, but thousands of other kids must have done the same——"

"Seven hundred forty-six thousand three hundred and twenty-four," Arthur Gordon said.

"See," Al said, "so how did you get to me?"

"Mr. Toolum, I could go into a long explanation, but I won't. All you have to know is that we *did* pick you—and nineteen others around the country. The Machine judged the facts sent in on the entry form, a panel of impartial judges looked over the pictures and twenty-five-word descriptions—in the case of your son it was a jingle that caught their eye—and . . . well, and here you are."

"A machine, huh? That I might understand."

John stood up. "Let's show him, Art."

Between the two men, Al was led out into a hallway and down to another room. This one, sterile in appearance with white walls and linoleum-covered floor, contained a small desk, a straight chair, and, across one entire wall, a huge gleaming monster eight feet tall and a dozen feet long.

"Meet the Machine," John Bell said.

"Wow," Al marveled. "I'd like to see what goes on behind those dials."

"Plenty goes on," Arther Gordon said, running one hand caressingly over the front of the Machine. "It took four years to build with some of the greatest minds of America working on it."

From the desk John picked up a double handful of perforated cards. "These are some of the rejects from the entries. Art, let's run them through for Mr. Toolum. What would you like, red-headed men?"

Al stared uncomprehendingly. "I'll show you what I mean," John said. "Redheaded men, Art."

Into a large opening Arthur Gordon fed the cards. Studying a chart for a minute, he then made several adjustments on the dials. He snapped a switch and stepped back. As the Machine whirred and hummed Arthur Gordon took a pose almost reverential, his eyes closed and his hands clasped at his chest.

In a moment the Machine spit forth the cards, but now they

were divided: three fell into one division, and the remainder were piled neatly at a different opening. John picked up the three cards.

"Here are three names of redheaded men," he told Al.

Al looked at the cards. "And those other guys. What are they?"

"Whatever they are, they're not redheaded. Now, how would you like the names of left-handed men who are accountants?"

Al held up his hand. "I believe you," he said. "Only—I still don't get it."

"You don't have to," John said warmly. "Just take the test. Then *if* you win on the basis of the Machine's totaling and weighing the facts, you'll see what an amazing thing has happened to you." They were in the hall again, and John held his arm as he explained a little further about the Machine's function in the test. When they were back in the office, John handed Al some sheets of paper, a pencil, and indicated that he was to sit at the desk. "Now, Arthur will show you how to mark the answers. When you're finished, just push the buzzer. Don't sign anything until I get back, because we have an affidavit form that you will swear to, saying that all the facts represented by you are true."

"What's the matter?" Al asked. "Don't you trust me?"

In John's eyes was the shadow of Miss One World. "It's—it's just a form," he said. "Of course we trust you."

Alone, Al stared out the window across the panorama of rooftops and loosened his tie. He chewed the pencil thoughtfully, wondering why he didn't have the guts to do what he'd set out to do. He'd planned that, once free of Sherman, he could talk himself out of this mess, and here he was . . .

Over the steeple of St. Patrick's Cathedral was the maze of windows in Rockefeller Center. There were thousands of people at work behind those windows now, people who had no earthly idea that so close to them was a man about to take a test that might make him Yankee Doodle '52. Yankee Doodle '52. If he said it a few more times it might not sound so stupid.

The great average American family head. Put that way it didn't sound half bad. Maybe all those people behind the windows were just average too; and if he were to turn out to be the *most* average—well, that was something.

Drawing a deep breath, he looked down at the stack of papers arranged neatly in front of him. Each question provided four choices, one of which he was to check as his answer. First of all they wanted physical description. The ages ran from 35 to 45, and he checked the space next to 40. Down the line he went on height, weight, hair and eye color until his complete description was given.

Perspiring as a result of his intense concentration, Al leaned back, removed his jacket and lit a cigarette. There must be a thousand questions, he thought. He began to enjoy himself.

When he came to preferences he had a little trouble.

Which one of the following artists do you prefer:

a) James Montgomery Flagg
b) Charles Dana Gibson
c) Norman Rockwell
d) Grant Wood

Al screwed up his forehead. The names were all familiar, but he couldn't think who painted what. Then the name Norman Rockwell struck a chord. He's that guy who does the magazine covers, Al remembered. Looked just like photographs.

He checked Norman Rockwell.

Next came composers, and the list was:

a) Victor Herbert
b) Irving Berlin
c) George Gershwin
d) Ferde Grofé

He didn't particularly like any of them; then he recalled a beer bust at the lodge when Ben Carroway, he, and two other guys had whipped up a darn good vocal arrangement of "Alexander's Ragtime Band." Nostalgically, he checked Irving Berlin.

In an adjoining office Sherman sat in a deep chair ogling Miss McClain who was typing busily and occasionally smiling at him in a quick, friendly way. In one hand Sherman held a tremendous lime lollipop and in the other he clutched a pair of sparkling new roller skates, the surprise that came with the compliments of the AAC.

Sherman had just about decided that Miss McClain was definitely his type, and he was desperately wondering how he could get around to asking her how old she was. It was always his fate to fall in love with an older woman; but Sherman, the poet, had learned to take such things quite philosophically. Like last year when he was in love with Miss Johnson, his teacher. She had been twenty-four at the time, a difference in age of almost seventeen years. He had asked her, and she had told him.

That fact had bothered him until he had brought up the subject at home, and Mama and Papa had seemed quite encouraging.

"As long as there's a meeting of the minds," Mama had said, quoting from a story she had read in the beauty parlor, "that's all that's important."

"I think we got that," he had said. "She gave me A in deportment."

"That's no meeting of the minds," Papa had said. "It's dishonest. You'd better grab her. After all, she's got a good job, hasn't she?"

This was then a sore point with Sherman, because he had not yet accepted the fact that it was necessary for a poet to be supported by his wife.

"Look at me," Papa had said, overriding his objections. "I could have had a life of ease if I'd married Edna Gerson whose old man died and left her the Buick agency."

"If I remember right," Mama had said, "you once walked Edna home from school, and she hit you with a geometry book."

"She was just jealous, because all the girls were chasing me."

"If only she'd been studying law," Mama had murmured. "The books are so much heavier."

Miss Johnson had proved a sore disappointment in the end when she turned around and married Mr. Gross, the shop teacher. Sherman had suffered for a whole week into his summer vacation.

Miss McClain stopped her typing. "Don't you like the lollipop?"

"Oh, sure." He licked at it mightily. "Uh—you been working here long?"

"A year."

That was encouraging. "Did you—did you go to college?" She smiled at him. "Uh-huh."

"Four whole years?"

"That's what it usually takes."

Sherman's hopes tumbled. That meant she was really *old*.

The door opened, and Mr. Bell came in. "Having a good time, son?" He handed some letters to Miss McClain.

"It's okay. When will Papa be out?"

"Pretty soon now. I just peeked in, and he said he was almost through." Turning to Miss McClain, he said, "Have a drink with me at five, Barbie?"

"I have a lot of work to do," she said shortly.

Mr. Bell seemed puzzled. "Please, Barbie . . ."

"Oh, all right."

Grinning happily, John Bell darted out of the room.

Sherman put down the lollipop. "He looks kind of dopey to me."

Miss McClain looked surprised, and then she laughed. "Oh, John's all right. He's just never gotten over being on the debating team at Harvard. He's a pretty good poet, though."

"Oh?" Suddenly Mr. Bell took on new importance. "I'm going to be a poet."

"Then you and John should get together."

"Does he enter contests?"

"No, he sends his work to little magazines. That's supposed to be a bit higher class."

"Do they pay him?"

"No."

"Huh. When you win a contest you get paid."

"So you do," Miss McClain said, and she resumed her typing.

Fifteen minutes later John Bell was back, and Al was with him. Al was tired, and he had forgotten to rebutton his shirt collar, but he felt very relaxed. With them was a man carrying a camera and flash equipment.

"No, it wasn't so bad," he said to John. "In a way, I'm glad I came."

"Of course you're glad," John said. "Why shouldn't you be?"

"Well . . ." Al looked at him wryly. "I kind of had the feeling you were making a fool of me. If it hadn't been for the wife and kids insisting——"

"Don't worry," John interrupted. "That's the last thing in our minds. If you get selected you'll remember this as one of the greatest days in your life. I promise you." He turned to the photographer. "Okay, George. This is just in case, Mr. Toolum . . ."

The man took four pictures. "Thank you," John said. "One way or another you'll be hearing from us."

Al nodded, and he took Sherman's hand. "Let's go, Sherman. Thank them for the roller skates."

"Thanks," Sherman said. He glanced sorrowfully at Miss McClain, wondering if it were the last time he'd ever see her.

Down on the street they paused at the corner to wait for a red light.

"I feel kind of funny," Al said.

"Why, Papa?"

"I don't know." They started across the street, weaving their way through a maze of honking traffic that clogged the intersection. "Maybe it's because all of a sudden I'd like to win that doggone thing. . . ."

At twenty past five Barbie McClain and John Bell sat in the dark cavern of a bar on Fifty-first Street. Two Manhattans, untouched, stood on the small table between them.

Digging into her purse, Barbie produced a cigarette and bent forward to accept a light. "I still say I feel sorry for him," she said, expelling smoke explosively from her mouth and nostrils.

"You said that when we came in."

"And you didn't ask me why."

"Okay, why?"

"Don't look so darn guilty, John."

"I am not looking guilty. You are getting smoke in my eyes."

"It's just that he looks like a very nice man."

"Who, Toolum?"

"Yes, Toolum."

"Sure, he's a nice man. Why shouldn't he be?"

"Because you and Mr. Welton share the same ideas of what the average man should look like, and even *I* was beginning to believe it."

"And how is this average man supposed to look?"

"Like a human receptacle for all the trash he reads, hears and——"

"Oh, Barbie, quit, will you?"

"All right, then, it's not Toolum, it's us. We are making a fool of him, aren't we?"

"No."

"John Bell, do you mean you *believe* all that malarky you've been putting out?"

"Barbie . . ." He looked around quickly. "Please, not so loud."

"You *do* believe it, don't you?"

He avoided her eyes. "We've been through all this before, on other things. Sure I believe it. It's my job to believe it. It's my job even to instigate it, invent it, foster it, nurse it. . . . You know that."

"But why, John?"

"For fifteen thousand a year plus bonuses, and Santa should bring lots of bonus this year." He bit savagely into a cherry.

She was silent for a moment. "It always comes down to that, doesn't it?"

"Did you study Money-hating 101 at Smith?"

"It isn't that, and it isn't what you do to yourself that matters. But when you involve innocent people like Mr. Toolum—and that nice little boy . . ."

"Toolum? Don't worry about him. The man who wins this thing will have the thrill of a lifetime. What average guy doesn't like to see his picture plastered all over the country, his word quoted as authority? What's wrong with bringing glamour into a person's life?"

"For what ends?"

"He gives a fair return for what he gets. No one can ask for more."

After another silence Barbie said, "You know, John, you made a big mistake showing me that book of poetry you wrote during the war. From it I got a picture of a completely different person from one who thinks up Yankee Doodles. Nice, honest—"

John's face reddened. He interrupted grimly, "It's awfully easy to be honest during a war. You're on the right side. You can write bitter stuff about an army and a war everybody hates. You can bite the hand that gives you three meals a day, a bed to sleep in and a check every month. Where else can you do that?"

"That's not what I mean."

"What do you mean? You want me to write sonnets against Paul Welton? Or do you want me to be a long-haired slob living in a Bronx basement now that rents in Greenwich Village are too high for poets?"

"When I first met you, you were going to get a foundation grant to translate Latin-American poetry."

He didn't say anything.

"Well, weren't you?" she persisted.

"They wouldn't give me the grant," he said.

"Did you try?"

"Of *course* I tried."

"It would be a lot better than what you're doing."

"*I said I tried.*"

"I bet you didn't try hard enough."

Leaning over the table, he shook his finger in her face. "Listen, Barbie, I'm getting damn sick of this. You sound like every other disappointed broad who once went to an intellectual cocktail party and can't get over the fact that it's necessary to eat. And if you want my opinion on something else," he said into her tightening face, "let me say that for a hundred bucks a week you're doing what I get fifteen thousand a year for—*plus* bonus. You aid and abet the very damn thing you're always screaming against. So *there*."

"Oh," she sputtered. "Oh, John Bell, you're a louse. An unmitigated louse."

"But a wealthy one," he said, and he drank his Manhattan at one gulp.

Five

"All I can say is, you're nuts," Ben Carroway announced.

Al, standing on a ladder outside the dining-room windows, ignored the statement. "You got beer in your refrigerator?" he asked.

"Yeah, I got some beer, unless Sadie's brother drank it all up last night, the muzzler. You're crazy."

"How about running in and getting a couple of cans. It's hot out here."

"I'm holding the ladder for you."

"So let go. I'll sit up here till you get back."

Lowering himself to the top step of the ladder, Al watched Ben go through the hedge that separated their two yards. He wished that Ben wouldn't hassle so much at him about the Yankee Doodle thing. If only Emily hadn't told Sadie. But, then, he and Ben had been friends, as well as neighbors, for almost fifteen years, and you don't keep a thing like that from a good friend.

He glanced distastefully at the storm windows. They'd need painting before he put them up again in the fall.

Ben Carroway returned through the hedge holding two opened cans of beer. He was a big, florid man whose hair was very thin except over his temples. His nose had been broken years ago when he played football in high school, and it still gave him trouble. He always spoke of having an operation, but as his wife, Sadie, said, "Ben's just a big, fat coward," a fact which Ben cheerfully admitted.

Al dismounted from the ladder, and together they sat on the grass, their backs to the house.

"I wish he'd go back to his wife," Ben said.

"Who?"

"My brother-in-law. This coming over every Saturday night and drinking my beer is getting me down."

"How come he left his wife?"

"How come, how come? How come anybody leaves their wife? She probably drove him nuts. Like I was telling Sadie the other night. 'Sadie,' I said, 'we've been married sixteen years. Aren't you tired of giving me hell all the time?'"

"And what did she say?"

"She said, 'That's what keeps me young, Ben.' Now is that any way to figure?"

"Maybe if you'd had kids it would be different. Kids keep a woman young." The last statement slipped out automatically, and, briefly, Al wondered about it. He'd read that someplace by some authority, but it didn't seem quite right.

"We'd've had some if we could've," Ben said morosely. "Maybe we'll adopt one yet."

Al made no comment on this, knowing that the Carroways spoke of adopting a child the same way that Ben spoke of having his operation.

Little Louie appeared from behind the house, peered at them a moment, and then disappeared again. A moment later they heard his voice from within the house, crying, "Hey, Mama, Papa and Uncle Ben are sitting drinking beer."

"Little sneak," Al said half aloud, and to Ben, "You can have that one if you want. I'll give him to you for Father's Day."

Ben shuddered. "No favors, please. With a kid like him, who needs trouble?"

Above their heads the window slid open with a bang, and Emily's head appeared.

"You drinking beer, Al?"

Without looking up, Al grunted, "Uh-huh."

"How about the storm windows?"

"We're taking a five-minute break. I figure since it's Sunday it's all right to do that. Even if there's no union around here——"

"Huh!" The window slammed shut.

"That's what I mean," Ben said, after a moment's pause. "And *you* don't have in-law trouble."

"What do you mean, I don't have in-law trouble. What do you call Emily's mother?"

"Ah, she's a nice old dame. And, besides, how much trouble can she give you living in the city?"

"An extra phone bill for about fifteen bucks a month's worth of trouble."

"Consider yourself lucky to get off with that."

"I guess so." Al chuckled. "It was Little Louie who made them decide to move back into the city, after all these years. One look at Little Louie, and they figured it was time to retire."

"I don't know," Ben sighed. "This Yankee Doodle business, for instance—do you really figure the average man puts up with this kind of stuff?"

"Hard to say, but I bet those fellows at the Consultants have the answer. Why, they got a Machine there gives an answer to any question you put in. Now"—he turned to Ben—"just suppose they do figure me for the most average guy. No mistake about that, see, because the Machine doesn't make mistakes——"

"But that's what I don't understand. How do they know what the average guy is? They have to know what the perfect average man is before they can find a human being who comes closest to him."

"On account of the polls——"

"Polls!"

"Yeah, polls. Fellow named Gordon down there explained it to me. Just suppose, for instance, they know that more people drink Schlepp's beer"—he held up his beer can—"than any other beer in the country. They *know* that because Schlepp's sells the most beer. So you can figure the average man drinks Schlepp's, right?"

"I suppose so."

"All right, so on the test they list four kinds of beer, and I check Schlepp's. They have about a thousand other things like that. So the guy who checks the most things that turn out to be what the average man drinks, eats, likes, thinks—he's the *most* average man. Isn't that right?"

"Yeah—but what for?"

"What do you mean, what for?" Al asked angrily.

"What for? That's all I want to know. So you get to be Yankee Doodle, what does it prove?"

"You know something," Al said. "I think you're jealous, that's what I think. You——"

"Jealous! Now you *are* crazy. What would I want to be a stupid Yankee Doodle for?"

"Stupid, huh. Listen, it's not so stupid. It's——"

"It's what?"

Al stared at the sweating beer can in his hands. "I don't know," he said. "But I do know," he said quickly as Ben looked triumphant, "what this guy John Bell said. He handed me a lot of stuff about Yankee Doodle and what it meant and stood for. Sounded pretty good too. And if you saw these offices the Consultants have you'd know they weren't kidding. That's big stuff." He paused. "And after a while, I got to thinking."

"About what?"

"Well, you know how you're always saying I sound off too much about what's wrong with the world."

"Sure, and I tell you either to shut up or run for Congress."

"And you're right. What good does it do a guy to make a lot of noise when he can't do anything about it?"

"So now you're gonna run for Congress, huh?"

Al shrugged.

"Oh, Al . . ."

"No"—grinning—"I'm not that nuts. But just think, Ben. Suppose I win this contest. Right away I'll be an important guy. The man said I'd be a *spokesman* for the average man. Boy . . ." He eyed the opposite hedge dreamily.

"And what would you say for us poor average men?" Ben asked lightly.

"I don't know yet. I'd have to give that some thought."

"Whatever you do, don't be like Sadie. These clubs she belongs to, they drive me crazy. All this running around, and nothing happens except I get a headache. You ought to be glad Emily got out of all that."

"She doesn't have time now with the kids."

Ben looked thoughtful. "Maybe you're right, Al. If somebody with the right ideas ever got to where he could say something—but it seems that every time somebody like that gets to that point he forgets what he wanted to say."

"It's a big responsibility," Al nodded.

He and Ben jumped guiltily as Emily's voice interrupted, "And right now, my fine average man, your responsibility is to get the storm windows down." She stood over him, arms akimbo.

Al scrambled to his feet. "I was just about to do that," he said, hastily climbing the ladder which Ben steadied for him. "Where are the kids?"

"Down playing ball. They wanted to go to the movies, but I said it was too nice a day."

"Why isn't Little Louie down there with them?"

"I wanted to keep him near the house. He didn't eat any breakfast, and he's in a state again."

"You coming over for the television tonight?" Ben asked.

"I suppose so," Emily said dispiritedly. "Can't miss Sunday—watch out, Al—night."

Ben grabbed at the teetering ladder and snickered. "If Al wins the contest they'll put him on television. Maybe with some pretty girls, huh, Al?"

"Faye Emerson," Al said. "Oh, boy." Gingerly he stepped down from the ladder holding a storm window. "Would you get jealous, Em?"

Turning away, Emily said, "More likely you go on puppet shows. That would make one more dummy added to the lot."

"That does it," Al said, leaning the window against the house.

"But you haven't done the upstairs yet."

"I have a personal rule. No insults while I work. If I get insults, I don't work. Let's get over to your place, Ben, and watch the ball game."

Ben shrugged and followed him through the hedge.

During the seventh inning it happened. Later, Al said it reminded him of Pearl Harbor day when he had been listening to a Giant football game, and the flash came over about the Japs bombing Honolulu. He could easily remember lying on the couch with the Sunday paper spread over his knees, a cold, gray day, and how the chicken Emily was cooking smelled so good all through the house. All he had to do was throw a little switch in his memory, and it came back to him, so clear and strong, like something etched out of hard metal.

Only this time it was spring, and, though it was again a Giant team, they were playing baseball, and the day was warm with the sweet smell of new grass coming strongly through the open windows. Ten years of progress had also brought the sight of the ball game into the home.

It happened at a crucial moment too, with the Giants a run behind; but Thomson was up with a man on . . .

Emily burst through the front door. "Al," she cried, "Al, the telephone."

Starting guiltily up from the chair in front of the television set, his mind was still absorbed in the fortunes of the struggling Giants.

"Hurry, Al, hurry."

"Wha' . . . oh, yeah." He started quickly from the room as he heard Emily say to Ben and Sadie, who had rushed from her kitchen, "I think it's those Consultants people," and they all followed him.

Little Louie was holding the receiver, and Al took it from his grasp. He stared at it for a long moment before putting it to his ear. Emily, Ben and Sadie watched him expectantly from the doorway.

"Hello. . . . Yes, this is Alfred Toolum. . . . Yes. . . . Yes. . . . Yes. . . . Yes. . . . Thank you. . . . What? Oh, sure, sure. 'Bye."

Dropping the receiver, he turned slowly to face his wife. "Em," he whispered, "I won."

"Oh, Al . . ."

Quickly Emily crossed to him and embraced him. "Oh, Al, isn't that wonderful?"

Al smiled at her. "Sure—wonderful."

Emily broke away. "We have to tell the boys. Little Louie, run right down to the park and get your brothers."

Little Louie darted from the room.

"And look out crossing the street," Emily cried after him.

Al turned to Ben and Sadie. "Well, what do you know!"

Sadie didn't look too impressed, but Ben, grinning, pursed his lips and began whistling a familiar melody.

Answering his grin, Al cried, "That's right, Ben, Yankee Doodle." He clapped his friend on the shoulder. "How about that, huh! I think it calls for another beer, don't you?"

"Al," Emily began, "don't you think . . . ?"

"My good woman," Al said, "according to a nation-wide survey, the average man drinks a hundred and six bottles of beer a year. Looks like I've got to catch up a little."

"What nation-wide survey?" Emily demanded.

Ignoring her, Al locked arms with Ben, and the two men

started out of the room. "Oh, and Emily," Al said over his shoulder, "if you're going to be the wife of a famous man you'd better get out the old home permanent. Your hair looks like hell."

"Oh," Emily gasped. "Oh!" And she and Sadie stared at each other as the two men left the house.

Though Al didn't get to sleep until three the following morning, he was wide awake at six thirty. For a long time he lay quite still, luxuriating in the warm comfort of the big double bed. With his cheek cupped in his palm he lay thinking what a wonderful life this was, after all. Just when you thought you'd go crazy with the rut you were in something always happened to jolt you into some exciting business.

It had been a great evening. At nine o'clock, when the kids were all in bed, Charlie Simpson, who owned the stationery store at the corner of Ninth and Main, had called excitedly to tell him that the morning papers were in from the city, and his picture was right on the front page of the *Mirror* and on page three of the *News*. Charlie himself had brought over a half-dozen copies of each, and from then on the phone had rung incessantly as friends saw the papers and called to congratulate him.

It wasn't everybody, after all, who got his picture in both the *News* and *Mirror* unless he was either a big-shot politician or sex criminal.

Slipping his feet from under the covers, he rose slowly, trying not to disturb Emily. Lord only knew when she had got to bed, because she'd insisted on cleaning up after everybody left, and he'd been too tired to stay up with her.

He groaned slightly as he raised his head. He should've taken Em's advice about the beer, but every time he decided to lay off someone else dropped in to toast his good fortune.

"Al."

He paused and saw Emily sitting upright in bed. "Go back to sleep," he whispered.

She waved him to sit down on the bed. "Al, how do you feel?"

"Pretty good. How do you feel?"

"Wonderful. You know, even though I got to bed so late it took me an hour to fall asleep."

He kissed her on the cheek. "Now, you just lie down and catch another snooze. I'll take care of the boys and breakfast and everything."

She nodded to him, and smiled as he left the room.

Padding down the hallway in his slippers, Al paused in front of the boys' room. Opening the door, he tiptoed inside and went to the double bunks occupied by Herman and Sherman.

"Pssst." He shook the figure in the top bunk. "Pssst, Sherman, wake up."

Sherman exhibited the buoyancy of youth by one moment being fast asleep, and the next being wide awake.

"What's the matter, Papa?"

Backing away and beckoning with his finger, Al whispered gleefully, "Come on downstairs, I've got something to show you."

"Watcha whispering for?"

Al looked over to the corner where Little Louie was peering up at him from his small bed.

"I didn't want to wake you up."

"You come bangin' in here . . ."

"I didn't bang," Al said. Walking to the bed, he reached down and thrust his finger into Little Louie's mouth. After a slight struggle he brought forth a wet mass of bubble gum. "I thought I told you the next time you went to sleep with gum I'd lick you."

Herman too was awake now. "You oughta sock him, Papa. He wanted water three times last night."

"A human camel," Al said, "right to his cud."

"I kept dreamin' I was thirsty," Little Louie protested.

Sherman was at the door. "What did you want to show me, Papa?"

"Oh, yeah. Everybody come downstairs."

The house was neat and clean again. Emily had done a good job, and the newspapers were piled carefully on the radio. Al passed them out, and he stood beaming at the consternation that followed.

"Boy," Sherman yipped, "there I am sitting next to Papa."

Al hooked his thumbs through the drawstring of his pajama trousers and rocked back and forth. "How about your old man *now,* boys!"

A chorus of yells answered him, and then he said, "Shushh, let's let your mother sleep. How about all of us pitching in and making breakfast. Maybe some French toast. Okay? I'll shave," he added, when the boys shook their heads.

When he emerged from his shower, Al found Little Louie sitting on a small stool next to the sink. He was reminded of their conversation the last time Little Louie had watched him shave.

"Still worried about this next year?" he asked as he lathered his face.

"Why?" Little Louie asked suspiciously.

"Well, I was going to say that now you had nothing to worry about. I'm going to be Yankee Doodle for a whole year—these Consultants *guarantee* it, and they're pretty powerful people."

Little Louie gave that some thought. "How many months until next January?"

The scraping of the razor ceased as Al counted. "Eight."

"Is my birthday at the beginning or the end?"

"Of what?"

"Of January."

"Right in the middle. January sixteenth."

"No it ain't."

"What do you mean it ain't."

"It's got a nine in it."

Al creased his brow. "That's right. I guess it's the nineteenth. It's Sherman who was born on the sixteenth. March sixteenth. I remember now, because I had to stall the income tax so I could pay the hospital bill." He winced as the razor nicked his chin. "Why are you wondering?"

"I was just figuring if I could go to school next year."

"Sure you will. You missed this year just by a couple of months. You might have gotten in then if the kindergartens weren't so crowded."

"Will I get a dog tag like Herman and Sherman have when I go to school? Those things they give out in case we get bombed."

"We're not going to get bombed," Al said.

"Then why do they give out those tags?"

"I don't know," Al said. "I don't know why they give them out except maybe because they have nothing else to do but go around scaring the hell out of people."

"I want a tag," Little Louie said, lowering his eyes. "If you have a tag you can't get lost. I don't ever want to get lost."

Rubbing his face dry, Al turned away from the sink. His skin burned terribly, almost bringing tears to his eyes. "You won't get lost, Little Louie," he said. "I promise."

Little Louie looked up at him, and then Al said, "Come on, you're supposed to be helping your brothers."

Emily came downstairs just as they were drinking their orange juice.

"Something's burning," she said.

At the sight of her, Al felt the irritation of one who offered a favor at personal sacrifice and was turned down. "Why aren't you sleeping?" he demanded.

"The flame under the skillet's too hot," Emily said, turning it down. "The toast is burning."

"Pour your mother coffee," Al instructed Herman as Emily sat down.

"I couldn't sleep," Emily said. "I'm much too excited."

"When do we get the presents?" Little Louie asked.

"Be patient," his mother said. "Al," she hesitated, "do you think I could—I mean, could I go to a beauty parlor sometime this week?"

He stirred his coffee. "What for?"

"Oh, I was thinking I might get a real permanent. You said my hair . . . Well, I want a *real* one."

"If that's all that's bothering you, go ahead. Get the works. I guess we can afford it."

"Will that make you pretty?" Little Louie wanted to know.

Herman and Sherman haw-hawed.

"What are you laughing at?" Al snapped. "Your mother doesn't need any beauty parlor to make her pretty."

He stood up. "Guess I'll get dressed and go now."

"It's early," Emily said. "You don't have to leave for an hour yet."

"Oh—I thought since it's such a nice morning I'd walk slow, maybe sit in the park a few minutes and look at the papers."

Emily smiled understandingly. "Have fun, Al."

Charlie Simpson was out in front of his store arranging papers in the rack.

" 'Morning, Charlie," Al called.

"Hi, Al, how do you feel this morning?"

"Great."

"That was a swell little party you had last night. Come in for coffee?"

"Just had some, thanks."

"Seen the *Times* and *Tribune?*"

Al shook his head.

"Page thirty-six of the *Tribune,* but no picture, and *nothing* in the *Times.*"

"Nothing in the *Times,* huh? Well, gimme a *Trib.*"

He handed Charlie a nickel. "Wonder what the afternoon papers will do," Charlie conjectured.

Al shrugged and yawned. "Who knows? See you, Charlie."

"Take it easy, Al."

He continued down the street, suppressing the urge to open the paper. "Nothing in the *Times,*" he muttered to himself. "I bet if it was about some rich millionaire . . ." And a couple of months ago he had even thought of taking a subscription. Just because Emily heard some guy lecturing who said that every thinking American should read the *Times* every day! And they don't even print important news like Yankee Doodle.

"Think it's going to rain today, Mr. Toolum?"

He looked up to see George Bower regarding him in a friendly manner as he opened the door of his department store. George Bower was a very rich man; he and Al rarely did more than nod to each other.

"Rain?" Al paused. "I hadn't noticed."

"I'll tell you," Bower said in a confidential voice, "I've got a sale starting today, and I'm a little worried. Thought you might have some advance word."

Noticing a *News* folded under Bower's arm, Al cleared his throat and stared into the sky. "Southwesterly wind," he said. "Hmmm. I guess it'll be okay unless we get a shift." His mind flashed to a news report he'd heard early the evening before. "Warm front on its way from the Great Lakes area. I think you're pretty safe, Mr. Bower."

Bower nodded, satisfied. Then he said, "Haven't seen Mrs. Toolum recently although she still has her charge account."

Automatically, Al opened his mouth to complain about the increasing cost of living, but he stopped himself in time. "You know, we were talking about that just a day or two ago, and Mrs. Toolum was saying she needed some new clothes."

"I'll wait on her personally," Bower said.

They nodded, and Al resumed his walk down the street, a feeling of well-being swelling his chest. Then he was overcome by slight shame at the lie he had told Mr. Bower. He and Emily had talked about her clothes, but when she had timidly suggested she needed something new he had reminded her that she'd already got a dress that year. Yes, she had said, but she'd gone to Fourteenth Street in New York for it, and here she was walking around with practically nothing to wear. Well, what about me, Al had told her, my *new* suit is so old you can see your reflection in it. . . .

"I'll send her down this week," Al promised himself.

Now Main Street was more populated, and at almost every step he was greeted by people, some of whom he didn't even know. By the time he got to the park he was wearing a broad smile that, when he realized it, made him look like some phony politician. But it was nice answering all the waves.

Sitting on a bench he turned leisurely to page thirty-six of the *Tribune*. There it was, all right, in two columns on the bottom left-hand side of the page.

FERNVALE MAN PICKED
AS NATION'S MOST AVERAGE

the headline read, and Al studied the story that followed. He was greatly impressed by its dignity and wondered where they'd gotten all that information about him. Then he remembered there was nothing they wouldn't know after seeing his answers to the test questions. Folding the paper carefully, he rose and turned toward the plant.

When he entered the front door of the Acme Tool & Die Works, Henry Muller, Pres., he punched the time clock as he had for the past sixteen years (with three years' leave for army service) and made his way toward the desk where, as foreman, he surveyed the workings of the entire first floor. But before he reached the large workroom, Henry Muller popped out of his small office.

"Al, wait a minute." He thrust out his hand. "Congratulations, Al."

"Thanks, Henry."

"I was going to call last night when I saw it in the newspaper, but I thought you would be so busy——"

"Oh, a bunch of people dropped in, and before you knew it we had a party going. You should have come over, Henry."

"Al"—Henry's thin face grew serious—"what's all this going to mean?"

"I don't know. What could it mean?"

"Well, will you have to leave us, or—or what?"

"Oh, *no*. It just lasts a year, and I don't think it'll take much time. Heck, I haven't any idea what I'm supposed to do."

Henry showed relief. "I'd hate to lose a good man like you, Al. But I should think at least you'd want to take the day off."

"What for?"

Henry clapped him on the back. "Okay, Al, then we go to work."

All morning people approached his desk to offer congratulations. At first they seemed embarrassed that one in their midst had gained such sudden notoriety, but when they saw how calmly Al was taking his fame, they loosened up.

"Maybe you have to stick a feather in your hat and ride around town on a pony," Paul Musiker called over from his bench.

Al grinned, but he was struck with sudden horror. Maybe he *would*. But, no, John Bell had assured him that everything would be on a very dignified plane.

At eleven o'clock Henry entered the shop. "Al, your wife just called. You gotta go home right away. She says there's all kinds of newspapermen there."

"Newspapermen! What am I going to do?"

"Go home. I said you could have the day off."

"I'm sorry, Henry."

"That's all right, Al. Just make sure they mention you work at the Acme Tool & Die Company."

He counted six cars parked in front of the house before he got up the nerve to go in. A harassed Emily spotted him sidling in through the front door and rushed to him.

"Al, I'm so glad you're here."

He surveyed the room. Of the eight or nine people there he recognized only John Bell. The others were gathered in a knot around Little Louie who was perched on top of Al's console.

"Oh, he's okay, I guess," he heard Little Louie saying. "He doesn't lick me *very* often."

One of the men, identified as a reporter by the pencil and notebook he held in his hand, said, "So the great average parent now believes in corporal punishment again. Well, that's one advance anyway."

"Depends on the kid," Al said, pushing his way through the group. "Get off there, Little Louie, before I belt you one."

"But he's so cute," a lady reporter said.

Al's arm was grasped firmly by John Bell. "I'm glad you could make it," he said. "Didn't the phone call yesterday make it plain we'd be out here today?"

Al shook his head. "If it did, I didn't hear it."

"You must have been too excited. All right, everybody, let's get set for some pictures. Mrs. Toolum, if you'll just stand with your husband in a natural pose."

"Some one give her a rolling pin," a voice said, and everyone laughed. Al's was a little hollow.

"Oh, I couldn't," Emily protested. "My hair . . ."

"I'm sure the housewives of America will understand," John said, urging her into position. "This is just a preliminary, anyway. The actual ceremony will be on Friday when Mr. Toolum gets his scroll. Someone very important will make the presentation."

"Who? The assemblyman from the district?" It was the reporter who approved of corporal punishment.

John eyed the man balefully, and while the photographers were getting set, he worked his way to the reporter.

"Take it easy, Mac," he said softly, "we've all got a living to make."

"What's the pitch here anyway?"

"No pitch."

"Then what's the pay-off?"

"No pay-off either. This is strictly on the level."

The reporter smiled. "Yes, sir, may I quote you on that?"

John looked at him thoughtfully. "Isn't your publisher on our board of directors?"

The reporter looked equally thoughtful, and then he began to write. "I am quoting you," he said.

The bulbs popped, and Emily winced as she saw the photographers tossing them carelessly into a corner. But before she could get to the bulbs and pick them up, the lady reporter was asking her questions.

No, she didn't have much time to herself with three children. . . . Yes, a little canasta now and then. . . . Milton Berle? Uh-uh, couldn't stand him any more. . . . That's right, they had no television set. . . . Well, she hadn't really thought of Al being so average. He'd always seemed special to her. . . .

"Oh, that's very sweet," the lady reporter said. Squinting at her notes, she said, "Herman, Sherman and Little Louie. How euphonious!"

"They are not," Al interrupted hotly. "They're perfectly legitimate family names."

"But I didn't——"

"Herman was my grandfather's name, Sherman my wife's brother's name in California, and Louis is her uncle's name."

A reporter tugged on Al's sleeve. "I heard your wife say you don't have a television set. How come?"

"That may be embarrassing," John said. "Perhaps Mr. Toolum's budget . . ."

"Oh, we could afford one," Al said. "I just don't want my kids jammed up in front of one of those things all night long."

"But the average man usually has a television set."

"I don't. And unless it gets better I won't. That awful stuff all day and night. Junk."

John Bell was getting nervous. "But the boys read comics, don't they?"

"Can't keep them out of the house," Al said sadly. "Tried for years, but it didn't do any good. It's like the creeping death."

"Nobody approves of comic books," John said confidently.

"And the radio," Al started loudly, "instead of getting better it gets worse all——"

"Well, that's all," John stated, even more loudly than Al. "I see that Mrs. Toolum is anxious to get to her housework."

In no time he had herded everyone from the room, but a minute later he was back alone. He was perspiring.

"Mr. Toolum, since you and I are going to see a lot of each other for the next few months, perhaps we'd better have a little talk."

"That's a good idea," Al said. "I kind of had the feeling I said something wrong at the end there."

"Oh, no," John said hastily. "It's just that those reporters— well, they're a pretty cynical bunch. Nothing they'd like better than to get you to say something that'd make us all look a little foolish. That's their business, you know?"

"Fine business," Emily said. Then an idea struck her. "Why

don't you come to dinner, Mr. Bell, and bring Miss McClain? Sherman was telling us all about her."

John nodded enthusiastically and then said he had to get back to the office.

"About Friday," Al hesitated. "What's my boss going to say?"

"Don't you think he'll be reasonable when he learns how much publicity he's going to get out of this? Anyway, he won't be required to pay you during your time off. That comes from us as a legitimate expense. What do you think?"

"I guess Henry'll be reasonable. As long as it's not too much at a time."

"Tomorrow, then, if that's all right with you, Mrs. Toolum," John said.

"Six o'clock," Emily nodded.

Little Louie blocked John's way at the door. "When are the presents getting here?" he demanded.

Grinning down at him, John patted his head. "I promise delivery tomorrow—Ouch!"

"He doesn't like people patting him on the head," Emily said apologetically. "He bites."

"Sweet," John murmured, rubbing his wrist. "See you tomorrow."

The door closed.

Al watched Emily pick up the flashbulbs. "Looks like we're really in for it now. I wonder . . ."

"It'll be all right, Al. Should I get a roast beef for tomorrow night?"

"Anything you like." He stared helplessly around the room. "No sense in going back to the shop. Maybe I should take down the rest of the storm windows as long as I'm home."

"After lunch you could watch Little Louie while I went to the beauty parlor," Emily suggested.

"Okay. Come on, son, you can hold the ladder." Stripping off his coat and tie, he put them in the hall closet. "And when I say hold it, I don't mean push it." They went out the door.

Walking briskly to the telephone, Emily dialed a number, waited a moment, and then said, "Hello, Armando, this is Mrs. Toolum. . . . No, I haven't been away, just too busy to come around. I'd like an appointment for one thirty. The works, Armando, everything. You're going to have to make me into a new woman. It's important. . . ."

A loud crash sounded outside the house, and Emily said, "Just a minute," and ran to the window. There was Little Louie scooting through the front gate as fast as his legs would carry him, and close behind was Al. Emily breathed a sigh of relief. At least they were both on their feet.

Back at the phone she said, "Better make that two o'clock, Armando. Something's just come up that's liable to take a little time."

Six

As he was preparing to leave the office Tuesday afternoon, John Bell was called into Paul Welton's office. Nervously reviewing events up to date to see where he might be called to account, he carefully cleared his desk and then proceeded slowly to Welton's office. His leisure was a studied thing, part of the protocol in AAC. Paul Welton professed to despise yes men, and eager rushing about in answer to a summons was condemned as part of the yessing process.

"Come in, Bell." Welton leaned back in his chair, locking his hands behind his head.

John noticed the pile of newspapers on one corner of the desk, and Welton, seeing the direction of his glance, said pleasantly, "Nice press."

John nodded, a touch of modesty balancing the triumph that was deserved. "With that base, sir, we can really build. About Friday——"

"Only one thing." The well-oiled chair snapped forward. "This reference to Toolum's attitude toward radio and television. Rather snide, don't you think?"

"Purely the reporter's fault," John said, reminding himself that he had planned to write a stinging letter to the editor. "Toolum has the average man's viewpoint toward these media; after all, he's conditioned by the constant hammering of the critics . . ."

"The critics," Welton snorted, making the word sound like a curse. "And what about his not having a television set? That's not going to sit very well——"

Certain of his facts, John felt safe in interrupting. "Strange as it may seem, sir, the lack of a TV set scored in Toolum's favor on our test. Latest figures show that, despite the fact that the coaxial cable's been in full operation for several months now, there are still wide areas that lack television in this country. There are less than twenty million sets in operation. The average man *doesn't* have a set."

"Still," Welton grumbled, "he lives in a TV area." He was struck by a sudden thought. "We'll give him one. He can't refuse it."

John nodded in agreement as Welton savored the idea. "We must remember, sir," John said, "that little things like this will crop up every once in a while. The Machine picked Toolum as the *most* average man, not the perfect average man, which, of course, would be impossible to find. Matter of fact, if we found the perfect average man we'd have no more contest. But polls show public taste changing all the time, so that next year a man very different from Toolum will be Yankee Doodle '53."

"Quite true," Welton murmured. "Now about Friday . . ." He looked questioningly at John.

John ticked off the points on his fingers. "I have the newsreels lined up and, of course, television. We have the scroll, but what remains is the person to make the presentation. Movie star or politician?"

"This has to be dignified, Bell," Welton said, after the proper consideration, "so I'd say a political figure. The average-man concept fits in with politics."

Remembering the reporter's crack about the local assemblyman, John hastened to say, "He has to be big, Mr. Welton."

Paul Welton made a steeple of his fingers. "Is it too late to rearrange things and go to Washington on Friday? I'm sure the President——"

Regretfully, "I'm afraid it is too late, sir."

"Then I guess a senator."

"Can we get one at this short notice?"

"Mr. Bell, all we do is say newsreel-television, and then step out of the way of the stampede." He nodded abruptly. "That's all then, Bell. You'll have Toolum briefed by Friday."

"I'm going to his house for dinner tonight, sir."

Paul Welton sighed. "You'll probably get an excellent home-cooked meal, something I haven't enjoyed in almost twenty years." He patted his stomach gently. "The price we pay, Bell. . . ."

Barbie was waiting for him. The invitation to Fernvale had been his first chance to mediate the quarrel in the cocktail lounge. From that afternoon until this morning Barbie had said nothing to him except what was necessary to carry out their daily business. He had done nothing to break through her anger, because, primarily, he believed himself right. There was altogether too much criticism of the advertising business, he felt; it amounted to near-hysteria. Everyone wanted to get in on the act, from within as well as without, to see who could knock the hardest and loudest. John had no more loyalty to the business than he would have given to any job that paid him a living, but he had made his choice, and he felt peculiarly unneurotic about his work. He was under no illusions, wanted to change nothing and quite happily thanked providence for giving him the talent that allowed him to make a lot of money without any struggle.

But whenever he tried to explain this to someone he found himself against a solid wall of prejudice, the thesis being that no honest man could actually do what he was doing without developing terrible guilt feelings (which he completely lacked), ulcers (which showed no signs of developing), and a desire to *do* something. Patiently he tried to explain that he *was* doing something: a job that paid him extremely well; and, though the business could be proved by its critics to be based in something slightly less than ideally honest, it was a business firmly a part of American culture, viewed with respect in the accepted order of things and not quite on the same plane with peddling dope. Until this changed, John was all for it.

He believed in Yankee Doodle, because it "had everything" as far as the advertising business was concerned, getting right to the core of the mass market. It was a gem of an idea, and would make him famous in the industry. Perhaps, he reasoned, Barbie resented this, because it was so perfect. She could punch no holes in his cloud.

He philosophically accepted the fact that she was accompanying him to the Toolums' tonight only because she wanted to be around while he worked on Mr. Toolum.

They left from a parking lot near the office in a car borrowed from Arthur Gordon, and little was said while John threaded through the late afternoon traffic. Once they were off the Fifty-ninth Street Bridge and the traffic had thinned, the atmosphere between them grew less strained.

"On days like this," he offered, "sometimes I wish I lived outside the city. Then, before I get too carried away, I think of commuting, lawn-mowing and the other accumulated joys of suburban life, and I thank heaven for my Eleventh Street haven."

"I agree," Barbie nodded, and glancing sideways she caught his look of exaggerated surprise. Analyzing the look correctly, she laughed. "Yes, we *do* agree on something."

"I like New York. Always have."

"You were brought up around here, weren't you?"

"Small town right over the Connecticut line. Used to have a nice atmosphere that's completely gone now. It's just far enough from town to make the trip in a chore, but close enough to come in when there's something worth while to do. I wanted to go to Columbia, but my father insisted on Harvard. I compromised by coming to New York every other weekend."

Barbie removed her hat and allowed the wind to whip through her hair; she stretched, feeling comfortable and relaxed. She stilled the small voice in her mind that told her she should be angry with John, and then she tried to picture him as he might have been living in a small Connecticut town. Barbie knew small towns all too well, having escaped, when she was old enough to go to college, the Ohio village where her father was still the only doctor. Except for short annual visits, she never wanted to go back. New York was wonderful, offering everything in fair return for what you gave. That phrase "fair return" reminded her that John had applied it to Mr. Toolum. Perhaps he was right.

She eyed him now, glad that he had asked her along, because in addition to wanting to see Mr. Toolum again, she always felt good with John when they were away from the office. He was an easy person to like because of his easy ways, and she often wondered why she continually baited him about his work. She didn't really want to, because of her feeling for John; yet she lived with the uneasy feeling that all her beliefs were negated when she abetted John Bell's work.

Her hand fell upon a small, neatly wrapped package on the seat between them, and she asked, "What's this?"

"Candy for Mrs. Toolum. With all the attention being paid to her husband, and the kids getting those prizes, I thought she might feel a little left out. So I picked this up at lunch."

She smiled at his thoughtfulness. "Johnny . . ."

"Yeah?"

"I have two tickets to the ballet Saturday night and no one to go with. Will you take me?"

"Say, that would be great."

"Maybe—maybe a bite at my place before we go, okay?"

"If I buy the wine."

"You buy the wine."

"Wonderful," he said.

She moved a little closer to him—to get out of the wind, she told herself, but when her arm came in close contact with his, she didn't take it away.

Meanwhile, preparations for the dinner were taking place in the Toolum household. Emily had spent the entire afternoon shopping and gathering the necessary implements for the special event. Soup dishes from Sadie, sterling salt and pepper shakers from Laura Brown and a flower arrangement by old Mrs. Pennyworth who, twice a year, lectured on flower arrangement at the Minute Maids.

Now, with dinner under control, Emily sat, with growing excitement, in front of her dressing table. The whole impact of Al's being made Yankee Doodle seemed to be coming to a climax this evening. Up until now Emily had been too confused by the array of events, the visit of the newspaper people, to realize that it was all actually true. But tonight important people were coming to dinner, strangers who, suddenly, without warning, had become a tremendous influence in their lives. Emily tried to delve into the rosy fog that was the future, but unable to see past immediate joy of the present, she decided to relax and enjoy the moment. That is, she could relax if only the success of the dinner didn't worry her.

A furious pounding out in the hall shook her into reality. Her own image in the mirror came into focus, and she realized that the pounding was now accompanied by Al's shouting. She ran to the door.

"Al, what's the matter? What are you doing?"

Al stood in front of the bathroom door. "Will you get those three kids of yours the hell out of the bathroom so I can dress," he demanded.

She knocked lightly on the door. "Boys," she called, "boys."

Herman's voice answered. "Yeah, Mama."

"What are you doing in there?"

"Washing like you said—only Little Louie doesn't want to."

"Well—hurry up and get out of there. Your father has to get dressed."

"Oh," Sherman said, "is that what he was knocking for?"

Al ground his teeth.

Emily made a helpless gesture and then patted his cheek. "They'll be out in a minute, dear."

She started away, and he grabbed her arm. "Hey," he said, grinning. "You look nice."

"Thank you. Or, rather, you should thank Armando."

"I will—next time I need a marcel. And, Em"—as he released her—"don't worry about tonight. Everything's going to be fine."

"I hope so," she said, as the bathroom door opened with a clatter, and three naked boys rushed past. Emily intercepted the third figure, and, clutching him firmly, inspected him with the eye of experience. Without letting go her grip, she passed him over to his father.

"While you're in there, Al—the ears and neck."

Al accepted his burden with exaggerated patience and disappeared into the bathroom. Little Louie howled.

Scrubbed, dressed, and with his hair almost slicked down, Sherman was the outpost who spotted John and Barbie driving up to the curb.

"Hey, they're comin'," he shouted, and the house sprang into action. The entire family lined up at the door to greet the visitors.

It was perfectly obvious to Barbie, as she came through the door, that this was a special occasion for the Toolums, for there was an electric tension in the air. When Barbie was introduced to Emily, Herman and Little Louie, the last-named was heard to whisper loudly to Sherman, "Aw, she ain't so hot," a statement which Al covered with effusive greetings, and John helped by handing Emily the box of candy.

Terribly pleased, Emily accepted the gift and told John he shouldn't have done it.

"I was telling Barbie on the way up, Mrs. Toolum, that you were probably feeling left out of everything. I thought the candy might help a little. Which reminds me, did the prizes get here?"

"A truckload of them," Al said from the closet where he was hanging up Barbie's jacket.

"It was only a small truck," Little Louie said.

They flowed from the door into the living room. "Your hair looks wonderful, Mrs. Toolum," Barbie said. "Do you have it done in the city?"

Emily made an unconscious gesture toward her newly waved locks. "No, we have a man in town who's very good. Armando, his name is. He used to be with Charles of the Ritz."

"They all used to be with Charles of the Ritz," Al said. "He must be like the Mayflower." He glanced at his wrist watch. "Three minutes after six, Em."

"Dinner is served," Emily said.

Al gallantly offered Barbie his arm as Emily hastened into the kitchen. "I should really help Mrs. Toolum," Barbie said.

Overhearing, Emily called, "Everything is ready. I'll only be a minute."

Barbie turned to Al and said, "I must congratulate you, Mr. Toolum. After all, I have a personal interest in you, since you're like the home team." She couldn't resist a significant glance at John.

Al moved her chair back from the table.

"What's Papa doin'?" Little Louie demanded of Herman.

"Helping her with her chair, stupid."

"Her arm busted?"

"Naw, it's polite."

"Hey, Papa," Little Louie called, "help me with my chair too."

"Sit down and be quiet—dear," Al said.

Carrying the roast, Emily set it down in front of Al and then surveyed the table. Everything looked good, from the gleaming silverware to the snowy cloth, and now she was glad she had done the work all by herself. For several wild moments earlier that day she'd considered hiring a girl to cook and serve, but she'd never had another woman in her kitchen before, and now, she'd decided, was no time to start. Then she thought that sometime during the dinner she might casually remark, "The maid got sick early this morning which is why I had to do everything myself," but such a statement would never sit well with Al, even if it got by unnoticed with the boys.

Now she felt better. Miss McClain looked very nice, and Mr. Bell seemed much more easygoing than he had the day before.

She sat down just as Little Louie, holding up his cloth napkin, said, "Hey, what's these things?"

"Ha, ha," Al laughed. "Always making jokes. You know that's your napkin."

"They make 'em outta this stuff now? Why ain't I ever seen it before?"

Emily was about to make some light remark to excuse Little Louie's excesses, but when she looked up she saw John and Barbie smiling understandingly.

"They've been away in the chest a long time," Emily said, "but I guess I didn't realize how long. We don't often have important company."

"I feel embarrassed," John said. "Frankly I'd much prefer eating in the kitchen off old china. Whenever I see beautiful plates like these I remember when I was a kid and my mother used to threaten me before a big dinner. She prized her best set of dishes more than worrying about my desperate fear of breaking a dish."

"Next time we'll eat in the kitchen," Emily smiled.

"Important company," Little Louie grumbled; "when *my* friends come——"

Al leaned over to him. "Little Louie," he interrupted softly, "for the next half hour the only time I want to see your mouth moving is when you are chomping on some food, or"—his voice dropped still lower—"I will stuff one of these beautiful plates right down your fat little throat. Understand?" Without waiting for an answer, he turned to Barbie. "Potatoes, Miss McClain?"

"Just one, please." Holding her plate, she turned to Sherman. "I was telling John about your poetry. He's very interested."

"That I am," John said. "Will you show me some after dinner?"

Sherman hung his head. "It—it ain't much."

"Do you read a lot of poetry in school?" John asked. 'Abou Ben Adam, may his tribe increase . . .' Did you have to memorize that?"

"I did," Herman said. "What a dopey poem."

"They don't learn anything these days," Al said. "They're too busy diving under desks."

"Diving?" John looked puzzled. "Oh, you mean——"

"Atom bombs," Herman said with relish. "When they drop 'em we have to get under the desks for protection."

"Or else everybody will get killed," Sherman added.

"They have special desks," Al said. "Atom bombproof."

"A dream world," John murmured.

Al regarded him questioningly. "I said people are living in a dream world," John repeated. "They talk in terms of *after* an atom war."

Al shrugged. "I was reading a story in the paper the other day by some old guy—they said he was a famous philosopher, but I'd never heard of him—and *he* said the world has always gone through these—he called them trumers——"

"Tramers," Emily said.

"Trauma," John said.

"Well, whatever," Al nodded, "and we all have to take the Long View. Aha, I said to myself, here's a guy with the answer, so I read on and find out that the Long View means that five hundred years from now people will still be around." He spread his hands in a gesture of disgust. "So this is a new idea? I could've told him that. The thing I'm interested in is *I* won't be around. *Now's* when I'm interested."

"The Long View has always provided philosophers with comfort," John said, "especially old ones."

"Old is right. On the bottom of the page in small print it said this guy is eighty-six, never was married and lives in California in a big house with two servants." His fork jabbed toward his three boys in quick succession. "See those three? That's why I can't take any Long View. Herman, there, had colic for seven months when he was born, and in that time Emily and I didn't get one good night's sleep. I walked the floor with that kid till my feet were worn down to my knees." He grunted. "What for? So he could be blown up by an atom bomb?"

John regarded him helplessly. "Mr. Toolum, yours is a question parents have been asking since wars were fought with people throwing rocks at each other. It's a little beyond me . . ."

Al looked a little disappointed. Not that he had any right to be, he supposed, but he had thought maybe a man like John Bell would have something important to say on the question. Nobody *he* knew did anything but grumble and look a little sick whenever war was discussed. "Only thing," he said, "you go on hoping. That Machine of yours—it's supposed to know all the answers, isn't it?"

"Only on the basis of the preknowledge we put in it," John said. "If we inject a formula the Machine operates with that. Where's the formula for stopping wars?"

"You'll have a chance to speak to a senator about it on Friday," Barbie said. "Mr. Welton's arranged to have one present you with the scroll."

Al's eyes lit up. "A senator! Boy, if Ben Carroway could only see that."

"He can watch it on television," John suggested; "or, bring him along. We'll have room for a couple of your friends—and, of course, your family."

Chewing contemplatively, Al said, "Better get a new suit, and, Em, you have to get a new dress. We can't meet a senator in old clothes. Hey, this is liable to run into money."

"You'll be reimbursed for legitimate expenses," John said hastily. "I want to talk to you about that."

"Eat now, and talk later," Emily said. "I can't stand to see all this good food get cold."

When dinner was finished, Barbie insisted on helping Emily with the dishes, and over Emily's voluble protests the two women disappeared into the kitchen. Al led John into the living room, pressed a cigar into his hand and urged him into an easy chair.

"Okay," he announced, "Music Appreciation. Let's go, boys." Turning to John, "We always play music after dinner. It's supposed to aid digestion. Besides," he added, from his position at the record rack, "it's pretty good music."

John relaxed, puffing happily at the cigar. Watching the boys arranging themselves on the couch he wondered if this were a put-up job to impress him. But the kids seemed perfectly natural about it.

A minute later he straightened up in surprise. The music that boomed out of the console was one of his favorite symphonies; whereas, he had expected—he didn't know *what* he had expected.

When the final note sounded, Al turned off the console and carefully replaced the record. "All right, boys, upstairs for a while." The kids scampered out of the room. "Usually we have more," Al said to John, "but I figured you wanted to talk."

"That was Beethoven's Sixth, wasn't it?"

"Yeah, I kind of like it." Apologetically, "That's the one thing we got some good out of when Emily joined a club. They took a course, and the ladies learned a lot about this stuff."

"Have you much of a collection?"

"Not so big." He glanced shamefacedly at John. "I got the lp attachment free when I bought twenty-five dollars' worth of records. Not a bad deal."

John cleared his throat. "Well, we'd better get down to business."

"There's one thing," Al said. "You have to tell me what to do on Friday. I don't want to look like one of those yokels in the newsreel who just won a sweepstake. I think they use the same people every year."

John nodded and said he'd have a statement prepared for Al to study. Then he said, "Here's the main story. You got a lot of initial publicity, Mr. Toolum, and there'll be more. You'll be known throughout the whole country as a result of this campaign."

"That's fine," Al interrupted, "but what for?"

"I'm getting to that. Once you're known, once you've been built as a figure of trust, you'll be—I won't say the word used, but, rather, employed—employed as a combination guinea pig for new products and endorser of old, *and,*" he emphasized, "for all this you'll be paid, and paid well."

Al showed bewilderment, and John scratched his chin thoughtfully. "Let me explain more fully. You see, the manufacturer in this country depends mainly on the average man—the mass market. Few products are directed toward special groups. You as the *most* average man will carry a lot of weight. People will believe you. We're getting away from the snob appeal in advertising. Just because some big shot drinks a brand of liquor is no reason for you to drink it."

"I don't drink liquor," Al said. "It gives me a headache."

"Well—beer, cigarettes, soup—it's all the same. And as a guinea pig you'll be employed to test certain new products. Say a company comes up with a new breakfast food. Usually they go through fantastic laboratory tests, spot checks all over the country, big expensive campaigns. You're their short cut. You taste it, like it and say so——"

"Suppose I don't like it," Al said in alarm.

"Then you say so," John smiled. "The manufacturer wants to know that too."

"And I can't say I smoke a certain kind of cigarette when I don't," Al said. "I hear that's done all the time."

"You won't have to do anything against your principles," John assured him.

Their chores completed, Emily and Barbie entered the room and made themselves comfortable as the two men continued their conversation. Emily thought how businesslike Al looked, weighing decisions, thinking out some of John Bell's suggestions. Al was meant for a real desk job, Emily decided. Not that she ever was ashamed of his work, she hastened to tell herself, but—but it would be nice if he had an important job in a big building like the one he described where the AAC offices were. Al had so much ability, but ability can only be measured against the opportunity a man was offered to use the ability. Perhaps this whole Yankee Doodle affair would bring him to the attention of people who would give him that opportunity.

There was a lull in the discussion, and Emily asked a question that had been bothering her. "I heard you say something about Al being paid," she hesitated. "How much will he get?"

John pursed his lips. "I would say, at an estimate, that this year will be worth anywhere from fifteen to twenty thousand dollars to you."

Al almost fell out of his chair. "Fif . . . ! Holy cow! Emily, did you hear that?"

"That's just an estimate," John said hastily. "It could be more, it could be less."

"I had no idea," Al said in wonderment. "I thought this was just some little thing where I got my picture in the paper a couple of times, and that's all."

"Hardly that," John said. "This campaign will be one of the most expensive we've ever run. But we expect the returns to be well worth it."

"Gee," Al said dreamily, "we can have the roof fixed."

Emily hardly heard him. She was too stunned. Fifteen or twenty thousand dollars. More money than they'd ever hoped to have at one time. How many times, when they were really broke, when Al's income was hardly enough to cover the expenses of running a house, had she lain awake worrying, torturing herself with the anguish of a future without money? And when all real solutions to their problems were discarded as too improbable, she would always succumb to the *most* improbable solution—a surprise windfall. It had always taken the form of an unknown relative's dying, because a family myth that Emily had grown up with dealt with a ne'er-do-well cousin who in the early 1900's had emigrated to South Africa. The myth—it was nothing else, since no one had ever heard from the cousin again—told how he had made a fortune in ostrich feathers. When ostrich feathers were no longer popular, it was said, the cousin went into the Kimberley diamond fields and made a big strike. This all was a nice family dream to have, and others, besides Emily, had used the cousin while in the throes of personal financial despair.

But here it was—and real! "And just think," Emily marveled, "all because of *Family Friend* magazine. Al, we have to renew our subscription."

A voice, Sherman's, interrupted from the stairs, pleading to be allowed to come down.

"Sure, sure," Al called, "come on down."

When the three boys trooped into the room, Al pulled Sherman to him lovingly and drew him to his lap. "Sherman," he said, "you are a very nice boy. If you were the only one I had I would say you were my favorite."

"And what a fine poet," Emily added.

"The best," Al said. Suddenly he rose, dumping Sherman from his lap. "Which reminds me," he cried, "what are you wasting time for? Write more poetry; enter more contests!"

"Chain him to his desk," John Bell suggested.

Al nodded, pointing dramatically toward the stairs. "A good idea, and who knows, in a year or so I can retire. Well"—nudging Sherman with his toe— "what are you waiting for?"

Seven

After work on Thursday Al walked slowly down Main Street toward the Bower Department Store. From all sides came greetings, both from people he knew and from people who, he figured, recognized him from his pictures in the paper. This was a new experience for Alfred Toolum, to be lauded by admirers, and his slow pace increased the enjoyment of the situation. Besides, he owed it to his public to give them a good look, and also to prove that fame could not swerve him from the course of democratic friendliness.

As he walked he compared his situation with that of other people he had seen and envied in times past. He remembered the welcome to Eisenhower to which, still in uniform, he had taken Herman and how the roaring millions had adored the hero. And Al, pushed and harried, his back almost broken from carrying Herman in a position where the boy could see, had experienced a moment of pure bitterness at the thought of the disparity between him and the general. They both wore the same uniform with only five stars and a few stripes to distinguish between them; they had both fought in the same war—well, they had both *been* in the same war, and yet Al was a nothing. Now he was no longer a nothing.

And he recalled a time twenty years before when his best friend, Jimmy Kane, and he had sat on a street corner of Fernvale for at least five hours in a burning hot sun waiting to see Lindbergh shortly after the flyer's return to America after his Paris flight. They had sat, along with dozens of their neighbors, telling each other how silly it was to spend a day doing this, but there had been a tremendous fascination in the thought of seeing Lindbergh, something Al could never explain. It was the kind of fascination that made him look at every parade, no matter what the cause, as long as there was the promise of band music, flying flags and, best of all, roaring motorcycle escorts. With Lindbergh there had been no band, no flags—and only two motorcycles flanking the open touring car. And the car had sped by so fast that Al hadn't even been able to distinguish between Lindbergh and the other men who sat with him in the car. He and Jimmy had gone home, empty and disappointed, telling themselves that they had been defrauded. A hero should take into consideration that his public has gone through hours of discomfort and at least wave even if he couldn't go more slowly.

So Al strolled down Main Street that Thursday afternoon, and for a little while he was an Eisenhower, a Lindbergh, a MacArthur —until his dream was exploded with atomic suddenness by Emily's urgent voice.

"Al, for *crying* out loud, what are you crawling along for?"

"Oh." He had reached Bower's, and there was Emily regarding him with asperity. "Oh, I didn't know what time it was."

"You're fifteen minutes late," Emily said, taking his arm, "and if you expect to get any alterations on your suit tonight we'd better get in right now."

As they walked into the store he ran over any number of retorts to her remark about his lateness: "I guess *you've* never been late," he could have said; or, "How about that time I was supposed to meet . . ." or "Remember that cold night I waited . . ." but he said none of them, and then they were being greeted by Mr. Bower himself as they entered the men's-ware department. Emily broke through his effusive welcome by saying that Al wanted to get a suit.

"Wonderful. What did you have in mind, Mr. Toolum?"

"Well, I was thinking——"

"Blue," Emily said. "Perhaps with a nice soft chalk stripe."

That's just what I was thinking, Al told himself.

George Bower asked what size.

"Forty-two," Al started to say, but Emily regarded him as though he were an idiot. "You take a forty-four, Alfred Toolum. You haven't been able to get into a forty-two since you got out of uniform."

Al shrugged. Forty-four.

They walked to a rack, and Mr. Bower pulled out a suit. "This is nice. It's, uh, eighty-five fifty."

Al started to shake his head, but Emily said firmly, "Try it on, Al."

He went into one of the small dressing rooms, thinking that it was nice of Emily at least to let him zip himself up. The suit seemed to fit fine, and he folded up the trouser leg ends. When he came out Mr. Bower led him to a three-way mirror. Boy, Al said to himself, what a great suit! It looked just like the one Mr. Welton had been wearing, and for a moment he pictured himself addressing a board meeting.

"How do you like it?" Mr. Bower asked, turning him so that he could see the sides and back.

Al could never get over how ridiculous he looked from the side. His head resembled an elongated melon, and he wondered why people didn't laugh when they looked at it.

"I like it fi——"

"No good," Emily interrupted. "The stripe is too harsh, and I think it needs more padding in the shoulders."

Al looked pained. "Padding? I don't need padding."

Bower took his side, gently reminding Emily that men's styles were getting away from padding. But Emily was adamant. "*He* needs padding."

A minute later he returned to the dressing room carrying another suit. Four suits later Emily decided that *this* was the one. Al didn't particularly care for it, but by this time he was resigned to giving up without a struggle.

When Mr. Bower promised that his tailor would get on the alterations immediately and the suit would be ready by eight o'clock, they went to the second floor where Mr. Bower turned them over to his wife.

"Something almost semiformal," Emily told Mrs. Bower. "An afternoon cocktail dress, but not exactly for cocktails. It's for Al's television show tomorrow afternoon when they give him his scroll."

Mrs. Bower looked properly impressed. "Are *you* going to be on it, Mrs. Toolum?"

From his position perched on a chair set in the corner, Al showed his disgust. Why Emily was positively simpering. "Who knows?" she said airily. "They *might* ask me, and I do want to be prepared."

"I have just the thing," Mrs. Bower promised.

Al didn't like the dress. It was black, and he never cared for Emily in black, but he didn't say anything until Emily had emerged from her dressing room. The dress was even worse than he had thought at first. It bulged at the shoulders and bulged at the hips— just too damn many bulges.

He stood up. "Em, I don't like it."

Emily pirouetted before the mirror. "Fits perfectly," she said. "It's wonderful to be back into a fourteen."

Fourteen! Al almost snickered aloud. These women—they would make a dress the size of a circus tent and call it a sixteen.

"I don't like it," he said again, louder this time.

Emily stopped pirouetting and looked at him sharply. "What do you mean, *you* don't like it?"

He lifted one shoulder. "I just don't like it, that's all."

Mrs. Bower and Emily shared the pity of the situation for a moment before Emily snapped, "Well, *you* have nothing to say about it. Now sit down."

He sat down.

At noon on Friday, Al arrived alone at the offices of the American Advertising Consultants. The ceremony was scheduled for two o'clock; Emily, the boys and the Carroways were to arrive at one thirty. He was supposed to be briefed and was to have time to read over his statement. Expecting to work in the office, he was surprised by being whisked out to lunch, despite his protests that he'd had a sandwich before leaving home.

"Have something light, then," John insisted. They were seated, with Arthur Gordon, in a tiny, crowded French restaurant. "Try the Vichysoisse."

Al nodded dumbly. In his mind was a faint suspicion of foreign-sounding foods, but if John Bell okayed it he was willing to take the chance. He just hoped it wasn't snails.

Al said he was almost too nervous to eat. "I'm scared," he wailed. "What am I going to do?"

Producing a piece of paper from his pocket, John said soothingly, "Now, now, there's nothing to worry about. Look over this statement, get the general drift of it and then you'll sound natural by saying it in your own words."

Al studied the statement. It was short, less than a page in length, and all it said was that he was honored, that he hoped he could live up to the spirit of Yankee Doodle, and he thanked everyone concerned for this great chance to bring recognition to the average American family head. When he had read the statement he felt better.

The Vichysoisse proved to be a soup, a white liquid with green specks floating around on top.

"Why, it's just cold potato soup," he said, when he'd tasted it. "My wife makes this all the time in the summer."

Arthur and John laughed. They were eating big salads, and Al was fascinated, never having seen grown men eating salads as a main course before. He forgot that his new suit was too prickly on his legs and began to enjoy himself.

Back at the office there were a great number of people hurrying about and, through an open door leading to the board room, Al could see newsreel cameras being set up. Wires ran in all directions, and men were shouting at one another. At one point Paul Welton emerged briefly from his office, surveyed the scene with obvious pain and then disappeared again.

The sight of all these activities caused Al's nervousness to redouble. He felt hot and cold flashes, and he wondered if his legs would hold him. John and Arthur had left him with the kind words that he should take it easy, and nowhere was anyone who looked like an ally. It was unfair, he told himself, that he, the focal point of honor, should be thus left to his own miserable resources.

He felt even worse when a man staggered by weighted down by a portable television camera strapped to his back. Pausing in front of Al, the man pleaded, "Got a match, buddy?" his eyes indicating a cigarette that dangled from his lips.

Hastily Al produced a match. "Thanks," the man nodded and then groaned, "For this I left a good job at Philco. Who is this Yankee Doodle jerk anyway?" Without waiting for an answer the man stumbled on his way.

With a feeling of hysterical relief Al finally saw the family and the Carroways edge out of the elevator just at one thirty. Greeting them joyously, he kissed Emily and the boys and wrung Ben's hand. Ben and Sadie, the latter topped with a flowery bonnet, looked unusually subdued.

"Gee, this is really something," Ben whispered. "The whole town is glued to their television sets, and somewhere I heard the town council's going to give you a big reception tomorrow."

Al licked his dry lips with an equally dry tongue, the effect feeling like sandpaper rubbing on sandpaper.

The elevator door behind them opened, and they were urged aside by a large group of people that surged into the room. In the center of the group was a stout, well-dressed man with a carnation in his lapel. White-haired and red-faced, he dominated the room with his booming voice.

"Well, now," he shouted, "where's my old friend Paul Welton? That scoundrel owes me twenty-five cents from an election bet."

The men around him laughed heartily as the group flowed into the board room.

"Hey, Ben," Al hissed, "that's one of the crooks we saw on the television last year."

"No, Al, that's the guy who asked the crooks a lot of questions. He's a senator."

"He's a crook," Al insisted. "I remember his face. Em, remember I said one look at that guy's face and he should get life."

Emily shook her head in confusion. "I can't tell the difference, Al."

John Bell hastened into the room. "Mr. Toolum, come and meet Senator Griffin."

"See, I told you, Al," Ben called as Al was hustled out of the room, and before Emily could stop him, Little Louie had scuttled after his father.

Becoming aware of Little Louie, Al whispered fiercely, "Go on back."

"I wanna see," Little Louie said, as the door closed behind them.

It was too late to do anything, because Senator Griffin's voice was booming its salutations. "So this is the great average man, Eh? It's a pleasure, Mr. Foolum."

"Toolum," Al said, accepting the moist, fleshy hand.

The thing that struck him about the senator was that the politician apparently paid no attention to walls; he had obviously developed his style of speech before the invention of microphones, for he always seemed to be addressing an audience somewhere off at a great distance. His eyes, even while he shook hands with Al, were directed to a point far beyond Al's head.

"I say to you, Mr. Toolum, that it is a great distinction to be allowed to shake your hand. That you, the great average American, should be so honored is only your due. *This could not happen in Russia.*"

Al allowed that it probably couldn't as John urged them all to get ready.

"We'll just run it through once," he said. Then to Al, "Would you like to have your family in the background?"

"I don't know. I'll have to ask." He opened the door to the reception room. He was forced to admit that the new black dress looked fine on Emily. "You want to be on the television, Em?" he asked, when he had her attention.

Emily opened her mouth to say yes. All the time she had tried to fall asleep the night before she had rehearsed how she would act and what she would say if offered this opportunity. But now she was completely terrified. Shaking off Sadie's hand that tried to urge her forward, she mutely expressed her unwillingness.

The senator was with John when Al reported, "She says no."

"I'll be in it, Papa," Little Louie said.

"What's *that?*" the senator asked pointedly.

"My youngest," Al said.

The senator smiled. For a moment Al was afraid he was going to pat Little Louie on the head, but some protective instinct prevented the move.

"You can read your speech on the run-through," John said to Al. "Now, if you'll just stand over here," leading him to a point a few feet in front of the cameras. The television cameraman who had asked Al for a light said suddenly, "Oh, brother," when he saw Al, and Al grinned weakly at him.

"You'll have to do something with Little Louie," John told him.

Spotting Barbie McClain in a corner, Al whispered, "Go over to Miss McClain, Little Louie."

"I don't wanna."

"Here, kid." It was the television cameraman, wanting to make up to Al. "You come over and watch how I work."

Little Louie showed interest. "Can I listen through your earphones?"

"Sure." He winked at Al. "My name's Kelly."

Doubtfully, Al said, "I don't know whether you should. He's liable to hurt your equipment."

"Ah-h, don't worry a second. I've got four of my own. Terrors every one of them. *I* know how to handle kids."

The run-through proceeded easily. First, Paul Welton made a short explanatory speech about the contest, and then he introduced the senator who, after a speech in which he dwelt on the meaning of the average American man, introduced Al and gave him a large framed scroll.

When it was over a man with a stop watch walked over to John. "Cut the old cornball down about half, and we'll be okay."

"Senator," John approached Griffin, "we're a little long, and if you'll just shave your speech down a little . . ."

"Can do, son. Course, there's a lot more I'd like to say . . ."

Giving the senator a friendly nudge, Paul Welton said, "This isn't the floor of the senate, Waldo."

Laughing heartily, the senator cried, "By godfrey, Paul, it isn't, is it?"

A voice called, "Two minutes," and there was a sudden hush. Then, "Places, everyone." Lights momentarily blinded Al; squinting he saw Barbie leading the family and the Carroways into the room.

At that instant Al was overwhelmed by panic; all strength left him, and he clutched John's arm for support.

"You all right, Mr. Toolum?"

Al gulped.

John moved away, saying, "Just take it easy."

I'm having a heart attack, Al told himself, and it could be true, the way his heart pounded, and his head buzzed from so much blood rushing up from his body. There was a huge cotton lump in his mouth and throat that threatened to choke him to death if he didn't die of anything else sooner.

"Oh," he cried to himself. "Help!"

But there was no help.

The voice, now one sounding doom, said, "Thirty seconds."

Then it started, and Al, through a rumbling sound in his ears, heard Paul Welton speaking in his deep, easy tones. Al's mouth was open, and his eyes stared directly into the cameras as though he were hypnotized. Tearing them away, he found himself looking at a horrible white mask that leered at him from beside the television camera. It was a few moments before Al realized that this awful mask was the face of Little Louie.

While the senator spoke, Al was aware of being on two separate levels of consciousness, a phenomonon he had never experienced before. One self was off somewhere surveying the whole scene in a purely objective way, and what it saw was hardly reassuring. The second self was a mind so chaotic that it couldn't remember the purpose of this whole ceremony. It was toward this second self that Al was forced to turn when the senator, a broad smile on his perspiring face, said, ". . . and so, Mr. Toolum, I say to you that you deserve the heartfelt congratulations of the American people. In a sense you are more representative of their beliefs and way of life than any elected official ever could be"—his hand rose with the scroll—"and with this token you are hereby officially recognized as the nation's most average family head—Yankee Doodle Fifty-two."

Scattered applause rang through the room as the senator thrust the scroll into one hand and shook the other. Al's voice came from somewhere out in left field. "Thank you," he heard it say, and then there was a deep, pregnant pause. The senator's eyes narrowed, while his smile remained. He was a veteran. "Haven't you anything to say on this occasion, Mr. Toolum?"

Al could think of nothing he could possibly want to say on this or any other occasion. "Just thanks," he repeated.

As the senator perspired more freely, Al watched two droplets of sweat run down the senator's nose, take a turn around the corners of his mouth and finally merge on his chin. Holding his breath, Al waited till they fell. "Uh—uh, I see your family is all here today, Mr. Toolum. I suppose they're very proud, as proud as *you* perhaps."

"Oh, yeah, real proud." He had a frightening desire to giggle, but successfully fought it down.

"Fine family. Real fine. *Every* average American family head should have a family. Uh—how many boys do you have, sir?"

Al gave the subject some thought. "Three . . . I think."

"You think?"

"Sure, three. Did I say 'I think'?"

"You did," the senator said grimly and caught the eye of the stop-watch man who nodded and waved his arm. "Well, then, Mr. Toolum, again I wish to congratulate you on this great occasion and wish you the best of luck."

"Thanks," Al said.

As the lights went out a hubbub of voices rose throughout the room. Standing rooted to the spot, Al wondered why Senator Griffin had looked at him with such naked hatred a moment ago, and then John, looking completely worn out, stepped up to him, and, firmly, he began, "Mr. Toolum . . ." He wilted. "Never mind, in a way it was my fault." He patted Al's arm. "Thanks anyway for a good try."

Slowly approaching Emily and the Carroways Al reached into his pocket for a handkerchief and his hand touched a piece of paper. "Oh, murder," he groaned, "I forgot all about my speech. I was supposed to make a speech." Suddenly he felt terrible, washed with shame. "Now I know why those sweepstake people look so stupid," he mourned.

"You were wonderful," Emily said sturdily. "I was so proud."

"Yeah, great, Al," Ben assured him. "Really great."

"Here, Emily, take the scroll. Where should we hang it?"

"How about over the fireplace?"

"Oh, no, I'd never want to take down the Jolly-Good-Fellow——"

A crash, followed by an agonized scream, broke off his words, and Al turned to see the cameraman, Kelly, standing with his hands at the sides of his head, and at his feet, toppled from its stand, was his camera.

Al ran over, and Kelly stared at him in utter shock. "Ten thousand dollars," he whispered, and then he regained his voice. "Ten thousand dollars," he shrieked.

Little Louie stood by the wreckage. "Did you do that, Little Louie?" Al asked sternly.

"I only wanted to see how heavy it was," Little Louie said.

"One second," Kelly murmured, "one second I took my eyes off this monster to put my earphones away." Tears filled his eyes.

Al felt terribly sorry for the man—but he'd been warned. "I told you," he said sadly, and then he felt he had to show Kelly that Little Louie wasn't going to get away with such behavior unpunished. "Come on, you," he said, roughly taking Little Louie's hand. "Just for that—no lollipop tomorrow."

Eight

In the Toolum household, the following three weeks came to be known as Operation Build-up, because that's what Al said was being done to him. In this hectic time he and the family saw little of each other, for Mr. Yankee Doodle, as Emily called him on the rare occasions that she saw him, was kept busy from early morning until late at night. There were pictures to be taken, radio and television programs, an official visit to New York's City Hall where he received the mayor's greetings, and other chores of that nature.

Soon, Al learned that making public appearances, though wearing, was quite easy and nothing to be nervous about. Reasoning that since people were anxious to see and/or hear him—or else they wouldn't turn on their radio and television sets—they were mostly sympathetic and easy to please. No longer did the sight of a television boom microphone remind him of a dentist's drill with the same accompanying horrors; instead, he came to regard it as a friendly object that gave him a chance to speak on any number of subjects on which he found, to his surprise, he was quite an expert.

It was this growing prowess as a pundit that got Al involved with the League to Free the Pacific Peoples, which, later, had wide repercussions, but the start of the trouble occurred on a daytime radio program noted for its purity and innocence, two qualities that matched the sponsor's products. The program happened to be the one listened to by more housewives than any other on the air, a tribute to the genius of its lady moderator, Emma O'Daniel, and when Al announced to Emily that he was to be on the program, she was terribly impressed.

"Be sure to get her autograph," Emily said. "Emma O'Daniel is my favorite. I listen almost every day and buy all the products she advertises. Is it this morning?"

Al nodded. "Then I'm coming with you," Emily said. "Sadie can watch Little Louie for a while. She won't mind if I come, will she?"

"I guess not." He was too tired to argue anyway, having got home quite late the night before after a dinner and pow-wow at the annual meeting of the Council of Eastern Indian Tribes where he had been made a blood brother and honorary chief of the Shinnecock Division. Imbibing freely of an innocent-looking purple punch, he had discovered, too late, that something potent had been added.

"Eat your eggs," Emily urged, and when he shook his head, she asked, "What's the matter with you?"

"Isn't it against the law to sell liquor to the Indians?" he asked. Then, to Sherman, "Take that horrible smelly thing off your head."

"You were wearing it when you got home last night," Emily said pointedly, "*and* you were singing a song that went 'Ugga walla walla.' "

Snatching the headdress away from Sherman, Al scaled it into a corner. "It's Ugga Walla *Woo*la, and it's my tribe's war song."

"Boy, you musta been awful loaded," Little Louie said.

Al ignored the remark. "You know, I found out something very interesting last night, something I've always wondered about. I betcha, Em, you don't know who the Indians root for in a cowboy and Indian picture."

Emily looked puzzled. "I'd never thought about it, but now that you mention it, who *do* they root for?"

"For the Indians, of course," Al cried triumphantly, "and there was a speaker last night from the Cherokee tribe out West who gave a long talk about this. *He* said that the Indians have been licked in movies so much that they have a terrible inferiority complex. And he said it's time something was done."

"They *could* let the Indians win for a change," Emily said thoughtfully.

"That's one thing they could do. Anyway, a resolution was passed that from now on every Indian who goes to the movies should hiss the cowboys and cheer for the Indians. This Cherokee said a vocal demonstration might bring some results. Maybe I'll try to work the discussion around to that on the program today."

"Emma O'Daniel's very fair about things like that. She's always saying how we should be kind to our neighbors."

"I can't stand that dame," Herman said. "I cough whenever I hear her."

"How can a radio program make you cough?" Al asked, in tones of disgust.

Herman said, "Remember when I was a little kid and had the whooping cough? Well, Mamma had Emma O'Daniel on every morning when I was home in bed, and now whenever I hear her I start to cough."

"You see," Al said, "they teach 'em about psychology in school now, so they have to be psychosomatic about everything."

"Psycho what?" Emily asked.

"Psychosomatic," Al said. "Didn't you hear that doctor talking about it on the Millicent Mulvanie show I was on last week? He said all diseases are caused by the mind."

"I didn't understand a word he said. And I assure you *my* mind hasn't anything to do with my knees trouble. *That* comes from scrubbing floors."

Al rose hurriedly. Whenever Emily's "knees trouble" was mentioned he knew the next item of discussion was when could they afford a woman to come in a couple of times a week for the heavy cleaning.

"I've got to get in a couple of hours' work before we go into the city. I'll take the car and pick you up here at eleven, Em. Be ready." He darted out of the house.

"Papa sure is a big shot now," Herman said when the door was closed.

"Don't believe it—and drink your milk," Emily said. "When all this is over you'll find your father is the same lovable old"—she paused —"dear he always was."

The boys all looked at her, and then they began to laugh.

Emma O'Daniel was a bland-faced, stoutish woman addicted to huge picture hats, and who, Al figured, was about sixty (she wasn't a day over fifty-five, Emily told him in tones mixed with reverence and indignation), whose flat voice with its Middle-Western twang was familiar to millions of American women as the Voice of Authority. On her two-hour program she discussed current events with her guests, usually authors, theatrical people and minor statesmen who employed publicity men. The discussion with each lasted from ten to fifteen minutes, and the rest of the time was spent eulogizing her sponsors' products with the aid of a young man named Merton Poole, whose chief duties consisted of reminding Miss O'Daniel of her commercial responsibilities. Housewives quivered whenever Merton's stern voice cut into the discussion as he "took Emma O'Daniel to task." And Miss O'Daniel always exhibited the proper amount of chastened spirit, reminding her listeners that if it weren't for the directive ability of the dominant male "we women would just chatter on and on and on."

Al knew nothing about Miss O'Daniel, although during the ride into the city Emily had tried to inject him with the respect that *she* had for the famous lady. To Al, Emma O'Daniel was just a vagrant voice he had often heard but to which he had paid little attention. Nevertheless, he knew, as John had impressed him with the fact, that to be on her program was a great accomplishment.

When he and Emily stepped into the studio they were approached by a thin, tired-looking man who said abruptly, "I'm Merton Poole. Sit over there, please."

"Fine way to be treated," Al grumbled, sitting on the indicated couch with Emily, but he felt better a moment later when Emma O'Daniel came over to greet them. She had an air of soft friendliness that was quite winning.

"And this must be Mrs. Toolum," she said, when she and Al had shaken hands.

He could feel Emily trembling at his side. "Yes, it is," he said, and then added boldly, "She's a big fan of yours. Talked my ear off about you on the way in."

Emily's face reddened, but Emma O'Daniel seemed quite pleased. "It's always a pleasure to meet the people who help make my program a success. Mrs. Toolum, I'm glad you could come this morning with your husband." Emily nodded a little numbly. "You know," Emma O'Daniel continued, leaning toward them, "most of our guests would wince at the thought of being called average men or women, but"—even lower—"*I* think it's something to be proud of, don't you, Mrs. Toolum?"

"Yes, I do," Emily said. "I certainly do."

"Come over and meet our other guest," Emma O'Daniel said.

He was a tall well-dressed man in his forties with a thin face and a deliberate accent that Al assumed was English; but the man, whose name was Bruce Benedict, was from the State Department in Washington—"Just returned from a tour of the Pacific Islands," Emma O'Daniel explained to Al and Emily. Benedict held a black Homburg in his hand and carried a cane. Al watched to see if he limped, but he didn't.

At Miss O'Daniel's insistence, Emily sat in one of the leather chairs placed around a small table, in the center of which was a microphone, and for a few minutes they discussed various matters that had nothing to do with the business at hand. Al tried desperately to engage Mr. Benedict in conversation, but the State Department man didn't seem in the least interested in the question whether the Giants could repeat or not. And he professed to having never heard of Milton Berle.

"That's a damn lie," Al told himself angrily. "He just doesn't want to admit he's ever heard of Milton Berle."

When he turned to talk to Miss O'Daniel he discovered that she and Emily were deep in the mysteries of fudge icing as opposed to plain chocolate icing, so he resorted to directing challenging looks at Mr. Benedict—who paid no attention to him.

When the program started he sat stiff and erect in his chair, but as the minutes droned by, and Emma O'Daniel exhorted her listeners to "rush right out," he began to relax. Finally Emma O'Daniel turned to him, and he found himself easily answering her queries about how it felt to be Yankee Doodle '52.

"Everything's happened so fast," he said, in answer to a question, "I haven't had time to catch my breath."

"And how does your wife feel about all this?"

"Ask *her*," Al said, grinning at Emily.

"And she's sitting right here, ladies," Miss O'Daniel told the microphone. "Mrs. Toolum is a charming, attractive lady who certainly doesn't show the affects of having three boys around the house. How *do* you feel about all this, Mrs. Toolum?"

It was a struggle to answer. "Fine," she eventually said hollowly.

"I'll bet you're very happy about your husband winning the contest, aren't you?"

When Emily showed extreme distress, Al, the veteran, rescued her. "She'd better be," he said, "because she talked me into it."

Emma O'Daniel expelled her famous chuckle as Merton broke in, "You're slighting Woof's Dog Food, Miss O'Daniel, and it's our newest product."

Al smoked a cigarette and held Emily's hand while Emma O'Daniel, with the aid of recorded dogs' voices, all howling for Woof's, fulfilled her obligations. Then it was Mr. Benedict's turn, and he launched into a description of his trip around the Pacific. He talked about various islands he had visited and the economic problems of the people.

To draw Al into the discussion, Emma O'Daniel said, "According to my notes, Mr. Toolum, I see you spent some time in the Pacific during the war. I suppose that qualifies you as an expert too. What do you think, Mr. Benedict?"

Mr. Benedict obviously wasn't too willing to open the doors to his fraternity. "I wouldn't say that the GI's view was an altogether objective one, Miss O'Daniel," he drawled, and then, to ease the sting, he chuckled drily.

Al stared at him. You stuffed-up pumpkin, he thought—I'll fix your little red wagon.

"I guess I'm not really an expert," Al said. "One thing I did want to know from Mr. Benedict was about the ice plant on Guam. Who owns it now?"

Benedict regarded him with vague bewilderment. "The ice plant? I'm sure I don't know."

"The reason I'm wondering," Al said, plunging the knife a little deeper, "is my battery was right near it, and while I was there some general had it rebuilt, and *he* owned it."

"Who owned it?" Emma O'Daniel asked, not too certain she was on firm ground.

"The general. I guess he made a lot of money with that"—he carefully avoided the knifelike glance directed at him by Emily. It was the one she always used when he sounded off too much at a party—"and the bus line and a few other things he had there. I sure put in a lot of hours on that ice plant. Working parties all the time. I helped put in the machinery. I wonder where he got it?"

"Got what?" Emma O'Daniel was forced to ask.

"The machinery. It was government property, but he sold the ice to the natives."

"That's ridiculous," Bruce Benedict said sharply. "That would be illegal."

"I thought so too," Al said innocently, "but he had a native there who was supposed to be the head of it, so nobody complained. Funny thing, too, because the natives were awfully poor——"

"They're doing much better now," Bruce Benedict interrupted coldly. "Our program is in full swing, and to use an old GI phrase, they never had it so good."

"Glad to hear it," Al said, leaning back. "I liked those people on Guam very much." He was pleased to see a fine film of perspiration on Mr. Benedict's forehead. *That* for you, Nasalhead, Al told him silently.

Suddenly he remembered his tribal duties. "Oh, say, I just thought of something. Talking about the Guam natives reminded me of it. It's about the Indians———"

"Time for Sillman's Salad Oil," Merton Poole said quickly.

"This'll only take a minute," Al insisted.

"Sillman's Salad Oil," Merton repeated, a note of steel in his voice. . . .

Some thousand-odd yards away as the pigeon flies, in his office overlooking Madison Avenue, Paul Welton snapped off the radio. He sat quietly for a moment examining the tips of his fingers.

"The trouble with the average man, Bell," he said to John, who sat nervously in a leather armchair across the room, "is that every time he opens his big mouth he puts his foot right in it."

"Yes, sir," John agreed, "but it's awfully hard to tell Toolum what to do under specific circumstances. He seems very vague about taking directions."

"Is he vague, or are the directions a little above his head?" Welton asked pointedly.

"I'm sure he understands," John insisted. "It's just that you never know what to expect from him."

The lines around Welton's mouth tightened. "John, one thing I've found out in my many years in this business is that the average man is completely predictable. Advertising is based on this one principle more than any other. We have formulae for this, John; we have the Machine. Without this predictability our whole structure would totter."

"You're probably right, sir," John hesitated.

"I *know* I'm right."

"But don't you see," John argued, "the predictability depends on control of the contributing factors. For example, we can determine what Toolum will do if we hold all the reins. But we didn't know that this Benedict would be on the O'Daniel show today, and that he'd lead the subject around to something Toolum decided he'd carry the sword for."

"Then we'll have to keep tight control from now on," Paul Welton said. "Call a halt to the preliminary build-up. From now on our returns are on a diminishing scale anyway."

"I agree, sir. There's just one thing tomorrow night—the Penelope Parsons show. We're committed, and I wouldn't want to foul up our connection there."

"Okay, let him go on that. Just make sure that Parsons keeps the talk on movies or his likes in women's clothes. I want no more slip-ups, John."

"I assure you there'll be none," John Bell said.

At eight o'clock the following evening Emily went over to the Carroways' to see Al on the television. In spring and summer she never worried about leaving the boys in the house alone when she was next door. Their room faced the Carroways' living room, and by leaving the windows open she could hear any sounds of mayhem.

Ben was relaxing, reading the paper, and Sadie was ironing.

"I hardly see Al any more," Ben complained. "He hasn't been bowling in three weeks."

"This is the last program," Emily assured him; "then we all see him for a while."

"We've slipped to third in the league standings. Charlie ain't near the anchor man old Al is. Hope we can pick up when he gets back."

"*If* he gets back," Sadie said deliberately from the alcove where she had set up her ironing board. "Maybe Al won't feel bowling is up to his new way of life." Sadie was in a snit about Emily's being on the Emma O'Daniel program.

"You know Al better than that," Emily said.

"Sadie's jealous," Ben said good-naturedly. "She thinks I'm much more average than Al."

"That's not what I mean," Sadie said hotly, putting down her iron. "You know, Emily, what happens to men when they get famous. First thing you know they're running off with some chorus girl and leave their wife and family."

"Not Al," Emily said, "he'd miss my cooking too much."

"So he'd eat in all the fancy restaurants. Look what happened to Cyril Carruthers and his wife the minute he got to be a movie star."

"I didn't kow Cyril Carruthers was man enough to have a wife." Ben said. "Every picture I ever saw him in he looked like he should be carrying a lace hanky in his sleeve."

"That's how much *you* know, Ben Carroway. I was reading in *Super-Screen Magazine* how for ten years Cyril tried to break into Hollywood, and all that time his wife supported him by working in a department store, and the *minute* he became a star, he divorced her and is going to marry Jennifer Jeffries."

"Maybe when she came out of the department store he got his first good look at her," Ben muttered.

"Fame sure does funny things to people," Emily admitted.

"That's what I mean about Al," Sadie said, taking up her iron again. "You keep your eyes on him, Emily."

"He is getting famous," Emily said thoughtfully. "Just this morning a man named Gomez called up who heard Al on the Emma O'Daniel program yesterday. He's the president of an organization called the League to Free the Pacific Peoples. Al's seeing him at lunch tomorrow."

"What did he want?" Ben asked.

"Wants Al to be a sponsor, whatever that is."

Ben whistled, very much impressed. "Maybe Al wasn't so crazy about going into politics after all."

"I just hope it doesn't cost any money," Emily said. "The word sponsor scares me. You think it has anything to do with putting a program on television?"

Ben rose and turned on the set. Finding the channel that carried the Penelope Parsons show, he adjusted the picture to his liking. "I don't know," he said. "Now you take this program—it's called 'What's My Weight?'" The screen showed four blindfolded panel experts poking a giggling fat lady. "You'd think the sponsor would be a reducing company, wouldn't you?"

"I should think so," Emily said.

"But they advertise a hair coloring. Hey, Sadie, how much did it cost to get that stuff washed out of your hair?"

"Ben!" Sadie warned.

"She had to go to the beauty parlor, and they were real mad. Her hair was purple."

"*Ben!*"

"Fifteen dollars, they charged."

Sadie stormed to the television set. "The picture's too dark." She twisted a knob.

"Now you've got it jumping," Ben complained, reaching forward to turn another knob.

"Now it's too light," Sadie said, reaching out.

"Leave it alone," Ben snarled, grasping her arm as they faced each other murderously. "I'm going blind with this damn thing," he shouted, standing up. "I'll throw it out the window."

"Please," Emily begged, "not till after the Penelope Parsons show."

The Carroways sat down, breathing hard, and Ben muttered, "This is what's supposed to be saving the American home. It's ruining mine."

"Humph," Sadie sniffed, her disdain indicating that there was little left to ruin.

Emily was about to suggest that the picture was too grainy, and could Ben make it less dense, but the dark look on his face caused her to remain silent.

Four film commercials later the Penelope Parsons show began. It was one of the more informal interview programs where both Miss Parsons and her guest sat on a couch in a set resembling a living room.

"Wow!" Ben gasped when the camera focused on Penelope Parsons. "She's wearing one of those topless evening gowns."

It wasn't quite true, as Emily saw with a second glance. It only looked that way.

"Haw, haw!" Ben whooped. "Look at Al. His eyes are almost as big as her——"

"Ben Carroway!" Sadie snapped.

"This is a free country, isn't it?" Ben demanded.

"Too free," Sadie said, "when you look at what that hussy is wearing."

Hussy is right, Emily told herself indignantly. She could barely hear what Penelope Parsons was saying to Al because of the anger rising in her at seeing how much Al was enjoying himself. Moving his hands around as though he didn't know what to do with them. The nerve of Alfred Toolum, sitting with a woman like that in public, letting millons of people see how lecherous he was.

And then the anger turned into a great sadness as Emily suddenly and honestly realized that it was not Al, and it was not Penelope Parsons. It was against herself that she should really direct her anger. And at that moment she hated all women like Penelope Parsons, symbols of all the glamour that to Emily was an unattainable dream. She had settled into her comfortable rut, certain of Al's unshakable loyalty—and now she was seeing him with someone who could show him how drab his life actually was.

". . . and how do you like my dress?" Penelope Parsons was saying, as she rose and whirled in front of Al. "I want to get the average man's opinion."

"That's more than my wife does," Al said.

"Really? Well, *I* want your opinion, Mr. Toolum."

Al crossed his legs. "It's—I guess it's okay."

"Okay?" Miss Parsons tinkled her famous laugh that was so contemptuous of all men, and looked directly into the camera. "Why, Mr. Toolum, this is an original made by the famous designer Laurene Lupin—her shop, ladies, is on East Fifty-seventh Street, consult your directory for the exact address—and you say it's just *okay?*"

Al shrugged, and Miss Parsons sat next to him again. "Tell

me," she said, "how would you like to see your wife in a model like this? It could be arranged."

Al squinted thoughtfully. "I don't know. On you it looks pretty good; on her—I don't know."

"What do you mean?"

"Well"—Al gestured with his hands—"with my wife there's a little too much here, and maybe not enough here, and——"

"Turn it off," Emily cried. "Turn it off."

With alacrity Sadie switched the knob, and the screen went dark. "Well! If I were you, Emily, I'd have a thing or two to say to Alfred Toolum when he gets home."

Emily nodded miserably.

"Gosh," Ben mourned, "it was just getting good."

Actually, what Ben didn't know, was that by turning off the program, they missed the best part. . . .

It was a quarter to ten, and around a small table in a Sixth Avenue bar Al sat silently with John Bell and Barbie McClain. In less than twenty minutes he and Barbie had watched John put away four old-fashioneds in the manner of a man waiting for execution. John was beginning to feel slightly numb, but no matter how numb he got, he didn't think he could ever look at Alfred Toolum again without shivering.

"It was my fault," he groaned for the sixth time. "All my fault, and I will take full blame tomorrow. But, Mr. Toolum, how could you have done it?"

Al shook his head unhappily. He didn't quite know what he was being accused of having done. All he knew was that the television show had ended somewhat chaotically, and all people concerned had looked at him as though he were a carrier of the plague.

"I can't *figure* it," John said, almost to himself. "I thought I had everything covered. She had all the questions she was supposed to ask, and you knew what they were. There was no chance for a slip-up. I even sat right in the studio myself and watched. Didn't you see me waving to you?"

"Oh, that. Well, she kept asking me, didn't she?"

"She brought it on herself," Barbie interjected. "Don't go blaming Mr. Toolum, John."

"But did he have to *bite* her?" John pleaded.

"I didn't," Al insisted indignantly. "I only said I wanted to. When she kept asking me what I thought of when I looked at her dress——"

"You were going to bite her," John accused, "if she hadn't gotten out of the way."

Al was horrified. "I never would've done anything of the kind. Who goes around biting ladies?—especially on television. She just kept asking me . . ."

John waved a hand sadly. "I know, I know. Oh, well—at least, it's the last time *that* can happen. For a couple of weeks we're just going to relax and then start the second phase of the campaign. Do you think you can keep out of trouble for two weeks?"

"I've never *been* in any trouble," Al answered truculently. "Anyway, not until this Yankee Doodle business." He rose. "I'm going home. My wife is probably wondering where I am. At least with her I've got peace and quiet—most of the time."

"Good night, Mr. Toolum," Barbie said. "And don't worry."

"No, of course he shouldn't worry," John muttered, as Al left the bar. "Let *me* do the worrying. Barbie, how should I kill myself painlessly—sleeping pills or a shot gun in my mouth?"

"Here," she said, pushing her untouched old-fashioned across the table, "drink yourself to death."

Nine

If there was one thing about Al that annoyed Emily it was the fact that he never seemed to realize when he was getting the cold, silent treatment. Long ago Emily had been forced to resort to this method of showing her displeasure when the level of noise around the house rose to such heights that to make *more* noise was impossible. She secretly suspected, however, that Al actually enjoyed the silent treatment.

This time the treatment lasted only a short while, because it was on the Saturday following the Penelope Parsons show that Emily was forced to go to Al with the fact that their problem with Little Louie had again reached a crisis, and now it was time to join forces. She found him in the basement where, for the past hour and a half, he had been "fixing" the washing machine.

"Al, could you put down your magazine for a minute."

Startled, he looked up from the story of spacemen versus bug-eyed monsters and guiltily returned to the twentieth century. Scattered about him were his tools, and reaching hastily for a wrench, he said, "I almost have this thing licked, Em. In ten-fifteen minutes . . ."

"Never mind, I called the man from the repair shop. It's something else." In answer to his questioning look, she continued, "It's Little Louie. He won't get out of bed."

"What's the matter, he sick? You take his temperature?"

"No temperature."

"Then what's wrong?"

She shook her head unhappily. "The same old business. He must have had a nightmare last night, and he says he's scared to get up."

"I'll talk to him." He gathered his tools and thrust them in the chest. "Frankly, I think he's just lazy. Takes after your father."

"My father is not lazy," Emily said hotly. "He's a genius."

"If sitting around on your prat all day is proof of being a genius, I agree. Now he's retired he has an excuse. But what was he doing all those other years?"

"He was thinking," Emily said weakly, as they started up the stairs. "He was inventing things."

"An inventor! If I live to be forty-one, which I sometimes doubt, I'll never forget him wanting me to invest money in a nonreflecting mirror for people who hated the sight of themselves."

"He never—" Emily started angrily, but Al's laugh, trailing down the stairs made her break off and say to herself, "Oh, that *man!*"

"Here—Little Louie." Al shook the blanket-covered mound. "Get up."

Little Louie peered up at him and shook his head.

Al decided to play it cheerful. "Come on, you haven't any temperature. It's a beautiful day." But there was no response, and Al sat down on the bed. "You feel bad? . . . Got a tummy ache? . . . Mad at anybody? . . . Anything hurt at all? . . . Something you want?"

The only response was negative shakes of his head, and Al got mad. He gritted his teeth. "You get up, or . . . or . . ."

"Don't hit me, Papa."

Al expelled his breath. "Who said anything about hitting you?" Running his hand lightly over the blanket, he said, "You get up, and—I'll get you an ice-cream soda."

"I don't want one, Papa."

"You *are* sick. Maybe we'd better call the doctor."

That word frightened Little Louie. "I'm not sick. I just don't wanna get up."

"Your brothers are at the park playing ball. I bet they'd let you be bat boy."

"I don't wanna be bat boy. I wanna play."

"You're too little to play. You'll grow up soon enough, and then you can play."

"How do you know I'll grow up?"

"*Everybody* does."

"They blow me up," Little Louie said.

"Who blows you up?"

"Herman and Sherman. They play atom bomb, and I'm the enemy."

"Well, when you're little you have to put up with stuff like that." Noticing some comic books spread on Herman's desk, he said brightly, "Here, suppose I read you a comic, and then you get up.

This is a good one. Look, it's Uncle Gotrocks and Little Winnie Waif." He shuddered, but continued bravely, "And what's this? Somebody's going to hit Uncle Gotrocks with an ax. Boy, Little Louie, do you think he'll be saved? Little Louie, get your head out from under the cover. I'm reading."

"I hate Uncle Gotrocks," Little Louie wailed.

Al put down the comic book. "So you're afraid to get out of bed, is that it? You think if you get up something might happen to you. Answer me, Little Louie, is that right?"

Little Louie nodded slowly.

"Well, I've got news for you," Al told him. "Latest insurance figures tell us that more accidents happen in the home than anywhere else, and the *worst* place to be is in bed."

"It *is?* What can happen?"

"Well—you can set fire to the house while smoking in bed; plaster could fall on you—oh, lots of stuff. So come on." He reached down and, blanket and all, picked up Little Louie, who didn't resist. "I'm a bright one," Al told himself as he carried Little Louie downstairs. "Now he won't want to go to bed."

"Ben," Al said, "in a way I figure you're lucky not having any kids. With kids all you have is trouble. Outside of the fortune they cost with *normal* things, they get sick; first they eat you out of house and home, and then they don't eat at all. You have cops coming around, teachers calling up, neighbors complaining." He shifted the bowling ball from one hand to another as they crossed a street. "Sometimes I wonder what the percentage is."

"How about the joys of parenthood?"

"An invention by people without kids. Maybe if you have one who leaves home at the age of six to go to work—and supports you too . . ."

Turning into the cool, darkened bowling alley, they were greeted by the owner who summoned a pin boy and lighted two of the alleys. Al and Ben sat on a bench changing from street shoes into sneakers.

"What brings all this on?" Ben inquired.

"Little Louie. Something's the matter with him. He's scared about things. It comes up once in a while usually after he's had a bad dream. Twice this week it's happened. This morning he didn't want to get out of bed."

"Spring fever." Ben ambled to the bar, calling over his shoulder, "Have a beer, Al?"

Poised for a practice shot, Al said, "No thanks," and he made his approach, released the ball and watched it curve into the one-two pins and sweep through for a strike. "Whappo," he said aloud.

"Good shot." Ben returned with his foaming bottle of beer. "Old eye, Al."

"Think we ought to take him to a doctor, Ben?"

"Who, Little Louie?"—shrugging—"What could a doctor do?" His ball spun down the alley.

"I don't know. Oh-oh, you got the seven-ten split. No, I guess a doctor couldn't do anything. No symptoms. No seven signs of this, eight signs of that like it says on the posters." He sighed. "He's always been a difficult kid."

"Difficult!" Ben snorted. "That Little Louie is a first-rate gangster."

"Let's say he's high-spirited," Al said unhappily.

"You have your opinion, and I'll have mine. Come on, Al, begin the game. You should relax for a while."

Al nodded, but he couldn't divert his mind from the picture of the way Little Louie first looked up at him from under the covers— as though he had been hopeful for something that he knew wasn't there. . . .

That night, while they were preparing for bed, Al and Emily discussed the problem.

"But you make me feel guilty," Emily said from her chair in front of the dressing table, "like it was all my fault."

"I haven't said that. Damn it, this sock has a hole in it. I've got no socks any more."

"I *mean* to darn them, but I don't have time. He's your son as well as mine."

"So I'll go barefoot."

"What did you say?"

"I said, sure he's my son. Who denies that? I just want to know what we do about it."

"I don't know. He's always been so hard to handle, and now on top of everything else——"

"Em, what in *hell* are you putting on your face?"

"I won't tell you."

"That means it costs forty-three dollars. Did that extortionist Armando sell it to you, that bum? Someday I'm going down there and muss up his permanent. Em, you look awful—like a—a person who's been tarred and feathered."

"It's what I look like when it comes off that counts. Don't you want me to be pretty?"

"Oh, Em, at your age . . ."

"Is that so!"

"What I meant," he said hastily, "is you're pretty enough right now to suit me—always have been."

"As pretty as Penelope Parsons?"

"In a different way, Em."

She patted her face harder. "Little Louie thinks I'm prettier than she is."

"That proves—" He cut himself short.

"What were you going to say?"

"Nothing." He folded his hands behind his head. "Em, remember a couple of years ago Little Louie busted Sadie's kitchen windows, and you read about the Child Guidance?"

She turned. "You think we ought to take him there?"

"I've just been wondering. There's nothing really shameful about it, is there?"

"Should there be?"

"I don't know—but when you have to get help it means you've failed as a parent. That's not very nice to face."

"Times have changed, and maybe the world's too complicated for parents."

"I think you're right. If I gave my old man trouble, he took a stick to me. I figured I never wanted to hit a kid of mine, and with Herman and Sherman it worked okay. But that Little Louie —sometimes I get so crazy I want to wallop the daylights out of him."

"The book says it's better to hit a child in anger than to keep it inside and get to hate them."

"But it's unfair. I'm so much bigger than he is. He can't hurt me the way I hurt him."

"He takes advantage in his way too," Emily assured him. "The book says——"

"Forget the book. It's all so simple when it's down on paper, but, my God, you have to have the patience of a saint to do what the book says. I'm no saint, so we're in trouble with Little Louie. So let's get help."

"And where do we get that?"

"I don't know. Look in those magazines of yours."

"They don't tell you where to go exactly."

"How about asking at school. They should know."

"That's a good idea. I'll go Monday." Standing up, she walked to the closet to hang up her dressing gown.

"Hey, Em, while you're there look in the pocket of my gray jacket. There's a letter in it from that Pacific League."

When she brought over the letter Al unfolded it. "Look, Em," he said proudly, "they already have my name printed on new stationery. See, here I am listed as a sponsor."

"Look at all those names," Emily admired.

"Mostly professors," Al bragged. "There I am in alphabetical order."

"It's kind of small."

"No smaller than anyone else. If the names were bigger there wouldn't be room to write letters."

"What does the League do?"

"I don't know exactly, but this guy Gomez explained that they're working to get the Pacific natives a square deal. You see, whenever a lot of advanced people go into a native culture there's always a conflict where the natives suffer."

Emily thought for a moment. "Say that last again. I didn't understand."

"That's what the man told me."

"But what does it mean?"

"It means," Al said, "that whenever civilized folks go into a place that isn't so civilized they louse up the works."

"Oh," Emily said, understanding. "Al, do you think I'm getting fat?"

"Fat! What's that got to do with what we're talking about?"

"It made me think of sarongs. I wouldn't look well in one, would I?"

"Who does? Not even Dorothy Lamour. Say, what ever happened to her, anyway?"

"I'm going to start a diet again, and maybe if I take off ten pounds . . ."

"Em," Al said gently, "what are you so worried about?"

"I'm having trouble getting into a fourteen."

"In that case you'd better take off ten pounds." He reached for the lamp. "You going to take that stuff off your face?"

"I have to keep it on all night."

"Oh, fine," Al said. "The man kisses his wife good night and she says, 'Here's mud in your eye.' " He scrunched under the covers. "What a life."

"Your feet are cold," Emily said.

Al had insisted that he be allowed to sleep late the next morning, and because the weather turned gray and chilly there was no occasion to regret the fact that no Sunday outing had been planned.

In the kitchen Emily was rolling out crust for an apple pie when the door opened and Sadie, first tapping lightly on the door as a gesture of politeness, entered briskly. She looked around and seemed surprised at the relative peaceful air in the kitchen.

"Where is everyone?"

"Al's still in bed, and Herman and Sherman promised to take care of Little Louie for the afternoon if I gave them movie money."

"Al's still in bed, eh?" Sadie's tones were loaded with hidden meaning as she made herself comfortable at the kitchen table. "I suppose these late nights are finally catching up with him."

"He is a lot busier than he used to be," Emily confessed. "This Yankee Doodle business is quite wearing."

Sadie sniffed loudly, and then she said, "Are you using cinnamon?"

"Can't. Al's allergic to it."

"I wouldn't bake an apple pie without using cinnamon."

"I like it better without," Emily said firmly. Then she said, "I'm glad you dropped over, Sadie, I was going to come over later and ask a favor."

"And I came over to ask *you* one."

"We'll trade," Emily said. "What I wanted from you was to take care of Little Louie for a while tomorrow morning. I have to go to the school and see Mr. Harkness."

"Herman or Sherman, this time?"

"Neither one. It's—it's something else." Without wanting to go into details about Little Louie's problems, she said quickly, "Now what did you want to ask me?"

"It's about the Minute Maids. Some of the girls were wondering if you'd be willing to become active again."

"They were?" Emily allowed a moment to feel flattered. "That's nice of them, but I don't see where I could possibly get the time. That's why I had to drop out before."

"Al seems to have a lot of time to do extra things," Sadie said pointedly.

"That's different. He has to do these things. Besides, he gets money for it. You know how much Yankee Doodle is going to be worth to us."

Sadie did know, and it irked her. "People are beginning to talk," she said primly.

"About what?"

"Well—about the way Al goes around town as though he's suddenly been elected president of the United States, or something."

"He does not," Emily cried in surprised anger. "You shouldn't say that, Sadie. People are just jealous, that's all—the same people who were so quick to congratulate him when it happened," she said bitterly, "now they talk behind his back."

"I'm just repeating what I hear," Sadie said quickly. "Don't think *I* say things. But you have to admit Al's changed ever since this happened. All this running around . . . Remember what I told you, Emily: First, Yankee Doodle business, then, monkey business."

Emily pressed her lips together. Sometimes she wished that Sadie would mind her own— "You're wrong," she said quietly. "I trust Al. I've trusted him all these years, so why should I start being the suspicious wife now?"

Sadie shrugged slightly, and Emily, trying to rationalize for herself, spoke her thoughts aloud. "After all, no matter how prominent a man becomes, he still respects his wife. Not out of duty, but because of what she is. I—I've been thinking about that lately. Being a wife and staying home, you're always in competition with the women your husband meets every day. He's always comparing in his mind."

"And now he sees a lot of slick women."

"Well, I can't help that," Emily said defensively. "And I certainly can't try to come up to some—well, like Penelope Parsons, even with Armando's help."

Seeing a chance to make a point, Sadie cried, "But you *can* keep up in other ways. You can be important too; you don't have to be left behind."

"I wasn't worried about . . ." she started, and then paused thoughtfully. "How can I be important too?"

"By getting active again in the Minute Maids."

"Oh," waving her hand, "what's so important about that?"

"*Well,* maybe it isn't as important as being Yankee Doodle, but if you head committees and things you'll get your picture in the paper. It wouldn't be the city paper, of course——"

"But it would show Al I was doing things, wouldn't it?"

"It certainly would. And we have so many things to combat these days." Sadie used the word "combat" often, it being a favorite of visiting lecturers.

"I could make the time," Emily said thoughtfully. "After all," she said with growing spirit, "I have as much right to do things as Al has. These aren't the old days when a woman was chained to the kitchen and wasn't allowed out. If I can't do outside work and housework too, why we'll just have to get a girl to come in a few hours a week."

"Right," Sadie exclaimed, rising to her feet. "Better Yourself, Better Womankind, Better the World," she cried, quoting the slogan of the Minute Maids International.

At that moment Al, in dressing gown and slippers, shuffled into the kitchen. "What's all the hullabaloo?" he demanded. Then he saw Sadie. "Oh!"

Walking toward the door, Sadie said happily, "We'll talk about this later, Emily. There's an important meeting this week. Al"—she paused—"you'd better keep your eye on Emily. She's going to be a new woman." The door slammed.

Al sat down, scratching his chin. "New woman, huh? What's the matter with the old?"

"Nothing—but maybe I feel like a few changes around here for myself." She reached toward the herb closet.

"Hey, what are you putting cinnamon on that pie for? You know I'm allergic to cinnamon."

"So you've told me all these years," Emily said, sprinkling cinnamon on the apples liberally, and thinking how she loved cinnamon. "What happens when you eat it?"

"I—well, I—I'm just *allergic,* that's all."

"We'll see about that," Emily said firmly.

"That Sadie," Al said unhappily, sensing the source of his trouble. "Every time she and you get together there's a revolution. There should be a law against women like her."

Emily didn't answer. "Where's my coffee?" Al demanded.

"You'll find the pot on the stove, and the coffee is in the canister. I'm busy," she said.

He stared at her in hurt surprise. This could be serious.

As Monitor of the Money, Herman kept his hand thrust in his

pocket all the way downtown. He wasn't afraid of losing the price of their admission to the movie; he just liked the comforting feel of hard silver. It gave him a sense of power, and he wondered how far ninety cents would take him if he decided to leave town.

"What'll we do till the show opens?" Sherman asked.

"How much time we got?"

The library clock told them there was still forty minutes.

"We wanna be first on line," Little Louie offered, "so we can sit in the front row."

"You don't wanna sit in the front row." Herman scoffed. "It ruins your eyes." He had quit sitting in the front row when he was ten.

"Who cares?" Little Louie muttered.

"Anyway, we hafta be in the middle of the line to work our act," Sherman reminded them.

They passed Willnick's Bar & Grille, and Ed Willnick, engaged in lowering his awning, paused to watch the three boys. Of all the children in Fernvale he liked only Little Louie. There was an expression in the small boy's eyes that aroused admiration in Ed Willnick's heart.

"Hello," he called, ignoring Herman and Sherman, "where you going?"

"To the show," Little Louie answered. "Double feature with Roy Rogers and Wild Bill Elliot." He paused, and his brothers, knowing of Ed's favoritism, gracefully accepted the snub by moving slowly on. Little Louie scuffed the sidewalk. "I don't *haff* to go—if you got something else I could do."

It being Sunday, Ed could easily make an excuse for refusing Little Louie's services. "The horses aren't running today. Come around tomorrow, and maybe I'll have something for you." He never did, but Little Louie never seemed to mind the postponements.

"If I can get away," Little Louie said importantly. "You got any peanuts for me?" he asked.

Ed nodded and disappeared. A moment later he returned and handed Little Louie a sackful of bar peanuts. "See you later, Little Louie."

Herman and Sherman were still discussing what to do in the remaining time before the show when he caught up to them. "How about it, Little Louie," Sherman suggested, "you wanna play space ship?"

"Oney if I can be an earthman," Little Louie said.

"You can't be an earthman. You gotta be a Venutian so that Herman and I can conquer you."

"Nope," Little Louie said.

A five-minute argument couldn't break him down, and Herman was disgusted. "What's the matter with you? When I was your age I was always the enemy. I oughta smack you." That gave him an idea. "Say, how's your tooth?"

Little Louie clutched his mouth possessively. "It's okay."

"Ain't it loose yet?" Little Louie shook his head. "Not even a little bit?"

Panic crept over Little Louie as he wondered whether Herman had seen him secretly working on his tooth. Just yesterday he was certain he'd detected a slight wiggle. Little Louie was of the opinion that a boy's front tooth was his own, to be worked to the full measure of satisfaction. He was determined not to allow his first tooth to become a community project.

"It hasn't started to move," he lied.

Sherman produced a wadded knot of string from his pocket and began straightening it out. "If we tied this around and both pulled," he began.

Little Louie, still holding his mouth, quickened his pace. "I don't wanna."

"C'mon," Sherman wheedled, "it'll be lots of fun."

Tears sprang to Little Louie's eyes. "Wah-h-h," he cried in muffled tones.

Herman, imitating his father, heaved a big sigh, and in his father's manner said, "All right, all right, don't be such a crybaby. Put it away, Sherman."

Sherman obeyed, saying, "It's time to get on line anyway." They were two blocks from the theater now, and his voice carried a threat. "And you'd better pay attention today, Little Louie. If you get caught again, that's the last time you come to the movies with us."

Little Louie nodded bravely.

In front of the theater a line of small boys and girls had already formed, and the three Toolums stood patiently in their place, not joining in on any of the horseplay and loud chatter. Each was immersed in his own thoughts—then Herman became aware that one voice dominated the over-all sound, and the words were directed at them. Leaving the world of Roy Rogers where he himself was Roy engaged in foiling a particularly villainous group of rustlers, he returned to the present and saw a large boy facing him who was saying:

"Yah, your old man's crazy."

Herman recognized the boy as a seventh grader from the opposite end of town; his instincts immediately informed him that the older boy was an inch taller and ten to twelve pounds heavier than he.

"What's'a matter?" Herman, sparring for time, asked the boy.

"Yankee Doodle, yah-yah-yah." Grinning kids drifted toward the center of activity.

Herman said, "Your mother wears army shoes." Sherman, he noticed, was working his way into position.

"Oh yeah?" demanded his opponent pugnaciously.

"And your uncle is a garbage man," Herman said, adding the crowning insult.

At that moment Sherman shouted, *"Hey!"* and belted the boy in the kidney.

"Ouch!" the boy cried, turning to meet this unexpected attack.

As he did, Herman brought around a vicious right, catching the enemy on his left cheek. The boy went tumbling back, aided in his journey by Sherman's foot thrust between his legs. A moment later the three boys were a scrambling, flailing heap on the sidewalk. Soon, however, the attacker, realizing his desperate situation, disengaged himself and retreated by crawling into the surrounding crowd.

Herman and Sherman got to their feet and dusted themselves off. "Nice going," Herman congratulated his brother.

"I almost didn't get my foot in there," Sherman puffed.

They turned to a wide-eyed Little Louie. "You gotta get into the act, punk," Herman growled. "You're getting old enough."

Little Louie's answer was cut off by the sudden surge of the line toward the box office, and the smallest Toolum drew between his brothers until he was almost unseen. When they reached the cashier Herman handed over sixty cents and picked up two tickets. The three boys held their breath as they approached the ticket taker, a tired, white-haired man who was extremely bored.

Handing him the tickets, Herman said, "Two," and as the old man took them Herman, suddenly covering his eyes with his hands, cried, "Oh, oh—ow!"

Startled, the old man said, "What's the matter, kid?"

"Oh, my eyes," Herman moaned. "Something's in my eyes."

"Let me see." Herman, feeling Little Louie slip past him, allowed the old man to peer into his eyes.

"I don't see nothing," he said.

Herman grinned relievedly. "I guess it was just some dust," he said.

"Been watching television too much," the ticket taker said disgustedly. "All right, move on."

They found Little Louie waiting at the entrance to the right-hand aisle.

"Good for you," Herman said. "You did a good job, Little Louie," and they walked down the aisle, secure in the thought that they faced a wonderful double feature that they could see twice if they wanted, and when they came out, there was money left for three ice creams. Sunday was undoubtedly a success.

But Monday was much less of a success. At least, it was for Al and Emily; and any day that Herman and Sherman had to go to school was not too successful from their standpoint. For Emily, it was the day when she had to go to see Mr. Harkness at the West

Side grade school, a chore she never particularly enjoyed. There was something about the faint odor of chalk dust, disinfectant and fresh paint, a mixture that repelled her and always made her feel a little ill. Emily had never enjoyed school much. She had gone when all the world except her own enjoyed the wild Twenties, but Emily had never known a boy who wore a raccoon coat or drank from a hip flask or raced around town in a zebra-striped jalopy. And whenever she entered a school, and walked down the cool impersonal corridors, and climbed the worn steps that clinked metallically under her heels, a memory of these gray times would sweep over her, and a memory of the depression that would bring back a gnawing emptiness in her stomach.

For Al it was a day when everything at the shop started out wrong. Instead of getting on with his regular work he spent most of his time struggling with machines that refused to work. He was stripping a recalcitrant press when Henry Muller thrust his head inside the shop door and called:

"Hey, Al, telephone."

Without releasing his stranglehold on the machine, Al said, "Tell whoever it is I'll pay him the first of the month."

"It's your wife, and she wants to talk to you."

"Okay." He stepped back and wiped the grease from his hands on a rag. "Cursed thing," he muttered, taking the machine's refusal as a personal affront. He kicked hard at its base before he joined his boss. "Henry, I recommend you throw every one of these miserable things out and start all over."

"Al, I'd sure like to," Henry said apologetically, "but you know what these shortages are doing to us."

"Shortages," Al snorted, "a couple more years, and this whole damn country breaks down. Hello," he said into the phone.

"Hello, Al, you busy?"

"No, no, I'm not busy. Henry and I were just sitting around smoking cigars and reading racing forms." He grimaced at Henry Muller who grinned nervously and averted his face as he fumbled with a pile of invoices.

"Now, Al, don't get sarcastic. I've had a hard morning."

"Did you see Harkness?"

"I spent over an hour with him."

"Well, what happened? Does he have any ideas, or is he like all the rest of those creeps?" All morning Al had been fighting an anger that bubbled close to the surface.

"He was very nice, and when I told him the whole story he was very helpful. He says we should take Little Louie to the Child Guidance."

"Oh, he does, does he? How does he know what we should do? Does he know what a nice little kid Little Louie really is?"

"Please, Al"—he could tell she was close to tears—"it was your idea I go to the school."

"Okay, okay. I'm sorry, Em. What will they do for us there?"

"The first thing," Emily hesitated, "is they would give Little Louie a Roaring Shock test."

"A—a what?"

"A Roaring Shock test. It costs ten dollars."

"But what is it?" Al asked, in extreme bewilderment. "It sounds terrible, like he was crazy, or something."

"No, no," Emily interjected hastily. "He said it's a very simple test that will give definite clues as to Little Louie's hidden personality."

"Who the hell cares about that?" Al said angrily. "It's his outside *I* want something done about."

Emily's voice carried the authority of recent knowledge. "It's what he is inside that makes him act outside, Mr. Harkness said——"

"Oh, brother," Al muttered.

". . . and when they know that they can fix him up. I'm going to——"

"Don't do anything," Al interrupted. "Don't make a move till I get home."

"But, Al——"

"You hear me?" he said ominously. "I'll stop in the library, and I'll look up this—this Roaring Shock test. Nobody's going to cut away part of Little Louie's brain before I know what's what."

"Cut away part of his brain?" Emily repeated faintly.

"Sure. Don't you read the *Reader's Digest?* That's what they do to people these days."

"Oh, I don't know," she wailed. "I don't know."

"Well, just hold on. Anything else happen, Em?"

"No, nothing—oh, yes, the Consultants called a few minutes ago. They want you to come tomorrow in time for a cocktail party. Mr. Bell called. He said I could come too. Six o'clock at the Consultants."

"How can you go? Who'll feed the kids?"

"I'll get Mrs. Begun to come over."

He was too confused to argue. "All right, if you want to. 'Bye, Em." He hung up and turned to Henry Muller. "Can you imagine those butchers? Right away they want to operate on Little Louie."

"Tsk-tsk. I didn't know he was even sick, Al."

"He's not. He's just—just— Oh, hell, I don't know what he is." He stamped into the shop where he was surprised to see the machine he'd been working on humming along perfectly.

"Hey, when did this start up?" he asked the man working at it.

"Right after you left. You got the magic touch, Al."

"Magic touch," he said to himself and regarded the machine malignantly. "Fine thing. All your skill, everything you know doesn't do any good. To get something to work these days you've got to kick it."

All during dinner Al didn't say a word, and with the deepening silence Emily grew increasingly nervous. Desperately she wondered what was contained in the pile of books on the living-room table. Actually, on closer outer inspection, she saw that it was only one book. But such a *thick* book. It had to be bad.

Only once did Emily try conversation, but Al's pained expression told her he was in no mood to indulge in trivia. Then she worried about the fact that Little Louie wasn't eating any dinner. If there was anything that enraged Al it was seeing food wasted, but tonight he seemed to be fighting down an urge to admonish Little

Louie. Finally, when dinner was over, Al said, "Never mind the dishes for a while, Em. Everybody inside."

The whole family trooped into the living room after him, and when they were settled, he said, "No Music Appreciation tonight."

"What are we gonna do?" Sherman asked.

Walking to the table, Al hefted the big book. "You are going to get a lesson in advanced psychology, *and* how to save ten dollars. Remember, boys, education begins at home." He turned to Emily. "You know, sometimes I wonder about you."

Alarmed, she said, "What did I do?"

"It's what you *didn't* do. Roaring Shock test!" he exclaimed with aversion.

"Mr. Harkness said——" Emily began righteously.

"He did *not* say Roaring Shock test. The lady librarian must have thought I was the most prize schmo in history." His face burned with remembered shame. "For fifteen minutes I argued with her—and on *your* say-so."

"All I know——"

"It's *Rorschach,*" Al shouted; "R-O-R-S-C-H-A-C-H, Rorschach."

Emily was hurt. "So I added an ing. Is that so bad? One little ing," she appealed to the boys.

Al also addressed the court of appeals. "One little ing, she says. You boys have read how a comma, one lousy comma, has changed history, and she tries to sneak out from under an ing."

"Where?" Emily asked.

"Right here. Right in front of all of us."

"No, I mean where has a comma changed history?"

"Lots of places, isn't that right, Herman?"

"If you say so, Papa."

"I *do* say so. Ignoramuses. I'm surrounded by ignoramuses. What do I pay school taxes for? This town doesn't even have enough money for extra kindergartens so that Little Louie can go, and when kids do go, they don't get taught anything."

"Never mind trying to weasel out," Emily cried. "You don't know either."

"I do know."

"Prove it. Prove it by tomorrow, and I'll make you a chocolate cream pie. Don't prove it, and you get me a new hat."

Al's mouth watered. "I'll bring written proof," he said with dignity. "Better get ready to make that pie." Then he slapped his hand on the book with finality. "Now! to get down to business. Emily, have you any idea what a Rorschach test is?"

"No, just that Mr. Harkness said Little Louie should have one."

"Well, *I* know what it is. Everything is explained in this book, and it's just another example of the fraud perpetrated on the public by *educated* phonies. Ten dollars," he snorted.

"It's not the ten dollars," Emily said. "The person who gives the test has to be highly trained."

"Highly trained! For what? To make ink blots."

"Who said anything about ink blots?"

"I do, and this book does. That's what a Rorschach test is. You show people ink blots, simple little ink blots, and then you know what's wrong with them."

Emily's face showed such disbelief that Al opened the book to a place he had marked and said, "See, what are those?"

"Ink blots," Emily admitted.

With an air of satisfaction, Al closed the book. "There. Now, isn't it awful what a state this world has come to? A guy goes to school for thirty years, his poor parents pour out thousands and thousands of dollars—and for what? So he can make bigger and better ink blots."

Emily still showed doubt. "But this is the age of specialization, Al. You're always complaining how the day of the honest craftsman is done, how there's no room for the little man any more. It must be that everyone can't make ink blots the correct way. You need training."

"Do you need training to splash gravy on your tie?" Al asked.

The analogy was so obvious that Emily gave up.

Then Herman raised a problem. "But, Papa, it's against the

law to practice medicine without a license. You can get twenty years."

"Who's practicing medicine? Enough of this horsing around. Little Louie, get some paper and ink."

For once Little Louie obeyed with alacrity. His eyes even glinted.

Al sat on the couch with the book opened on his knees. Upon order, Herman and Sherman cleared the tea table for the paper and ink.

"Now here's what happens," Al said, when he was handed the proper materials, "we make ten ink blots, and Little Louie looks at them and tells us what he sees in them. The interesting thing about this is, the person who is emotionally disturbed sees different things than the well-adjusted person."

"My!" Emily exclaimed.

"I'm reading from the book," Al said, somewhat apologetically. "But, anyway, you can see how easy it is."

"You're right, Al. To charge for that is a gyp."

"You have to be pretty careful these days to catch con games on all sides. Little Louie, are you ready?"

"Yes, Papa." Little Louie was fascinated.

Everyone drew closer as Al said, "Remember, the important thing is what he sees in these ink blots. Interpreting the reading is intricate, it says in the book. I doubt that, but we'll see."

Carefully he poured ink onto a piece of paper, and with a deliberate gesture, folded the paper in half. Closing his eyes, Al then counted to ten and opened the paper again.

"Now what do you see in there?" he asked solemnly. "Careful, take your time and don't jump to conclusions."

Little Louie studied the paper for a moment, and then, without hesitation, said, "I see three big bad ogres eating a little boy."

"He sees three big bad ogres eating a little boy," Al repeated sarcastically. "Oh, Little Louie, what am I going to do about you?"

"But you asked me what I saw in there?" Little Louie said sullenly.

Al waved the paper. "Haven't I been telling you for three years there *are* no such things as big bad ogres? How can you see them if there *aren't* any? Now, look here." He spread the paper out and peered at it for a moment. Then in surprise, he said, "For gosh sakes, big bad ogres."

"Eating a little boy," Little Louie said in satisfaction.

"It looks more like a calf," Al started to say, and then, crumbling the paper, "Emily, get away, I'll try another one."

"Are you sure you're doing it right?" Emily asked.

"How can I do it wrong?" Al demanded, making another ink blot. "You have to give ten before you get a clear picture of your subject anyway." He stared at Little Louie. "With this kid, maybe it'll take twenty. Here, read this."

Little Louie judiciously studied the offering. "Communists," he said finally, with pursed lips.

"Communists!" Al shouted, snatching the paper away from him. "That's the stupidest thing I ever heard." He lowered his voice. "I mean, when you look at this thing all you see is what looks like two guys in hoods and a hammer and sick——"

"Better try another one," Emily advised.

"What did you say was so important about this test?" Herman asked. "About the nutty people seeing other things from the sane people . . ."

"Never mind," Al ground out as he prepared another ink blot.

By number seven Little Louie had seen a succession of goblins, cities devastated by atom bombs, and Officer O'Malley arresting Mr. Willnick for bookmaking. Although Al differed privately on one or two small points, he had to admit to himself that he had got a helluva likeness of Ed Willnick.

On number eight Little Louie announced that he saw a big snake swallowing Herman and Sherman. Afraid to look at the ink blot, Al slowly tore it to small pieces. He was in the classic pose of a broken man.

"Emily," he said sadly, "I'm admitting defeat."

"But, Al, you haven't finished."

"Sure, it was just getting good," Sherman protested.

"No," Al said; "no, it looks like I was wrong. Take him to the Child Guidance, even pay the ten dollars. And, Emily"—he looked up briefly—"Emily, ask if they have family rates . . ."

Ten

At Emily's suggestion he parked the car in front of Willnick's Bar & Grille, because she said she "had something to do" that would only take a few minutes and didn't want him along. It was just five o'clock when he stepped into Ed's. He was showered, shaved and dressed in his new suit. The front part of the bar was almost empty except for two or three customers who had paused on their way home from work for a quick one; but from behind the innocent-appearing door leading to the back room Al could hear the slight rumble of voices which he attributed to horseplayers awaiting the results from the Western tracks. Al didn't bet on the horses, and he had never been in Ed's back room. Not that he held anything against people who did frequent the horse room—he just wasn't interested.

Bald, white-jacketed Ed whistled as Al ambled to the bar. "Hey, Al, that's a sharp-looking suit."

Hoisting himself onto a bar stool Al fingered the cloth of his new suit, then reached into his pocket, drew forth an unopened pack of cigarettes and stripped away the cellophane.

"I got it a couple of weeks ago. They want a lot of money for suits these days."

"This Yankee Doodle business must be paying off. Draw you one, Al?" Al nodded, and as he worked the beer spiggot, Ed said, "How's Little Louie?"

Al shrugged. "Something's eating that kid, and his mother and I can't do anything about it. We're taking him to the Child Guidance over in Mineola tomorrow morning. Maybe they'll know what to do."

Ed's face expressed sympathy as he placed the beer on the bar. "It's tough to know what to do about kids these days. Everything is so fouled up in this world it's no wonder." The phone rang, and Ed said, "Excuse me, Al," and hurried to answer it.

Watching Ed through the glass of the phone booth, Al was aware of the vague envy he held for the man, and in his mind he reviewed the story that had made Willnick one of the town heroes—at least, to the male half of the population.

Years ago—well, eight or nine, anyway—Ed's bar had been an ice cream parlor, one of the old-style kind with a marble fountain, white tile floor and wire chairs with figured backrests. Both the ice cream parlor and Ed had been ruled by his wife, a stout, imposing woman who sat, frozen-faced, at the cash register while her husband dispensed the fountain products. Children were warned by a large sign on the wall that "Ice Cream Cones Are NOT To Be Eaten On Premises!!" and at slack moments Ed was always to be seen sitting at a corner table playing solitaire with a torn greasy deck of cards. The Willnicks, who lived in the rear of the store, were a neighborhood scandal, for at night noises were heard that could only mean that Mrs. Willnick beat Ed.

Then one day, with no prior announcement, Mrs. Willnick disappeared. When questioned, Ed stated vaguely that she had left to take care of her aged mother in Kansas, and, although this story was hardly believed, there was no proof of anything else nor was any other explanation offered.

Perhaps the normal suspicions of the neighborhood might have been quelled with time had not Ed, only two months after his wife's disappearance, closed down the ice cream parlor and boarded up the front, the only hint of inner activity being a sign reading "Closed for Extensive Alterations," and then, some weeks later, a large banner announcing the gala opening of Willnick's Bar & Grille.

Al believed with everyone else that somehow Ed Willnick had

murdered his wife and collected the insurance. Still, against Emily and the other women who accused Ed, he always came to Willnick's defense, quoting the unbreakable argument that had Ed really killed Mrs. Willnick, the police and insurance company would certainly have uncovered the crime. Though few held faith in the police, it was a generally accepted fact that insurance companies were infallible. Yet how could one explain both the disappearance of Mrs. Willnick and Ed's sudden wealth?

To add to the ladies' chatter, Ed's metamorphosis was complete on the personal level too. Never again did he play solitaire, although one could always get a poker game in the back room. Ed had quickly given up these quarters and now resided in a bachelor apartment where, it was rumored, he entertained women of loose character. And for months the gambling activites supported the establishment, for Ed, in an orgy of camaraderie, gave away many more drinks than were bought. Hiring a bartender, he perched himself each night on top of a special stool that in a way was a faint mockery of his departed wife and greeted each customer with increasing friendliness as the evening wore on. By closing time Ed was always pie-eyed.

Then, just as suddenly, Ed quit drinking, and from then on Willnick's Bar & Grille was conducted in a totally businesslike way. Al suspected that he and Ben were mainly responsible for Ed's going on the wagon, because it had been to them that Ed had almost spilled the story of what had happened to Mrs. Willnick. Perhaps he had become frightened, afraid that if he drank any longer he *would* talk. At any rate, he'd been sober for a long time.

His and Ben's near discovery of the truth had happened one night when they had dropped in for a late beer after bowling and had found Ed in a joyous alcoholic haze, sitting, in a departure from his usual practice, next to the jukebox and beating time to a Muggsy Spanier record. Greeted effusively by Ed, they had sat down with him and, protesting weakly, accepted the free beers pressed on them.

When the record ended, Ed shouted, "Put another nickel in, Al. Boy, I sure love that ricka-ticka-ticka music."

Ben grinned and said innocently, "It sure is a lot different around here, Ed, than it used to be."

"You can say that again," Ed cried. "Say that again, boy. Have another beer." His eyes glazed slightly, and he was overcome by the shudders as he pictured what the bar had formerly been. "Tell you something, boys," he said, leaning over the table, "you'll never know how I hated that ice cream parlor. Remember that sign I had up? I put it there because I couldn't stand kids. Seeing kids eating ice cream cones made me sick to my stomach. Their little, grimy paws . . ." He closed his eyes and seemed about to expire with the memories of the past, and Ben quickly tilted the bottle Ed had in front of him. The drink revived him enough so that he could look at them again. "It got too much," he said. "Too much. Man wasn't made to stand such torture." He raised his finger and shook it pedantically, "Comes a time when *something* has to go."

Al and Ben looked at each other, but Ed didn't notice the exchange. "My wife," he muttered, "how I hated that woman. But she did me one favor—one favor——"

"And that was?" Al asked eagerly.

Ed regarded them owlishly. "All those years we were together," he said slowly, "all those years she wouldn't let me spend a nickel—and when it came time for me to count it up, it came to"—he tapped the table—"seventeen thousand dollars."

Al whistled. "So that's how you paid for the bar, huh?"

"That's how."

"But what about"—Ben paused, licking his lower lip—"what about Mrs. Willnick?"

Ed looked at the bottle of whisky in front of him and quickly took another drink. "I hated her," he said. "I hated her so bad—and like I said something had to go. Twenty-two years of hell with that woman. Then one night I said to her, 'Norah—[this was the first time Al had ever heard her first name] Norah,' I said, 'either you clear outta here, or I will kill you with an ax.' I had an ax, too, you can bet your life."

"Uh," Ben grunted.

"Yeah, that's what I said. You boys have another beer. First she thought I was kidding. But I wasn't. Honest I wasn't." He tilted the bottle again. "She says, 'You kill me, and you get the chair,' an'

I say, 'For killing you the chair would be a pleasure. Now clear out,' I tell her—" He broke off suddenly.

"Well, did she?" Al prompted breathlessly. "I mean, did she clear out?"

"You boys have another beer," Ed said, and as the record on the jukebox ended, his face relaxed into the look of a sleeping man lost in a beautiful dream, and slowly he slumped forward—out cold.

Of course, there was no more out of Ed that night—or any other night thereafter. That was the end to the strange affair, but the strangest thing was that Al, though he had all intentions of doing so, never told Emily of Ed's partial revelation. Without any spoken agreement, he and Ben kept Ed's secret.

The sound of the phone booth as it clattered open brought Al back to the present, and as Ed waddled across the floor to take his place behind the bar, Al wondered briefly what he had done with the body. Then he said to himself, No, it couldn't have happened that way. She must have left—and how wonderful it was for Ed that things had turned out well for him. And though Al couldn't quite clarify the thought to the full realization of why he admired Ed so, it was the knowledge that so rarely did a man triumph completely over tyranny and adversity, that when it happened it was to be revered like a perfect jewel or some other miracle of individuality——

And again his thoughts were broken into, but this time by Emily's voice, and as he looked up to see her standing in the doorway of the bar, he noticed that something about Emily's appearance had changed since they left the house. He puzzled over it as Emily and Ed greeted one another.

"Ready, Al?" Emily asked. She seemed to be posing, holding her head in a funny position.

"In a minute." He lifted his beer and drained the glass. Then he slammed it to the bar. "Hey," he said, "you got a new hat."

She smiled. "Like it?" She turned like a model. "Do you like it, Ed?"

Ed nodded admiringly.

"It cost a lot, but it's a present from my husband. Al's so generous."

"Generous! Boy, you don't waste any time, do you?" he complained, and then he turned to Ed. "Willnick, how about it, when you were a kid in school don't you remember learning where a comma changed history?"

Ed's expanse of forehead wrinkled as he concentrated. "Sounds familiar, Al, but I can't really say. That was so long ago," he apologized. "Wouldn't the library have it?"

"Too late," Emily cried triumphantly. "You said you'd bring written proof by today."

He got off the bar stool and took her arm. Rather than tell her he'd spent his whole lunch hour in the library, he decided to keep quiet. "Even though you take advantage," he said piously, "I never welsh on a bet." They started out the door, and Emily leaned over and quickly planted a kiss on his cheek.

"There's a chocolate pie in the refrigerator," she whispered. "You can have a piece when we get home."

He grinned as he helped her into the car. It was an awfully pretty hat.

Ascending to the upper reaches of the building at 462 Madison Avenue an hour later, Al was grumbling about it being a silly time for parties, and Emily was telling him that if he read magazine stories he would know that this was the proper time for a cocktail party; but when they emerged on the twenty-third floor, they were surprised to find the office quiet and seemingly deserted. Just as they were about to retreat, however, Barbie McClain came from behind one of the doors leading to an inner office.

She greeted them warmly. "I've been waiting for you, Mr. Toolum, and I'm so glad you could come along," she said, shaking hands with Emily.

"Where is everybody?" Al asked, suspiciously. "I thought something important was supposed to be happening."

"It is," she assured him, "but it's happening at the Thirty-three Club. John thought—well, he didn't want you to become confused, so he thought you should come here."

Al laughed shortly. "He doesn't trust me, I guess."

Barbie smiled at Emily. "You *have* given John a few bad moments." She pressed the Down button. "He thought you *might* get lost, and that would be disastrous. You're a very integral part of this afternoon's activity. A lot of our press releases involve you."

Al had parked the car in a lot, so they hailed a cab. "This Thirty-three Club," he echoed, after Barbie had given the address to the driver, "it's a night club, isn't it? Why are we going there this time of day?" Emily, he noticed, had perked up considerably at the mention of the 33 Club. Now, seated on his left, he could feel her trembling in what he interpreted as delight.

"Publicity cocktail party," Barbie explained. "A lot of the fancier ones are held there. The press is more likely to show up if the food and liquor promises to be good."

"Free loading, huh?"

"In return for publicity. This party is to start the Miss Schlepp contest."

"Pardon me?"

"The Miss Schlepp contest. You know, every year Schlepp's beer chooses a girl to be Miss Schlepp."

"I don't read the advertisements," Al said apologetically.

"I do," Emily said. "She's always very pretty."

The cab had made a U-turn under the baleful gaze of a traffic cop and was now heading north. "Be sure and keep that quiet, Mr. Toolum, when you meet Mr. Schlepp," Barbie said drily.

"Oh, it's my favorite beer," Al said hastily. "Not that I guess there's much difference between them," he added thoughtfully, "but Ben Carroway—he's my best friend—he buys it all the time, so I got into the habit. Uh—what have I got to do with this?"

"Mr. Welton thought it would be a nice tie-in to introduce you to one of the candidates. She's a New York girl, and because you're a famous contest winner from around New York you might be her sponsor." She glanced sidewise at Al. "Take sort of a fatherly interest."

"What it this, a beer-drinking baby?"

Barbie laughed as the cab swung west and slowed to a stop in front of a green-and-brown-striped canopy. Al felt terribly uncomfortable as Barbie pressed a dollar into the driver's hand. He'd been wondering about the protocol of paying, but she didn't give him time even to make a gesture.

"Speaking of being a sponsor," he said, reaching for the door, "a man got me to be a sponsor for an outfit that has to do with——"

"Thank you, Mr. Toolum."

". . . the natives of the Pacific. It's called the League to Free——"

"That's nice, Mr. Toolum. Now we just go inside."

". . . the Pacific People. Do you think that's all right?"

"Leave your hat right here. Yes, yes, I think that's fine. Let's see, where's John?"

"Oh, this is so wonderful!" Emily quivered, as Barbie led them into a larger room. "I never expected *ever* to see the inside of this place."

The anteroom had been dark and heavily carpeted, but the room in which they now found themselves was brightly lighted, and the walls were gaily decorated with dancing antelopes. A maze of people milled about in total confusion.

"The Antelope Room," Emily sighed. "Don't be surprised if you see Clark Gable."

"I wouldn't recognize him in this mob," Al said.

Actually, as he stood studying the scene, it took on some order. In one corner stood a knot of men surrounding a long table laden with food. Some of them carried cameras. A number of well-dressed men and women flowed about, their voices pitched brittlely over the general hum of conversation. Two other small groups were formed, one around a short, fat man who was almost completely hidden by his satellites, and the other paid court to a tall, strawberry-blonde girl who seemed frightened. Almost everyone carried a glass of beer, but Al could see whisky bottles placed unobtrusively in different parts of the room.

"Hello, Toolum." John appeared, looking slightly wild-eyed. Al wondered whether he had been drinking. Wiping perspiration from his face, John exclaimed, "What a rat race. I'm going crazy trying to get everything to go off all right. You *will* co-operate, won't you?" he begged.

"Sure," Al promised.

"Then come over and meet Jean Wilcox. Mrs. Toolum, I'm sure you can find someone to talk to." He led Al away, saying, "We'll get some pictures, and then maybe I can relax awhile."

Al experienced a moment of apprehension. "No speech this time, I hope."

John grinned. "Not this time. Just look fatherly."

"What's this fatherly?" Al asked, but the question was unanswered.

Jean Wilcox, New York candidate for Miss Schlepp, smiled at him quickly and, Al thought, mechanically as they were introduced. She was taller than he and quite thin, and her movements were constricted by a stiff, black taffeta dress that crackled as she moved. It was so low-cut that Al glanced guiltily toward the spot where he had left Emily, but she had disappeared.

She looks awfully worried, Al decided, studying Miss Wilcox. Her face, pretty enough, was imprisoned behind a layer of make-up, and what was wrong with her, Al thought, was that she was desperately trying to make a good impression on the people who counted, and since she couldn't separate the ones who counted from the ones who didn't, she was forced to turn her charms on everyone.

They stood in the uncomfortable position of two people left alone who had nothing in common, suspended in thought and motion, as John tried to round up the photographers.

"Are you—are you with the Schlepp people, Mr.— Mr. . . . ?"

"Toolum," Al said. "No, I'm not. I'm Yankee Doodle."

There was a brief second as Jean Wilcox's eyes reflected something approaching madness; then they cleared. "Oh, yes, yes, Yankee Doodle. For a minute I didn't—quite understand."

Her voice was soft, and under the make-up she was quite a pretty girl. Al patted her hand, acting fatherly. "Sometimes I don't understand myself," he confessed. "All this happened because my son is smarter than I am. Who got you into this?"

She laughed shortly. "I got myself into it. The head of my model agency thought it was a very good idea."

"Well, if you make a living at it," Al nodded.

"Oh, it's very worth while, Mr Toolum, honestly. I'd be terribly lucky if I won."

"Then I hope you do," Al said stoutly.

John arrived then, and for the next several minutes Al and Miss Wilcox were subjected to flashing lights that caught them in varying poses: shaking hands, smiling at each other, mutually admiring an oversized bottle of Schlepp's beer, and Al planting a very fatherly kiss on Miss Wilcox's forehead.

"Thank you, Mr. Toolum," Jean Wilcox said, when they were released.

Al's lips were slightly coated with powder, but he liked the flavor. "That's all right," he said. "I hope you win, and if I can help you . . ."

Miss Wilcox's eyes were beyond Al, pinned on a columnist, from whom a mention was tantamount to sanctification. She murmured, "I'll call on you," as she drifted past.

Al's smile froze to a grimace as he saw that he was being regarded from across the room by Emily who did *not* look particularly gay. Emily was standing with the fat, little man, and as Al approached she turned to the little man, ignoring her husband.

"Anytime," she said, "anytime you want I'll be glad to make you some goulash."

"On my yacht?" the little man asked happily, and then he sighed. "Goulash. Those fool doctors—and ever since my wife died——"

"What yacht?" Al demanded.

Emily turned slowly. "Are you through with your kissing?"

"Oh, now, Em, for crying out loud . . ."

They were surrounded by the same knot of people who tended the fat, little man whose face was red, and whose hands moved constantly as though he were shooing flies. He held Emily's arm like a drowning man, and suddenly began waving wildly at the young men who, with amoebic movements, flowed around him.

"Go away," he cried. "Go away. I can't breathe any more."

The amoebas dissolved. "Now we talk about goulash some more," the little man said to Emily. He fixed a stern glance on Al. "Who are you?"

"This is my husband," Emily explained.

"I'm Schlepp," the little man said. "So you're that Yankee Doodle dandy," he accused. "Ain't you too old for such foolishness?"

Al flushed, then he answered spiritedly, "No more foolishness than this contest you've got here."

"You're right," Mr. Schlepp admitted sadly. "But"—leaning toward Al—"I can't do nothing about it. I don't own myself any more. Used to be when I was a young feller I made a little beer, gave it to my friends, sold a little here and there. I was happy, hein? No more. I got breweries, board of directors, agencies—agencies!"

"You've got money, too," Al said.

"Money! You think money makes you happy?"

"You're damn right," Al said, "and if it doesn't, I'll trade a little of that unhappiness for the unhappiness I've got now."

"What's the matter with what you've got now?" Mr. Schlepp cried. "Look at your beautiful wife—she says you got three boys." He pressed Emily's arm smiling at her tenderly. "And if she's half the cook she says she is——"

"I'll vouch for that," Al said, "but you misunderstood me. I was talking about my troubles, not my family."

"Phooey," Mr. Schlepp exclaimed. He pursed his lips, and as a young man in a blue flannel suit passed, he transfixed him with a fat forefinger. "You! Go pour Mr. Toolum into a glass some beer."

The young man nodded and hurried off.

"That's all they're good for—waiters," Schlepp murmured. "You drink my beer, don't you?" he asked Al.

"Yes, sir," Al answered, glad it was the truth. Schlepp beamed, and Al reached into his pocket. "Have a cigar?" he offered.

"Cigars! You smoke cigars? Don't you know smoking ruins taste? How can you appreciate good beer if your tongue is paralyzed?" His face quivered with indignation.

"I like it," Al said, puffing heartily. "Sometimes a good cigar is better than a good beer. Depends on how you feel."

"Feh!" cried Mr. Schlepp.

The beer was delivered. "Look at him," Mr. Schlepp referred to the retreating figure. "Saying yes, sir, yes, sir, all the time, and behind my back they give the newspapermen liquor."

Al sipped the beer and smacked his lips. "Good. Really hits the spot."

Mr. Schlepp's face cleared. "I can see you're a man with taste. You can come on my yacht with your wife."

"The boys would love it too," Emily said.

"Bring them all," Schlepp cried. "I have a special trip. Leave Seventy-eighth Street and sail around Manhattan. From one point in the North River you can see my breweries in Brooklyn, Queens and Manhattan all the same time." He pinched Emily's arm lightly. "I got a galley on board. That's nautical for kitchen. You cook dinner, huh?" He smacked his lips. "No doctors allowed on my yacht."

"I'd be glad to," Emily smiled.

"Tonight. What do you say tonight?"

"We can't," Emily apologized. "We have a sitter, and . . ."

Mr. Schlepp showed his disappointment. Then he snapped his fingers. "Hey, you," he shouted, and immediately they were ringed by the knot of young men. "Enough already," Schlepp instructed. "They drank enough liquor. Throw 'em out."

He nodded to Al and then kissed Emily's hand lingeringly.

"Looks like you have a boy friend," Al grinned, as Mr. Schlepp drifted away. "He's no Clark Gable, though."

"He's very nice," Emily defended, and then John stepped up to them.

"I was hoping Mr. Welton would show up," he said, "because he wanted to talk to you. But he just called and asked if you could come down to the office tomorrow morning."

"I don't think so," Al hesitated. "We have to take Little Louie somewhere." He looked helplessly at Emily who came to his rescue. "That's all right, Al, you go ahead. I can take Little Louie alone."

"Okay, then I can make it," Al said, feeling strangely relieved that he didn't have to go to the Child Guidance.

"Fine. You can go home now, if you want to, Mr. Toolum. Thanks for coming."

Al nodded. "It was fun," he said.

In the cab they took to the parking lot Al studied a handsomely printed brochure about the Miss Schlepp contest that he'd been handed as they left the club. He peered at the pictures of the other five contestants, and after long deliberation, decided that, even allowing for his natural prejudice, Jean Wilcox was the prettiest of the six girls.

"The winner is determined by popular ballot," he read. "Each purchaser of a bottle or glass of Schlepp's beer is allowed to place a vote in the ballot box found in every bar and store that handles Schlepp's beer. Well,"—he looked up at Emily—"looks like I have to do a little electioneering."

"Oh, you do, do you?"

"Look, if you can cook goulash for Mr. Schlepp, I can vote for Miss Wilcox." There was no answer to this, and he added, "And, besides, it's every American's duty to vote. It's the democratic way."

He leaned back into the seat cushions and grinned. He'd line up Ben to help him, and between them they'd get plenty of votes for Jean Wilcox.

Eleven

Although Al made a big fuss the following morning about being sorry he couldn't go to the Child Guidance, Emily was perfectly aware of the fact that he wasn't sorry at all. He knew Little Louie had to go, but as the time approached he became more and more distressed at the fact that it was necessary. Al felt that a visit to the Child Guidance was an admission of failure and was something to be ashamed of, and he hated the idea that somewhere along the line he and Emily had failed.

He could, he told Emily, take the whole day off and call the Consultants to tell them he'd be in that afternoon, but he was beginning to feel guilty about all the time he was stealing from Henry Muller. Not that Henry was complaining, he hastily added; on the contrary, the publicity given Acme Tool & Die had already brought in new business, and Henry was very pleased, still . . .

Emily said she understood perfectly, and she didn't mind going alone with Little Louie. As a matter of fact maybe it would be better.

What did she mean better? Al wanted to know. Who else but a boy's father should take him to the Child Guidance? he demanded.

Well, Emily told him, Al might get sore at people who pretended they knew more about Little Louie than he did, and it would be better if she first sized up the situation.

Al thought that over for a little while and finally admitted that perhaps she was right.

So it was Emily alone, feeling an unpleasant emptiness in her stomach, who took Little Louie to the Child Guidance for his appointment. He was dressed in his best clothes, his hair was slicked down except for that little piece that never stayed put no matter how hard it was combed, and he went without complaint. Quite subdued, their hands clasped, Emily and Little Louie entered the cold, gray building that housed the Mineola division of the Child Guidance Bureau.

Immediate reassurance was theirs, for the inner offices of the Bureau were warm and friendly as was the manner of the middle-aged lady in a white silk dress who greeted them.

"I'm Mrs. Toolum," Emily explained nervously, "and I have an appointment for eleven o'clock."

"Oh, of course," the lady said and magically produced a card from a small file. "I'm Mrs. Goren, and this"—eying the card and then Little Louie—"this must be Louis Alvin Toolum."

"We call him Little Louie," Emily said.

From nowhere Mrs. Goren whipped a lollipop and held it in front of Little Louie's nose. "Do you think you can make away with this while you wait for Dr. Martin?"

"If you got a lime one, maybe I could," Little Louie said. He was willing to go part of the way with this lady who had that silly look on her face that grownups always got when they wanted kids to do something for them.

Before Emily could admonish him, Mrs. Goren produced the lime pop, and Little Louie sat down with it on a couch and thoughtfully surveyed his surroundings.

Before they were received by Dr. Martin, Emily was able to establish the fact that he was not a medical doctor but a PhD in psychology. Mrs. Goren imparted this knowledge in a whispered conversation that was supposed to exclude Little Louie.

"What's a PhD?" he asked, when Emily joined him on the couch. He had very sharp ears except when he was called on to do a chore, get washed or go to bed. At those times he was overcome by a strange hearing ailment.

"It means he went to school longer than most people," Emily said.

"Is he smarter than Papa?"

Emily hesitated. "In some things, I guess."

"But Papa says going to school don't mean you learn more."

"About life, no," Emily said. "About Roaring Shock tests, yes."

Dr. Martin proved to be much younger than Emily had imagined, but her worries on this score were partly settled after a look at the shelves of books that lined the walls of his office. If Dr. Martin, who had risen to greet them, knew just a fraction of what was in those books, he was very smart indeed. There was no couch, Emily also noted, and outside of a large screen that obscured one corner, the room resembled a well-appointed study.

Dr. Martin, who was thirty and slender, with thinning, sandy hair, removed his glasses as he rose. His voice was low-pitched and friendly. "So this is Little Louie," he said. "I've read about your father in the newspaper. I bet you and your mother are very proud of him."

Emily nodded vigorously, while Little Louie tried his best to look both disinterested and sinister at the same time. His sinister look told Emily that he was frightened, and as she sat in the chair indicated by Dr. Martin, she drew his stiff body close to her.

Expecting a preliminary talk without Little Louie's being present, where she could tell Dr. Martin all about Little Louie's silly fear of dying, she was surprised when Dr. Martin said, "Well, Little Louie, are you ready to look at some pictures with me?"

Little Louie said, "I guess so."

Emily was again surprised, because she fully expected her son to resist any suggestion. But the sinister look was disappearing.

"If you'll wait outside, Mrs. Toolum," Dr. Martin said cheerfully, "your boy and I are going to play a game."

"I know all about the Roaring Shock test," Little Louie bragged. "Papa gave me one the other night."

The doctor laughed. "Oh, he did, eh? I bet that was fun."

Emily was terribly embarrassed as Little Louie said gleefully, "I scared the pants off him."

"I'll tell you something," Dr. Martin grinned, "there's nothing you can say or do that will scare me."

Emily left, wondering if the doctor had said the wisest thing. There was a calculating expression in Little Louie's eyes that showed he would sure try.

Settling herself in the outer office, Emily remarked to Mrs. Goren what a wonderful way Dr. Martin had with children.

Mrs. Goren nodded. "Boys, especially, take to him right away."

"I thought he'd want to ask a lot of questions before he did anything. I could help him find where the trouble is."

"He'll find out," Mrs. Goren said with certainty.

"But how? If I don't tell him——"

"*You* don't know," Mrs. Goren said a little sternly, and then her voice softened. "What I mean is, you just suffer the results. If you had known the cause of the trouble, chances are there wouldn't be any trouble."

This seemed reasonable. "Still," Emily said, "what good does it do to get just one side of the story?"

Mrs. Goren regarded Emily thoughtfully. "Actually, Mrs. Toolum," she said, finally, "unless there's extreme disturbance in the family—if one or both of the parents show great unbalance—there *is* only one side, and that's the child's. Of course, the parents, average parents, that is—and certainly"—she smiled—"you and Mr. Toolum must be average—the parents have to come in for a little education to learn what happened to the child, and how they slipped up."

Emily hated the thought that she and Al had slipped up. "Maybe—maybe with three children a mother just doesn't have time," she said unhappily.

"Perhaps." Mrs. Goren's tone had once more become impersonal.

Emily spent the next few minutes staring out the frosted door that led to the hallway. The offices were arranged so that each one led off a central hall to insure a maximum of privacy. Then she switched her gaze to the door leading to Dr. Martin's private office. The silence, and the finality of the closed door made her anxious to know what was happening.

"He's just giving the Rorschach," Mrs. Goren answered her question. "It won't be much longer."

"What's behind the screen in there?" Emily asked.

"Oh, that," Mrs. Goren smiled. "A stenographer sits behind there who takes notes on everything the subject says. Dr. Martin just shows the cards and draws out the subject. Little Louie will say a lot more that way. It would cause him to freeze up if he saw the doctor writing down everything he said."

Emily saw the logic to that, remembering the times she had been polled by numerous public opinion people, and always, though she wanted to say a great deal, the sight of the pencil poised to take down every word, and the eager, expectant look in the interviewer's eyes had caused her to answer in stupid monosyllables.

"What happens after this?" she asked, wanting to anticipate Al's questions.

"When the boy is Little Louie's age we make an appointment for play therapy. Would you like to do that now?" She drew out an appointment book and leafed through it. "How about next Monday, the same time?"

Emily made some rapid calculations. "I'm afraid not Monday. I have an important meeting of the Minute Maids. Is Tuesday all right?" Mrs. Goren nodded, and while she made the notation, Emily asked, "What's play therapy?"

"It's a little complicated to explain; actually, through play we find out against whom the subject's aggressions are directed. You'll see when you bring Little Louie in next week."

A few moments later the door opened, and Little Louie strutted out, followed by Dr. Martin. To answer Emily's anxious gaze, Dr. Martin assured her, "Little Louie did fine. He and I are old pals now."

"He's better than Papa," Little Louie said. "His pictures have a lot more stuff in them."

Dr. Martin and Little Louie shook hands, and the doctor disappeared into his office. "Say good-bye to Mrs. Goren, Little Louie," Emily instructed.

" 'Bye," Little Louie said. He paused in the doorway. "Next time have cherry—" Mrs. Goren nodded. "And bigger," Little Louie said, then turned to his mother. "Hey, you know what?" he asked as they went out the door, "there was somebody hiding behind the screen all the time I was in there. Just like a spy story on television."

Emily closed the door, smiling weakly at Mrs. Goren, whose mouth remained wide open, expressing just the slightest awe.

Sitting in Paul Welton's office just about the time that Emily left the Bureau, Al was wishing that he could break away for a few minutes to make a phone call. If he called Emily it would ease his guilt a bit. But how could he say to Welton, "Do you mind if I call my wife to see if one of our kids is nuts?" This was obviously not the thing one said to Paul Welton, so he dismissed the idea from his mind and tried to concentrate on what Welton was saying.

"Now, Mr. Toolum, I've been thinking that all that's happened to you so far is what *we've* planned for you. Perhaps it's about time one of your wishes were fulfilled. Is there anything that you'd like to do as Yankee Doodle Fifty-two—say a realization of a lifelong ambition?" he concluded.

Al showed his bewilderment. "I don't get you. Like what?"

"Oh, I don't know. Isn't there something you've always wanted to do, yet have never had the chance? Maybe someone you'd like to meet. How about the President?"

"I saw him once in a parade," Al said. He thought a moment, and then he brightened. "There is someone I'd like to meet—or, what I mean is, I'd like my kids to meet him. Maybe even have their pictures taken with him."

Paul Welton chuckled. "And who is that? Gene Autry?"

"Who? Oh, no, no. Albert Einstein."

Welton stared at him, puzzled, and Al added, "You know, the man who invented the atom bomb—or, anyway, started it all."

"I know who Einstein is," Welton said, a little sharply. "But, for heaven's sake, why do you want to meet him?"

"Not me really. My kids. I read in a book where Einstein is maybe one of the ten greatest men who ever lived." Holding up his hand, he began to tick off on his fingers, "There was Aristotle, Mohammed, Buddha, Jesus—you know, men who had tremendous influence on the civilizations after them. That's something, isn't it? All these thousands of years, and there's only nine people as great as Einstein. Wouldn't it be wonderful for my kids to show a picture of themselves with him to *their* kids?"

"Einstein," Paul Welton said, and, turning to John, he said, "How about it, Bell?"

John shrugged. "From all I've heard he's a pretty hard man to reach."

"That's because he plays the violin a lot," Al offered, as explanation. "People who play the violin like to be alone. It helps them think."

"I'll get in touch with Princeton," John said, ignoring Al, "and see what we can do."

"Perhaps we could work a nice twist to it," Welton said thoughtfully. "The country's most average man meeting the world's most *un*average."

Al, glad to see his suggestion receiving acceptance, was about to bring up the Miss Schlepp contest, hoping he could be used again in some capacity, when Paul Welton said, "One more thing, Mr. Toolum," and Al noticed the stern lines returning to his face. He forgot the Miss Schlepp contest. "Yes, sir?"

"I—uh, I've recently received some information from Washington telling me there was a rather surprising response to the O'Daniel program where you"—his expression turned to one of distaste—"you expressed some views on the plight of the Pacific natives."

"Oh, that. They wouldn't let me finish. I had more to say, but about the American Indians. Do you know——?"

"To be sure," Welton interrupted, "but my informant says that a great number of letters were recieved asking for an investigation of your charges."

Al cringed deeper into his chair, and hoped he didn't show his sudden inner turmoil. Just goes to show you can't fool with the State Department. "I didn't charge anyone," he said, finally.

"Didn't you say that a general owned an ice plant and some other installations?" Welton asked coldly.

"Sure, but—is that really wrong? I thought all generals did that. They don't make much money, and——"

"Toolum, I simply want to explain that there's danger in expressing such half-thought-out opinions. Obviously the letters were sent by Reds who look for any chance to cause trouble. You want to get mixed up with them?"

Al was frightened. "Oh, no, *sir!*"

"I'm glad." Welton sighed. "Of course, there'll be no investigation."

"That's fine," Al said earnestly. "I wouldn't want to cause that general any trouble. After all, he saw to it that the enlisted men got two cans of beer *every* month."

Welton looked up sharply, but there was no hint of sarcasm on

Al's face. Softly, Welton said, "All right, Mr. Toolum, that'll be all for today."

Barbie was standing at John's desk when they came out. "Hi, Mr. Toolum," she said, "how's the family?"

"Fine," Al said automatically, and then, "I mean, not so fine. We're having trouble with Little Louie." He could call from here, he thought.

"I hope it's nothing serious," Barbie said sympathetically.

I'd better do it outside, he decided, and saying good-bye, he left, and when the door had closed behind him, John said, "You know, sometimes that guy scares me."

"Why?" Barbie asked.

"Well—it's really hard to put into words. He looks simple, but he isn't—or is he? All I know is that I'd hate like hell to be a lawyer and have him on the stand for cross-examination."

"He's *your* average man," Barbie said pointedly.

"I'm beginning to wonder," John said.

In a drugstore downstairs Al tried to call home, but there was no answer, and he left the phone booth feeling frustrated. First Reds and now no one home to answer the telephone. Debating for a moment whether he should have lunch here in the drugstore or wait until he got home, he decided on the latter. He had turned down an offer of lunch with John for a vague reason that he couldn't really define. He felt uncomfortable, he admitted to himself, whenever he was with anyone connected with AAC—except, maybe, Barbie. But this admission which led him to a further feeling of inadequacy made him angry. Smart talk about books and plays and things! Even when he had something to say he was afraid to say it, because everyone looked at him like he was going to come out with something freakish.

Leaving the drugstore, he walked toward the corner bus stop where four buses were lined up at the red light. Quickening his pace, he saw that the first two were crowded, so he stepped up to the third just as the light turned green. Slam! went the door as the driver pulled away from the curb.

"Damn!" Al muttered and whirled to get the last bus. The

driver was watching him blankly through the windshield. His door was already closed, and as Al tapped on it, the driver averted his head and started the bus.

"Open up," Al shouted, and in a sudden fury he kicked the side of the moving bus as it slid away. Two women passing by turned to observe this strange action, and Al exclaimed angrily, "I'll kill him."

The women looked away impersonally as they continued on their way, leaving Al fuming impatiently on the curb. All the way up Madison there wasn't another bus in sight.

Deciding to walk to Penn Station gave him little satisfaction other than knowing that he was depriving the bus company of his dime and two cents for a transfer, but as he walked he told himself sternly that he would never ride that bus line again. This decision seriously limited Al's transportation in the city, because he already had similar feuds with the Fifth Avenue, Broadway and Eighth Avenue lines. There were any number of bus drivers suffering under a gypsy curse that Al had once wormed out of Emily's great-aunt early in his marriage. He often regretted that these unfortunate men didn't know the source of their continued ill luck that was a certain result of the curse.

"No wonder," he told himself, "people become bolsheviks or anarchists or something," and this thought reminded him of Paul Welton's warning. He wondered if the League of which he was a sponsor had written any of the letters—and decided that it had, for that was one of the functions of the organization as explained to him by its president, Mr. Gomez.

Al began to feel uncomfortable. Only Reds wrote letters to stir up trouble.

Bringing out the letter he had received from the League, he studied it as he walked along. Nothing suspicious about it at first examination. All those professors and everyone listed on the side— they couldn't be Reds.

The League, he saw in the heading, had its offices on Forty-third Street, and, on sudden whim, Al decided he would go up there and see what it was all about. Once more his pace quickened as he swept down Madison Avenue, a man with a purpose.

The office of the League to Free the Pacific Peoples was a distinct disappointment. Al had imagined a spacious, luxurious suite to match the lofty purpose of the organization; instead, the League was housed in a building so narrow that he walked back and forth three times before he spotted the correct number in a recessed hallway between a bar and a clothing store. There was an elevator that creaked and groaned and was hardly big enough for another occupant besides the rheumy old man who operated it. The hallway floor was worn, and the frosted glass that identified the League office was milky-dirty and scarred.

A girl in a black dress regarded him suspiciously in the small anteroom, and her look of suspicion wasn't dispelled when he announced his name.

Yes, Mr. Gomez was in, and, yes, she'd call him.

Tomàs Gomez greeted him with pleased politeness. He was a wispy brown man, so tiny and dry that he gave the appearance of one whose appointment on earth is merely temporary. On their first meeting he had explained to Al that he was a native of Guam who had been educated at the University of Hawaii. During the Japanese occupation of the island from the winter of 1942 until July 16, 1944, he had lived, as did his fellow islanders, in passive acceptance of the invader, but with the beginning of the bombardment that preceded the landing of the Americans, he had been a leader of those Guamanians who risked their lives by lighting lanterns at night in the critical target areas.

Gomez had told him about this during their lunch together, and though Al had heard the story many times while on Guam, it sounded particularly heroic coming from Tomàs Gomez, mainly because Gomez told the story in a very unheroic manner. But he must be a hero, Al had decided, or why else would he leave Guam to come to a country where he was looked upon as inferior because of his color? And why would he knock his brains out in a fight that had so little chance for success? The world was like a man being eaten up by a lion, and who was going to pay attention to a gnat like Gomez?

Gomez told him that it did a man good to fight a good fight, no matter how futile, and that's why Al should become a sponsor. Al accepted this, and said, Okay, he'd be a sponsor, but later he shame-facedly admitted that the main reason he wanted to be one was to get his name listed along with the professors.

Now, after apologizing for the appearance of the office, Gomez asked him if he'd had lunch, and Al explained that he was on his way to Penn Station and just thought he'd drop in.

"I'll walk you there," Gomez said.

Over Al's protests, Gomez insisted that he always took a walk around lunchtime, and he welcomed the chance to get out.

They walked west until reaching Broadway and then turned south. Little was said, because Al was arguing with himself whether he should speak to Gomez about Welton's warning. Now that he was with the little man he felt foolish about the whole thing.

Finally, he said bluntly, "Somebody told me today that a lot of letters were written on account of that broadcast asking for an investigation."

"Oh, yes," Gomez said happily. "I am glad to hear that."

"But nothing's going to happen," Al added, turning to see what effect this would have on Gomez.

But if his companion felt disappointed, he didn't show it. Instead, he shrugged philosophically. "Like water dripping on rocks," he said. "To see it one notices no effect." He eyed Al slyly. "But have you ever seen the Grand Canyon?"

Al grunted. "No, but I read where it took millions of years to make."

"Your senators and other lawmakers are less than stone," Gomez said.

Reaching the station, they descended to the Long Island level. When Al saw that he had over ten minutes until the next train left for Fernvale, he and Gomez sat on a bench.

"Look, Mr. Gomez," Al said, after a pause, "this guy—the one who told me about the letters—said the only people who wrote things like that were Reds. That scared me. I—I can't afford to get mixed up in anything. I have a wife and three kids . . ." He broke off, waiting for a reply.

Gomez took his time, and when he did answer, he said, "Mr.

Toolum, haven't you ever written a letter to your congressman?"

"No, why should I? I vote—sometimes. That's enough."

"It's more than most people do," Gomez admitted, "but it isn't enough."

"I want to write letters when I get real mad, but, what the heck, they don't pay any attention."

"It's your voice," Gomez said, "a means of action—your way of being heard." He smiled. "But that doesn't answer your question, does it?"

Al shook his head. "I hate to ask you, like I'd hate to ask a man his religion."

"Well, I'm not a Red," Tomàs Gomez said. Al sighed with relief. "But that really doesn't mean anything," he continued. "To the general—the one we both knew on Guam—I am a Red. Anyone who opposes him is a Red—you too."

Al stared at him in horror. "Me?"

"Yes. It's an excellent way of keeping you quiet, don't you see?"

"No, I don't see," Al said hotly. "What you told me about wanting to give the people in the Pacific a square deal—it all sounded good to me. It's stuff written right in our own constitution."

Gomez answered with a helpless spread of his hands.

"I don't want to get caught in any mangle," Al said. "I made up my mind a couple of years ago that if the world is going to hell in a barrel there's nothing I can do to stop it. I can only relax and enjoy myself, as the lady said."

"But maybe the world isn't going to hell in a barrel."

"If it isn't, it's giving a darn good imitation. I wouldn't mind for myself, because I've lived a pretty good life. But I get awful sad when I look at my kids. If something happened they wouldn't know what hit 'em, and they wouldn't even know why. Once"—he shifted in his seat—"I saw an old woman right after she'd been hit by a car. She was almost blind and had been walking against the light. I didn't know her, so I couldn't feel sorry for her the way I'd feel if she were a friend—but I remember thinking how awful it was, because she hadn't had a chance."

Tomàs Gomez nodded slowly. "Would you have tried to pull the old lady out of the way if you'd seen it happen?"

Al started to answer, and then he saw the reason behind the question. "I don't know," he said slowly. "Maybe I would've, maybe I wouldn't've. I'm no hero—and anyway, saving an old lady from getting hit by a car isn't the same as trying to save the world. I wouldn't know how to do that."

"Perhaps you do. Perhaps everybody does, but it's just too simple to be believed."

There was a deep pause, and then Al stood up. "Okay, you win the argument. I'm still a sponsor of the League. Yeah," he admitted a little ashamedly, "I was thinking of ducking out, but you haven't cost me anything yet, so I'd just be running from shadows if I quit now."

Gomez, who had risen with him, bowed slightly and smiled. "Thank you, Mr. Toolum. I appreciate your confidence."

When the dispatcher called the Fernvale train, the two men hastily shook hands, and Al walked briskly to the gate. Turning, he half raised his arm for a final wave, but he saw that the Guamanian had already begun to walk away. It would be awfully easy to lose a little man like that, Al thought to himself.

Twelve

The rest of the week passed quickly as Al worked hard at the plant, even going in on Saturday to make up for time lost. He even suggested to Henry that perhaps he might pass up his vacation this year, but Henry wouldn't hear of it.

"You'll want those two weeks, Al, when you and the missus go on your prize trip. You figured out yet where you're going?"

They hadn't discussed it past Emily's mentioning California.

"Maybe the West Coast," he told Henry.

"Might as well go the farthest you can long as it's on their money."

Al agreed. Inwardly, however, he debated whether to tell Henry that the real reason he wanted to pass up his vacation was so he could take time off for Little Louie and the Child Guidance. It didn't seem fair to leave Emily alone with the problem. But how could you tell a man that maybe your youngest son was crazy?

On one of the few nights that week when he came home reasonably early, he and Emily discussed the problem.

"On the days I have to go with Little Louie you could call Henry and tell him I'm sick," he suggested.

"With what?"

"Oh, something—diphtheria."

"Don't even say that, Al Toolum," she cried. "I don't want to go through *that* again. Besides, with the drugs they have nowadays, I don't think you can get diphtheria."

"I bet *I* could," he said morosely. "Everything happens at once," he complained. "A man doesn't have time to work with all that happens."

Emily, lost in thought, was humming and wasn't paying attention. "What the heck song is that?" he demanded.

"What? Oh, that." She creased her brow and hummed two or three bars. " 'You Go to My Head'—remember, Al?"

"What made you think of that?"

"I guess—your mentioning your diphtheria. It made me think of that dreadful week when I'd sit up with you all night long, and sometimes I'd play the radio. That was a song hit then, remember?"

"No, I don't remember," he said. "Come on, Em, concentrate."

"If you feel bad about leaving me alone," she said, "don't. You can come to the Child Guidance with me just next Tuesday, and I'm sure Dr. Martin will tell you Little Louie is going to be okay, if that will make you feel better."

"Well, okay," he said, but he wasn't convinced.

Other nights that week, when he left work long after dinner-time, he would stop off at Ed Willnick's for some corned beef and cabbage and a glass of beer. It was on one of those nights that he discovered Ben Carroway's perfidy.

The bar seemed no more crowded than usual for a Saturday night when he stepped through the door, but the noise was far out of proportion to the number of imbibants present. He grinned with understanding when he saw that the center of the hubhub was his friend Ben. Good old Ben.

"Hey," he called, elbowing his way to the bar, "I guess I know whose wife is out for the evening."

"That makes two of us," Ben shouted, "and they both went to the same place."

"Emily didn't say anything," Al started, but he became quiet at the look of interest on Ben's face. In all fairness, Emily hadn't a chance to tell him she was going out, since he hadn't phoned all day. "That's right, I forgot," he lied. "First Saturday I've worked in years, and I got a little mixed up. But she didn't say *where* she was going."

"To the Minute Maids International, that's where. Flimflam these blasted women anyway," he cursed. "I'm gettin' damn tired waiting for 'em to take over the world. Why don't they do it, if they're going to do it?"

Losing interest now that he know Emily was engaged in harmless activity, Al asked, "What was all the noise about when I came in?"

Ben's attitude changed immediately from one of warmth to a calculating hardness, and his answer was lost to Al, who had caught Ed's eye, and by hand motions ordered the corned beef special. "What was that, Ben? I didn't hear you."

"I said I was electioneering."

"Huh? What for?"

Ben's arm described an arc that took in the opposite wall. "For that!"

His eye following the pointing finger, Al saw a huge poster

that announced the Miss Schlepp contest and below that another poster with pictures of the girls.

"Oh, boy, it's started. How many votes you got for Jean Wilcox?"

"I got *none* for Jean Wilcox, and seventeen for Mimi Cartright of Kansas City, Missouri."

Starting to say something congratulatory, Al gasped in an involved double-take. "You got—what! Mimi Cartright of Kansas City. You—you double-crosser. You traitor, you," he sputtered.

In his eyes the grinning Ben changed into a fat monster and no longer his buddy. To be sure, when Al had proposed they get votes for Jean Wilcox, Ben had studied the pictures and hesitantly had said maybe Mimi Cartright of Kansas City was better-looking. But Al had attributed this minor defection to Ben's being a little jealous of his adventure in the 33 Club and the fact that his picture kissing Miss Wilcox had been in the papers. But this!

Ed Willnick moved uneasily to the center of the dispute. "Now, boys," he urged, "take it easy."

"Take it easy, he says!" Al shouted. "Take it easy! How can I take it easy when my best friend, my buddy of over ten years turns into a prize heel?"

Ben's face reddened in anger. "Prize heel, eh? You dictator. You Hitler. Just because you kissed this floozie you think you own her." He turned to Ed for support. "See, Willnick, I told you this crumb would get sore. This is a free country, isn't it? You can vote for who you want, can't you?"

"Sure, sure, Ben," Ed Willnick soothed. "He's right," he said to Al. "If he likes Mimi Cartright of Kansas City he can vote for her."

Ed's voice penetrated Al's anger, and the words made sense. Never mind the fact that Ben was acting out of pure jealous spite. He, Al Toolum, had to smother his anger; so fighting down his inner seething he coldly and analytically studied the problem. From the grins of the men who surrounded them, Al assumed that Ben had already made progress. It would take a bold move to offset Ben's initial advantage.

He nodded slowly, his eyes narrowed. "Okay," he said softly, "if that's the way you want it," and then, turning from the bar, he announced, "I'm buying for anybody who votes for Jean Wilcox," and without a backward glance at Ben, he slid to the opposite end of the bar to set up his command post. A solid movement of customers followed him, and this mass desertion precipitated a shriek of protest from his erstwhile friend, Ben Carroway.

"Foul!" Ben bellowed. "No fair buying."

Paying no attention, Al counted his followers. "Set up nine," he directed Ed, "and hand me a pad of votes." He settled down on the bar stool, his mind clear and determined. Never mind how much this night would cost him. This was one of those times when a man had to rise above the mundane consideration of money.

From the alacrity with which Ed drew the beers Al realized he had the tavern owner behind him, and as Ben kept up his background chant, Al slammed his palm onto the bar. "All right, let's have a ruling. Ed, a ruling."

Grinning, Ed set the beers down in front of Al. "I rule it fair and aboveboard. Maybe it's dirty politics, but where do you find any other kind?"

Dispensing the beers to his eager constituents, Al made out nine votes for Jean Wilcox. "Set 'em up again," he instructed, as Ben became silent.

But if Al, in his flush of victory, thought he had won the final victory, he had underestimated his most worthy opponent, for within a few minutes, from the corner of a suspicious eye, he saw Ben in whispered consultation with Ed Willnick. His fears were answered when, a moment later, Ed disappeared into the kitchen and soon returned with some plates.

"Free peanuts," Ben called. "Eat free peanuts with your free beer. Step right up, men, and vote for the prettiest girl in America."

With sheepish glances of apology to Al, most of his contingent drifted toward Ben, leaving only one supporter, a stranger, who said, "I'm with you. I hate peanuts."

"I hate Ben Carroway," Al ground out. "Ed, let me see you a minute," but he had to wait impatiently while Ed set up the opposing camp. "Ed," Al said, when the proprietor was finally free, "how's my credit here?"

"Fine, Al," Ed said happily.

"Then I want bread, cheese, hard-boiled eggs and anything else you have set up at this end. A regular old-time free lunch. That'll fix the bum."

"Sure, Al, right away."

The free lunch brought back most of his followers plus a few late additions who had wandered into the bar and joyously drank Schlepp's beer and voted for Jean Wilcox, never questioning the issues but taking quick and full advantage of the windfall.

By midnight, however, a stand-off occurred, for Ben also had his free-lunch counter, and most of the lucky voters, not caring any more from which source came their refreshments, wandered back and forth between the two camps. Only a hard core of supporters who showed an admirable political conscience remained loyal to each side, and the smoky air rang with their lusty campaign slogans. But since their numbers were about equal, neither faction showed any real gain.

The stranger who hated peanuts proved to be Al's most loyal supporter. He had a fabulous capacity for beer, being able to drain a glass as fast as the liquid flowed from the upended stein.

"Don't have to swallow," he modestly told the admiring group that watched him, and because he was somewhat of a freak, Al allowed him to perform only for those who voted for Jean Wilcox. But soon even this advantage faded when the novelty had palled.

By one o'clock Al and the stranger were exchanging confidences like lifelong friends, and Al poured out the whole bitter tale of Ben's double-cross.

"He doesn't know it," Al ended darkly, "but he's busting up the bowling team—and we had a great chance to win the town championship."

The stranger shook his head sadly. "Shame. It's a nice town too. I travel for wholesale groceries, and I never came across a more friendly town. Where else could this happen?"

Al drank from his glass (Was it his fifteenth or sixteenth?—he had lost count) and he felt a tear burning the corner of one eye. "It is a nice town," he said in a rush of patriotic emotion, "but look at that louse! Dividing up the whole place. Just because he's jealous."

The stranger looked puzzled. "Jealous? How come?"

"Because I'm Yankee Doodle, that's why, and he isn't."

"Oh." The stranger quickly drank another Schlepp's, and then he leaned toward Al. "You know, traveling on the road like I do gets pretty lonesome, and sometimes I pass the time making believe I'm different people." He winked. "I guess you know how that is, huh?"

"Differ'nt people. What d'ya mean?"

"Oh-h, I never got around to being Yankee Doodle, but sometimes I'm a movie star, and other times I'm a general or a big-shot Wall Street banker."

Al stood up, weaving slightly. "You crazy?"

"Who says I'm crazy?" the man demanded indignantly. "If you can be Yankee Doodle, I can be Paul Douglas, can't I?"

"I *am* Yankee Doodle, and you don't look anything like Paul Douglas." The man had made an unfortunate choice, since Paul Douglas happened to be Al's favorite.

"Okay, you're Yankee Doodle," Paul Douglas shrugged.

"You still don't believe me? Hey, Ed, tell this guy I'm Yankee Doodle."

"That's right," Ed nodded, "he's Yankee Doodle, all right."

Paul Douglas regarded them blankly. "Gotta get back to the hotel," he stated.

"Trouble with you," Al shouted at the retreating back, "you drink too much. He drinks too much," he repeated to Ed Willnick in a normal tone. "Ever since there aren't many farmers' daughters around, these traveling salesmen hafta spend their time in saloons."

Ed leaned on the bar. "Al, don't you think it's enough for tonight?"

Al had been thinking that for a half-hour. "I won't go till *he* goes," he insisted stubbornly.

"I'll talk to him," Ed said and went off to confer with Ben. In a moment he was back. "He says he'll go if you go, but he won't walk home with you."

"Who asked him to? I'd probably beat him up," Al threatened.

"Take it easy, Al." Ed stared at the ceiling thoughtfully. "How about if one goes out first and walks on the other side of the street?"

"That's okay, but who goes first, and who says that the second guy doesn't sneak in a couple of votes?"

"I do. I'll close the bar for five minutes."

"Okay," Al said gladly; then his pride intervened. "But I won't be first."

"He says he won't be first either. Al, look, here's your chance to show everybody what a big guy you are. You go first without any argument, and he'll feel like two cents."

The idea was appealing. "It's a deal. I'll show up that lowlife." He turned his pockets inside out. "No more money, Ed. Lemme know what I owe tomorrow."

Ed nodded, and Al, his head high and his chin thrust out, strode toward the door. A loud sniff from Ben didn't cause him to break stride, but when he reached the door, he turned. "Contest continues at eight o'clock tomorrow night," he announced. "Everybody come." There was the satisfaction of seeing a stunned look come over Ben's face. "That'll show the fourflusher," he told himself happily as he walked out to the street followed by loud cheers. He felt so good all the way home that he didn't once feel his feet on the pavement, and this was such an elevating experience, both literally and figuratively, that he began to sing. While he tried to fit the key into the lock, an operation that seemed to take hours, he amused himself by keeping up his vocal efforts. Finally, he discovered that the door was unlocked all the time.

Up the stairs he went, and to his joy there were Herman, Sherman and Little Louie bunched in the doorway of their bedroom waiting for him. A man didn't see his kids often enough, Al told himself, and the sight of his boys, so angelic in their pajamas, with their sleep-heavy eyes staring at him was so overwhelming that he almost cried.

"Boys," he said, his arms outstretched. "My boys."

At least he had them, he thought, come what may with Ben

Carroway or anybody else who wanted to stab him in the back.

"Holy roger," Herman exclaimed. "He's blind."

An indignant reply died on Al's lips as Emily appeared from their bedroom, and as her fingers tightened over his ear he felt a sharp pain.

"Come on, Ezio," she said patiently, "beddy-by time."

"But, Em," he protested as he was drawn inexorably into their room.

"But Em, nothing," she exclaimed and pushed him onto the bed. "Get your feet up so I can take your shoes off." He complied. "Get your dirty shoes off the bed," she cried sharply.

"Whaddaya wa . . . ?" He tried to struggle to a sitting position.

"Lie back and be quiet. Oh, you should be ashamed of letting the boys see you in this condition. What is happening to you, Alfred Toolum?"

"But I'm cold sober, Em. Watch, I'll walk a straight line."

"You'll walk nothing. Why didn't you tell me you were going to a tribal meeting?"

"Don't blame this on the Indians. They got trouble enough. It's Ben. Wait'll you hear what Ben did to me."

"It'll keep till morning. There, your pants and shirt are off. Now, go to sleep."

There was sudden darkness. "But I want to tell you what Ben——"

"I said go to sleep."

He did.

Emily heard about Ben from the lips of Sadie Carroway at nine thirty Sunday morning when she went next door. Sadie, sitting at the kitchen table reading the papers, waved her through the screen door and wordlessly poured another cup of coffee. The fact that there was only one breakfast setting told Emily that Ben, like Al, had not yet joined the world of the living.

"What time did yours come in last night?" Emily asked, taking the coffee.

Fingers beat a sharp tattoo on the porcelain top. "Five after two, *and* he kept me up till quarter of three describing some ghastly event that took place at Ed Willnick's." Rapidly she told Emily an approximately accurate, though highly colored, version of what had happened.

Emily was silent in the face of Sadie's obvious disapproval. She resented the fact that Sadie blamed Al, and although Emily was quite willing to admit to herself that at some later moment that morning she was likely to flay Al alive, there was no cause to make him the scapegoat.

"What is this big love affair Ben's having with Miss Kansas City? You sure he's never met her, Sadie?"

"Of course, he never met her. He's just baiting Al for acting the fool over this Jean Wilcox."

Emily saw pitfalls in pursuit of the subject, so she changed her course. "Are you sure that's what happened last night?"

"I made several phone calls this morning, and, Emily, I'm ashamed to say that the story is all over town, *and* Al promised that the voting would begin tonight again at eight o'clock."

"Oh, he did, did he? It will start without him then, unless he gets there over my dead body and on crutches besides."

Sadie's thin-lipped expression of approval boded the same fate for the sleeping hulk on the floor above.

"At their age," Emily said indignantly, "carrying on like grammar-school kids."

"It's disgusting," Sadie said. "However, I have a plan. Instead of starting a big business with them that can end up in who knows what, I have a way of solving the whole problem with no pain involved at all."

"Good," Emily breathed. "Tell me about it."

"It strikes at the source—right at Ed Willnick." She paused for dramatic effect. "As you know, Paul Gorham is Assistant Commissioner of Licenses in the county, and Bea Gorham is a past Molly Pitcher of our Minute Maids chapter——"

"Oh, you wouldn't have Ed's license taken away from him, Sadie."

"No, no," Sadie said hastily. "I like Ed—even if he did murder his wife. It's just a—say a word to the wise."

"That's it," Emily said, "a word to the wise."

At eleven thirty Al carefully made his way down the stairs. In strange contrast to last night when he had felt so buoyant, he now found it difficult to navigate a body that had taken on so much weight he had to hold onto the bannister to keep himself up. He had been awake for some time, but had just got up the nerve to rise and face the inevitable.

He sidled into the kitchen, still in his bathrobe, and Emily, standing at the sink, said, "Good morning, dear."

"I just want to explain . . . What?"

"I said, good morning, dear."

"Uh—good morning."

"How would you like your eggs?"

"I guess—boiled."

"So were you."

"What did you say?"

"I said, I'll put them right on. Will you watch your toast?" She handed him two slices of bread.

"Yeah, sure, sure." He sat by the toaster, a puzzled look on his face.

"Did you have a nice time last night?" Emily inquired.

Al winced. "Fine—I think." Clearing his throat, "I want to tell you what Ben did to me."

"I've already heard—from Sadie."

"From Sadie! That's like hearing why Harry Truman is a good guy from Senator Taft."

"You'd be surprised. I got a very clear picture of what happened, deducing a few things here and there. Personally, I think it's very childish."

"My best friend," Al muttered. "What d'ya mean, childish? You'd think after all these years he'd stick by me. Boy, am I sorry I helped him paint his garage last year. That's the thanks I get."

Turning down the gas under the boiling water, Emily popped in two eggs "I understand you're going back tonight."

Al cringed slightly. "Well, I . . ."

"You go right ahead, dear. Sadie and I have Minute Maid business anyway. We have to draw up a report on the high-price-of-food situation for the next meeting. I'm the chairman of the committee, and that reminds me : Next week I have two meetings, both in the afternoon. We'll have to get a girl to come in to clean up—maybe permanently." She paused. "Were you going to say something, Al?"

"No, no. You get the girl. That's okay."

"I was sure you'd see it that way."

"Just don't make it a habit," Al said automatically.

Sharply, "What did you say?"

"I said—I . . ." Her eyes bored right through him, and he took a deep breath. "I said it would be nice if you could make it a regular thing."

Emily's voice softened. "I knew you'd understand, Al. You're always so sweet about things like that."

The kitchen door slammed open, and Little Louie poked his head in the door. "Hey, Mama," he complained, "Herman just smacked me."

Emily strode to the door. "Herman," she cried, "you leave Little Louie alone."

Herman's voice came from afar. "Aw, Mama, he's a pain in the neck."

"I'll give you a pain someplace else if you don't watch out," Emily cried, shaking her finger. "You get outside, Little Louie."

He scuffed his feet. "I don't wanna. Can't I stay with you?"

"Fresh air and sunshine, Little Louie," Al said. "Now go on."

Little Louie disappeared, saying something under his breath, and Al half rose to his feet. "Did he call me balloon head?"

"I didn't hear," Emily said calmly. "Eat before everything gets cold."

"Maybe the Child Guidance can straighten him out," Al said. "I give up. Did you tell them about his business where he doesn't think he's going to live until he's six?"

"They didn't give me a chance," Emily said. "I told you about that."

"What are they doing?" he complained.

"Let's give them a chance," she said. "After all, what else can we do?"

By suppertime, after a long nap, Al felt greatly refreshed, although he was quite apprehensive about the evening coming up.

"What are you kids doing tonight?" he asked, when Emily was clearing away the dinner dishes.

"We're going to Carroway's and watch the wrestling," Herman said.

"Miss Flemish is on tonight," Sherman said.

"Oh, that should be interesting. Wait a minute—isn't Miss Flemish your fourth-grade teacher?"

"Sure, but she wrestles under the name of Mad Maggie."

"You just *think* it's Miss Flemish," Emily said. "You never really got a close look at her on the television."

"Couldn't be two women that ugly in the same way," Herman said. "It has to be Miss Flemish."

"What teachers won't do to supplement their income," Al marveled.

"I don't think women wrestlers are ladylike," Emily said.

"Ah, ah," Al waggled his finger. "Remember the Minute Maids, Em. Women can do anything men can do."

"I don't think men wrestlers are menlike," Emily retorted. "They're disgusting."

"I'd sure like to see Miss Flemish," Al said. "I remember the run-in I had with her that year when Herman punctured the tires on Harkness's car. She said Herman was going to grow up to be a criminal. If I'd known she could wrestle, I wouldn't've said what I did to her."

"Come on over to the Carroways', Papa. The wrestling starts in ten minutes."

Al's face darkened. "I would drop dead before . . ." Emily's warning glance caused him to stop. "I mean, I have something else to do."

It was seven forty-five when Al slowly made his way toward Willnick's, and in his heart he deplored the fact that Emily had let him come. If only she had pleaded with him not to spend the money, even threatened him. . . . What the hell was the matter with that woman? Didn't she care what happened to their budget?

Looking around surreptitiously, he saw that Ben was nowhere in sight. Maybe Sadie had laid down the law, he told himself happily. If that were true, he would buy a quick round for everyone and come right home. It would be a moral win.

But his hopes were dashed as he turned onto Main Street and saw Ben's bulky figure just ahead of him. Ben was unaware of his presence, and, matching him stride for stride, Al kept apace. Once when Ben looked over his shoulder, he quickened his step and Al felt a return of the righteous wrath of the night before.

Instead of going right into Ed's, however, Ben stopped and was staring at a sign hung on the door when Al drew abreast of him. The sign read: NO ELECTIONEERING WITHIN 100 FEET OF THE POLLING PLACE.

Al gasped. "How do you like that!"

"Yeah," Ben growled darkly, "how do you like that!"

Both men strode into the saloon which, except for Ed, reading a racing form at the bar was empty.

Al took up the attack. "Hey, Ed, what's the idea?"

Ed looked up from his literature. "You seen the sign," he said grumpily.

"Sure, but what does it mean?"

There was an obvious struggle going on within Ed Willnick. "It means what it says," he retorted finally.

"You mean we can't get votes for our candidates?" Al asked wrathfully, while inwardly he rejoiced.

Ed stood up. "That's right. And you, Al, you owe me eighteen fifty, and Ben, you owe sixteen thirty."

I got more votes after all, Al told himself joyfully. "I'll pay you next week," he said. "S'long, Ed. No sense hanging around, I guess."

"S'long," Ben said too, and followed him out.

Al rid his face of a slight smile as he looked at Ben. "That sure is a lousy trick," he announced.

Ben nodded. "Wonder who promoted that?"

They stood silent for a moment, and then by unspoken consent, started walking slowly toward home.

"And I was all worked up for a big night," Al said sadly.

"Me too. We could," Ben paused, "go to another saloon."

"Yeah, I suppose we could," Al said.

They kept on walking.

Ben's next words were hard coming. "You know, I was thinking all day. And—and I came to the conclusion that you were right —in a way," he added hastily.

"About what?"

"Well, this Jean Wilcox is almost a home-town girl, after all, and maybe I shouldn't try to promote for Mimi Cartright—even if she *is* better looking."

"You vote for who you want," Al said sturdily. "This is a free country just like you said last night. And I was thinking today too. You were right calling me a Hitler. I shouldn't try to dictate to you."

"You had a right to be sore, Al. I pulled a dirty one on you."

"You never did a dirty thing in your whole life, Ben," Al protested. "I always said you were the most sportsmanlike guy in Fernvale—no matter what anybody said."

They found themselves in front of Ben's house. "I think I'll go in and watch the television," Ben said, half turning. "You—you wouldn't want to come in, would you, Al?"

"The kids are there looking at the wrestling."

"Oh."

"But—how about bowling a couple?"

Ben's eyes lit up. "That's a great idea. Why didn't I think of that? I'll run in and get my stuff."

"Meet you in two minutes," Al called, running across his lawn.

He bounded up the steps. There was nobody, he told himself, he'd rather spend a Sunday evening with than Ben Carroway. . . .

Thirteen

When Al, accompanying Emily and Little Louie, walked into Dr. Martin's office on Tuesday morning, he had no idea that two hours later he would emerge a broken man—well, if not broken, then pretty badly bent. For at the end of those two hours he learned that Little Louie hated him. Yes, hated him—that was the only way to put it, Al insisted stubbornly, even though Dr. Martin tried his best to explain that Little Louie, at five and a half, certainly didn't know what the word hate meant.

But Al, retreating into a shell of hurt feelings, refused to listen to any arguments that tended to ease the situation, and during the brief conference they had with the doctor, while Little Louie was being entertained by one of the social workers, Al kept saying, "Don't try to kid me. Didn't you say he took the doll who was supposed to be me and beat the hell out of it?"

"That he did," Dr. Martin admitted.

"I bet he enjoyed himself," Al said, almost tearfully, while Emily caressed his arm sympathetically.

"I'm glad to say he did enjoy it," was the answer. "He showed great glee, as a matter of fact, which is the healthiest possible sign. When you see a child at play therapy who exhibits guilt or fear, *then* is the time to really worry."

Play therapy! Al exclaimed angrily to himself. What a stupid thing for adults to spend their time thinking up. What was the idea of it anyway? Give a kid a bunch of dolls, each one supposed to be a member of the family, and then sit around egging the kid on to smack them around. Boy, he thought, I bet Little Louie gave them a run for their money. He probably asked for an ax.

Finally, Dr. Martin urged them to go out for some lunch while he finished up with Little Louie for the day, and when Emily dragged Al out of the Child Guidance, he was still burning like a fuse lit at both ends.

"And have a doughnut," she said calmly, when they'd ordered coffee in a near-by luncheonette. "You didn't eat much breakfast."

"I'll never eat again," he stated dramatically. "How can I eat when I know my kid hates me? He'll probably poison my food."

"Don't be ridiculous," Emily said, "and let's talk this over like grown-up human beings."

"You can say that," he accused, "because Little Louie loves you, according to the game he played. What have you been doing?" he sneered, covering up his hurt, "sneaking him candy on the sly?"

"Now, Al, don't feel that way," she said understandingly. "You know that Dr. Martin said this is a very common situation, and we're lucky it's caught in time."

"Lucky!" he raged. "Listen: *Every child is supposed to love their parents.*"

Emily began to get impatient. "That's such an outmoded idea. Who says Little Louie has to love us?"

"Who says? Everybody says, that's who!"

"Is this a law, a written law? And anyway"—she paused, and then continued softly—"did you love your father?"

He drew a quick breath. His father was a subject rarely mentioned in the house, even in private conversations between him and Emily. No, he hadn't loved his father. He had despised a man he remembered only as cruel, mean and furiously angry at the world. Even when he was older and his father was dead, Al never could think well of his memory, though he knew, with maturity, that what had driven his father was ignorance, bigotry and a gnawing poverty. His mother he couldn't remember at all, her place in his life had only been as a negative symbol of something he didn't have.

Emily was sorry she had asked this question when she saw the look of pain come over Al's face. She wanted to say the reasons for Little Louie "hating" him had nothing to do with the reason why Al had hated *his* father, that, where Al could never have done anything about that relationship, something *could* be done about Little Louie.

"All I want to know is—why?" Al asked softly. "What have I done to him?"

"Dr. Martin said it's too early to tell why, Al. But he did say there's nothing deeply wrong, and it can be straightened out without much trouble."

"It all has to do," Dr. Martin had finally said reluctantly, in answer to Al's insistence, "with Little Louie's position in the family. That's the source of most difficulties of this sort."

They had discussed Little Louie's periods of meanness—"aggression," Dr. Martin had named it—and his equally alarming periods of shyness—"extreme reticence," Dr. Martin called it—and the conclusion to be drawn was simply that Little Louie was trying to break down the walls of an established family circle that he thought had no place for him. This confused Al terribly and even made him angry, because, he insisted, Little Louie was as much a part of the family as anyone else.

"That's a matter for careful examination," Dr. Martin had said.

Emily finished her coffee now, and said to the silent Al, "What are you thinking about?"

"I was just thinking," he said, "how loused up things can get. Your bringing up my old man made me think of it. When I was a kid I used to lie in bed at night and wish I had an older brother or sister—mostly a sister. I used to make up imaginary games, even conversations. I knew what she looked like, my sister. Funny"—he smiled slightly—"she looked a little like you when you were in high school. Her name was—Susan, and she was big, so big that whenever my old man threatened to lick me she'd give him hell, and he'd have to leave me alone."

"Too bad you didn't really have a sister," Emily said.

"That's what I thought all those years, and that's why I say now I'm all loused up. When we got married and talked about having kids I said it was no good having just one. One kid gets too lonesome." He spread his hands. "Now I don't know. When Sherman was born Herman raised all kinds of hell——"

"But he got over it."

"Maybe he did, I don't know. And now Little Louie, because he's the smallest—he has *his* problems. What are you going to do?"

"First thing is to make Little Louie feel like he's more a part of the family the way Dr. Martin said."

"How do I do that?"

"First thing, I think, is to do things really special with him—maybe things only you and he do together."

"Then Herman and Sherman will be mad," he complained, "so we'll take them for Rorschach tests. Just a crazy merry-go-round."

"They're old enough to understand."

"Agh-h . . ." He lapsed into silence, a silence that deepened into gloom until a light appeared over Al's face. "Wait a minute," he exclaimed, "I have an idea. What time is it?"

A clock on the wall of the coffee shop told them it was twenty to one. Al got to his feet, reaching into his trouser pockets for change. "Wait right here. I want to make a telephone call."

He was gone for over five minutes, and when he returned there was a look of extreme satisfaction on his face. "I guess those Consultants are worth something after all," he said, without sitting down. "Come on, Em, let's get going. We don't have too much time."

"For what?"

"We're going to pick up Little Louie; then I'll drive you home, and then I'm taking Little Louie to a ball game."

Sliding out from behind the table, Emily asked, "But what have the Consultants got to do with it?"

"They're getting me box seats. I remembered the Giants are playing Brooklyn today at the Polo Grounds, and it would be hard to get good seats. Miss McClain said she'd have two tickets waiting for me at the ball park."

"That's wonderful, Al. But what about your going to work this afternoon?"

Handing the right change to the cashier, he turned away with a determined look on his face. "Forget my going to work. Dr. Martin says I have to become pals with Little Louie, so I'll be a pal. Even," he added with a trace of bitterness, "if it means we all starve to death. I wonder if those psychology books take into consideration a guy has to make a living . . ."

If it's every father's dream to take his son to a big-league ball game, sit in a box right behind the home team's dugout, have his picture taken with all the players and get their autographs on a brand-new baseball presented by the home-team manager, then Al's dream should have been fulfilled that afternoon. All those things happened plus he was almost decapitated by a foul ball hit by Jackie Robinson, and what disturbed Al was that only the last incident amused Little Louie.

When he had spoken to Barbie on the telephone she had wryly warned him that it should be kept a secret that he was a Giant fan— and not a Dodger rooter as every average man is presumed to be, so he was a bit concerned when he and Little Louie were taken in charge by the Giant publicity man. His fears were soon forgotten, however, in the ensuing glory of shaking hands with his heroes for the benefit of the press.

"Well, how do you like that, Little Louie?" Al asked, when the excitement had died down and the teams took the field. "Some stuff, huh?"

"I want some peanuts," Little Louie said.

The peanuts had to wait till after the singing of the national anthem, rendered by the lady star of the Broadway hit musical, *Goniff in Gomorrah,* and Al remained standing to look for the peanut man.

"Down in front!" a voice bellowed.

Automatically, Al ducked; then he saw that the command had come from a gloomy-faced man directly in the box behind them.

"I'm trying to get my kid peanuts," Al explained.

"So do you have to make a federal case out of it? He'll be around, he'll be around."

"He wants 'em now." He spotted the vendor. "Hey, peanuts."

A roar rose from the crowd as Al caught the bag and tossed the peanut man a dime. "What happened?" Al asked, turning around toward the field.

"That fella hit a home run," Little Louie said, pointing to the Brooklyn lead-off man.

"Boo, Maglie, ya bum," the gloomy-faced man howled at the Giant pitcher.

Al whirled, pained. "Give him a chance. Anyway, what are you booing for if you sit on the Giant side?"

The man unfurled a cloth sign that read: THE DODGERS STINK. "I hate both of 'em," he snarled. "I'm a Saint Louie Browns fan."

Al was horrified, and edged away. "You should see a psychiatrist."

Little Louie tugged at his jacket. "Hey, Papa, I hafta go."

"You just went as we left the Child Guidance."

"I hafta go again."

Maglie had struck out the next batter, and the one after that was thrown out at first. Going down the ramp Al was gratified to see Robinson pop out to the catcher. "Now hurry up," he urged Little Louie.

But it was ten minutes before they untangled the maze beneath the stands and were ready to come back. All that while there was a terrific furor from the crowd. Just as they re-entered the box, the Giants took the field again.

"What happened?" Al asked the gloomy-faced man.

"Thomson hit a homer with Lockman on," the man responded reluctantly.

"That's smackin' it, Bobby," Al cheered as Thomson passed the box.

"He's a bum," the gloomy-faced man said. He was holding a new sign that read: DUROCHER STINKS.

"Hey, Papa," Little Louie said, "I wanna hot dog."

Al ignored him. "Do you hate everybody?" he asked the gloomy-faced man.

"I'm misanthropic," the man said.

"Oh." Al subsided, wondering if it hurt.

"A hot dog," Little Louie demanded.

"Okay," Al sighed. "Hey, hot dogs!"

"DOWN IN FRONT!"

Al reached for the hot dog. "Take it easy. You want my kid to starve?"

"He looks like he's starving," the man sneered. "You rich bums."

Al was enraged. "Rich! I *work* for a living."

"Then what are ya doing out at the ball park?"

"What are *you* doing at the ball park?"

They had reached an impasse. "All right," the gloomy-faced man continued, "then what are they taking your picture for?"

"Because I'm Yankee Doodle Fifty-two, that's why. I represent the great American public that loves baseball."

For a moment Al was afraid that the man would haul out a sign reading YANKEE DOODLE '52 STINKS, but obviously he had not prepared for this emergency. Instead, the gloomy-faced man satisfied himself with another sneer.

A cheer rose from the Giant fans when Campanella hit into a double play.

"Oh, boy," Al chortled, "that guy should be a tailor."

He felt a tap on his shoulder and turned to see the gloomy-faced man staring at him coldly. "What's the matter with being a tailor?" he demanded. "I'm a tailor."

Al was disconcerted. "I didn't mean there was anything wrong with tailors. It was just a figure of speech. I meant he should be anything but a ball player."

"Uh-uh," the man said. "You used the word tailor, which means you don't like tailors. You think it's degrading to be a tailor."

"I do not," Al protested. "Some of my best——"

"I'm a respected man in my community," the gloomy-faced man interrupted. "I make a good living. I have four people working for me. You think that's so bad?"

Al held up his hand. "I apologize," he surrendered.

"Trouble with this country," the man muttered. "No tolerance. You stink."

Al shrugged, turning away, but the man persisted, leaning over his shoulder. "I got a brother who's a rug salesman. You got anything against rug salesmen?"

"I've got nothing against nobody," Al said patiently. "I love rug salesmen, I love tailors. I came out to watch a ball game. Is that all right with you?"

"Hey, Papa, can I have a Coke?" Little Louie asked.

Al stood up. "Hey, Cokes!"

"DOWN IN FRONT!"

The cry was icily ignored as Al obtained the Coke and handed it to Little Louie. "When are you going to get filled up?" he demanded. "And don't spill it on your good suit."

"Hey, Papa," Little Louie whispered, "look at that guy. He's nutty."

The gloomy-faced man was standing and waving wildly toward a booth high up behind home plate, almost falling over into their box in his anxiety.

Al pushed him back gently. "Take it easy, mister."

"I'm waving to my employees on the television," the man explained. "I always wave in the third inning." He unfurled a big sign that read: BON-TON TAILOR SHOPPE 39-42 72nd DRIVE ELMHURST. "Free plug," he said and looked pleased for the first time. "That guy on the television camera never swings away in time." Refolding the sign, he sat down, satisfied.

"That must make your employees feel real good," Al said. "Almost like being out at the ball park themselves instead of chained in a sweatshop."

"Sweatshop! You ever hear of a sweatshop with a television set?"

"Why not? They have 'em in jailhouses now, don't they?"

"Sweatshop!" The man was overcome.

Al turned back to the field, feeling great. He had scored.

"Hey, Papa, can I have an ice cream?"

During the next three innings Little Louie had: 1 bag of peanuts (his second), 1 orange pop, 2 hot dogs (his second and third, with mustard, no relish), and 1 box of popcorn. And while this was happening, both teams played hitless and errorless ball until the seventh inning when the dam broke, sending both Maglie and his successor showerward. During the deluge the Dodgers scored six runs, and Al's head was almost torn off by the foul ball. When the nightmare had ended and the third out finally achieved, Al clutched his forehead.

"I'm sick," he moaned.

"So am I," Little Louie said.

Al looked at him and saw that Little Louie was indeed not well; his skin was a light shade of green.

"I wanna go home," Little Louie said.

"Please," Al begged, "hold out, Little Louie. We'll get those runs back."

"Home," Little Louie insisted. "I don't like to watch baseball."

Opening his mouth to protest, Al saw by the look on his son's face that no argument would make any impression.

They stood up to leave.

"Ha, ha," the gloomy-faced man jeered, his first outburst since he had been silenced in the third inning. "Cowards who run because their team's behind."

This canard, Al felt, should not go unanswered, but as he tried to frame a reply Little Louie pushed him toward the ramp, and he was forced to leave the scene of battle, his last impression being the triumphant face of the Elmhurst tailor. . . .

The moment they were out of the ball park Little Louie made a surprising recovery, so complete that he even tried to promote an ice cream cone. But Al, his indignation at a high pitch at being forced to leave the game, refused, and Little Louie became silent.

"I never had to leave a game with Herman or Sherman," Al said, as they walked toward the parking lot.

"Baseball is dopey," Little Louie said. "Nothing ever happens."

"You're just not old enough to recognize the finer points of the game," Al said, and then, remembering something Dr. Martin had said, added hastily, "But that's all right. If you don't like baseball, you don't like baseball."

He handed the attendant his parking stub, and they waited for the car to be delivered. Al said thoughtfully, "Maybe there's something else we can do."

"What?" Little Louie showed interest.

"I don't know. Something."

"Next week, huh? Something Herman and Sherman never did."

Al nodded slowly. "All right, we'll do it. And maybe we won't tell anyone about it until it's all over."

"It'll be a secret," Little Louie said with satisfaction.

As the car pulled up, Al opened the door, and when he'd tipped the attendant, he and Little Louie climbed in.

"Say, Papa," Little Louie asked as they eased out of the lot, "what was wrong with that crazy man behind us?"

"He was a tailor," Al said.

"What's wrong with that?"

"I'll tell you," Al said; "a guy stands over a presser for a few years, and he piles up a lot of steam in his head——"

"Is that real bad?"

"Terrible," Al said. "As a result they're always blowing their tops." Darn it! he thought to himself—why didn't I think of that as a last shot at that guy?

Fourteen

When Al promised Little Louie to do the "something special" the following week, he had done it with perfectly good intentions, completely unaware that all his spare time had already been scheduled for him by the AAC. When this fact became apparent, Little Louie became quite outraged, much out of proportion to the importance of the situation, Al thought. But Little Louie kept saying *You promised, you promised,* and Al kept telling him for crying out loud quit making such a fuss. When all this is over, he said, we'll do something *extra* special. But it got so bad he finally had to tell Little Louie to shut up, Dr. Martin or no Dr. Martin. He was so busy that following week he didn't have time even to think of Little Louie, so that when the accident happened he felt terribly guilty, almost as though he had been the direct cause of Little Louie's bruises.

Actually, it wasn't much of an accident, and it happened on the day that Al and John Bell went to endorse Kandi Kola. This was the high point of a full week of such activity. Every day he had been transported in all directions for pictures and interviews. Al was quite cheerful about these endorsements, since John was careful to get his prior approval on all products. He was particularly overjoyed at endorsing Hashknife Harry Western clothes for boys, because for almost two years he had been propagandized by his sons to buy full Hashknife Harry outfits; and when he made this fact known to Mr. Gansevoort, president of the Double-H Company, three full outfits were prepared for immediate delivery. And best of all, Al had his picture taken with Hashknife himself who was in the city with his rodeo. There were maybe easier ways for a man to become a hero in the eyes of his children, Al figured, but they didn't come along often.

The afternoon that Al was at the Koola Kola company tasting Kandi Kola, Emily drove carefully up the Toolum driveway at four o'clock, stopped the car just short of the garage and climbed out, urging Little Louie to follow her. The day had been chilly and drizzly, and together they hurried around to the rear door and paused to wipe their feet.

Next door Sadie Carroway opened her side window and called, "The paper boy hasn't been here yet. I've been waiting."

"Come over for some tea," Emily said, opening the door. "We'll wait together."

"I really should do my work," Sadie said. The window slammed.

Emily had just got her hat and Little Louie's raincoat and rubbers off when Sadie appeared through the kitchen door. "Sit down," Emily said. "I'll only be a minute. Do you really think they'll run the story?"

"They certainly should. If the local paper won't run the story of a local housewives' meat strike, then I don't know what they *would* run."

"I'm so nervous," Emily said. "This is one of the most important things I've ever done. Little Louie," she said, in an aside, "would you like cookies and milk?"

"Okay. Then will you read me a book?"

"Not now, dear. I want to talk to Sadie."

"Aw, Mama, you're always talkin' about the Minute Maids. I wanna read a book."

"Not now," Emily said firmly.

Little Louie stalked out of the kitchen, and Emily shook her head. "I *guess* there's some improvement, but it's going to take a long time. I suppose I thought the Child Guidance would work a miracle."

"Things don't happen that way," Sadie said. "Like our battle to keep down prices. It's a long struggle. But, Emily, I think you're doing a wonderful job. All the ladies think so. I called the radio station in Hempstead this morning, and a man there said they might use the story on the five o'clock news."

Emily looked pleased, and then she said resolutely, "This is just the beginning. Even if we have to fight this thing all the way to Washington . . ."

"That's the way, Emily. And if Step A doesn't work, we're all set to go right on to Step B."

"I hope that won't be necessary," Emily said nervously. "Even though I proposed it, Step B seems terribly drastic."

"These are drastic times," Sadie proclaimed. "Fight fire with fire."

Little Louie reappeared. "If Papa was here, *he'd* read me a book." He seemed on the verge of breaking into tears. "I want my Papa."

"He misses Al," Emily explained needlessly. "They were supposed to do something special this week."

"He promised," Little Louie insisted.

"You'll just have to wait your turn," Emily said.

"Dr. Martin says I'm supposed to have my own place in the family group."

"So he did, but didn't he also say a family group was based on co-operation? Now, you be a good——"

"When did he say that?" Little Louie asked suspiciously.

"When you were breaking a chair over the head of the Sherman doll," Emily snapped.

"I'll bust his head," Little Louie threatened. "I'll *really* bust his head. Push me around . . ."

Emily closed her eyes, and, apologetically, she said to Sadie, "This is supposed to be a stage he goes through, like the swing of a pendulum. From"—she searched for the words—"from submission to aggression."

"When was Little Louie ever submissive?" Sadie scoffed.

"It's different now," Emily explained. "His aggressions are directed against the people who do him harm instead of just anyone."

"Psychology," Sadie said. "What's the difference as long as he's aggressive?"

"But the pendulum will soon stop swinging," Emily said,

without too much conviction. "They always do—don't they?"

"Clock pendulums, yes. Little boy pendulums, I don't know. And even clock pendulums don't stop—if you keep on winding them up."

Quickly, Emily changed the subject when Little Louie showed great interest in this last theory. "Oh, the tea water," she said.

Sipping their tea quietly and appreciatively, Emily said, "Today they're taking pictures of Al for *Life* magazine."

"That's really something," Sadie grudgingly admitted.

"*And* somebody from *Manhattanite* magazine has been interviewing him."

Sadie sniffed. "Oh, that magazine. They just make fun of people. I almost never read it except for the cartoons. I just *don't* understand their stories. The last one I read was about a man standing in the vestibule of a train and thinking."

"What happened?"

"Nothing. He just thought. At the end of five pages, the train whistled."

"I guess I like Faith Baldwin stories best of all," Emily said, "even though our lecturers are always telling us not to. At least, in them everything turns out all right."

The door clattered open, and Herman and Sherman burst in. Sherman was carrying the evening paper.

"Here, give that to me," Emily said. "And take your things off, boys."

"It's stopped raining, Mama," Herman said. "We're going out and throw a ball around."

"Then take Little Louie with you."

"Aw-w-w."

Little Louie had looked up eagerly, but when his brothers protested, he lowered his eyes.

"Don't argue," Emily said.

Herman took Little Louie's arm roughly. "Come on, jerk, get your rubbers on."

"I don't wanna," Little Louie said. "I want Mama to read me a book."

"Don't be a crybaby," Herman said. "Come on."

"Mama . . ." Little Louie pleaded.

"Please, Little Louie," Emily said impatiently. "Sadie and I have some business."

A minute later, when the three boys were gone, Emily and Sadie quickly searched the front page of the evening paper, and then hastily leafed through the entire sixteen pages. At the end, they stared at each other.

"Maybe we missed it," Emily said.

Slowly they turned back, page by page.

"It isn't there," Sadie cried disappointedly. "They didn't print it."

"What a shame," Emily said. "I wonder why?"

Compressing her lips, Sadie said. "I know why. The grocery stores threatened to take out their advertising. I have a good notion to call the editor—right now!"

Emily shook her head sadly. "That wouldn't do any good, Sadie."

"But why not? Didn't we agree that we have to fight fire with fire? They organize to fight us——"

"We're organized too. Don't we have our Fair Prices Committee?"

"All right—we'll wait until that five o'clock broadcast. If the story isn't used, we'll call the ladies and have them prepare for Step B."

At precisely five o'clock Emily switched on the radio for the news. Fifteen minutes later, as the announcer said, ". . . and now for a message from the Artful Armenian who brings you television at the lowest . . ." Emily snapped the switch, and sighed, "They didn't say anything about the Minute Maids." Outside there was a sudden squeal of brakes, a sound which cut into Emily's consciousness, but which was dismissed as Sadie proclaimed ominously, "Emily, it is time for Step B."

Standing up and starting toward the telephone, Emily nodded —as the front door burst open, and she was faced by a white and trembling Sherman.

"Mama . . ." he gasped.

Emily stood transfixed—twelve years of being a mother told her that something awful had happened. On legs that threatened to give way under her she started toward Sherman, as that little boy burst into tears, and cried, "Mama, he just ran out . . ."

The squeal of brakes, she remembered. Oh, God! And behind Sherman, through eyes misted with shock she saw Herman and a strange man, and in the man's arms was Little Louie. . . .

Fifteen

He isn't hurt, Al kept telling himself all the way out on the Long Island. He isn't really hurt. Yet he couldn't keep from torturing himself with the picture of Little Louie lying in the street—a little kid, not knowing what hit him. Running in the street like that, Al thought, and his anguish was transformed to momentary ire that shook him from top to toe. *How many times have those kids been warned?* he told himself fiercely, and then, just as quickly as it had come, his anger was dissipated in the surge of relief that he felt knowing that Little Louie was all right.

It had taken Emily some time to track Al down, finally locating him in the Koola Kola offices, and by that time the crisis was over. Nonetheless, Al insisted on coming right home. It was dark when he got off at the Fernvale station, and when he heard his name called, he turned and saw Dr. Martin from the Child Guidance. Al greeted him warily.

"I thought I might meet you and walk you home," Martin

said. "Mrs. Toolum called me shortly after the accident. She was told that Little Louie might be—well, hysterical, when the shock wore off." He grinned. "He was nothing of the kind."

They walked out onto the street. "Have you talked to him?" Al asked.

"We had quite a conversation."

"Then he *is* all right?"

The doctor nodded, and Al felt added relief at the professional assurance. "But it must have been awful for my wife," he said.

"These things are pretty shocking, but, of course, the fact that the boy wasn't hurt——"

"How did it happen?" Al interrupted. "And why?"

"How? Well, the other boys say they weren't paying much attention to him, which is perfectly normal, since Little Louie is old enough to take care of himself, and he ran into the street to chase a ball that Sherman missed.

"As for your why"—he took time to light a cigarette—"that's a different story. I assume he was trying to *show* them."

"Show them what?" Al asked, puzzled.

"Lots of things. That he could get the ball, that he was part of their game—and," he added cautiously, "perhaps he was reckless in a way to show you and Mrs. Toolum he resented the lack of attention."

"I had business," Al protested. The doctor nodded, and Al said angrily, "I *had* to be in the city."

"Your wife is blaming herself," Dr. Martin said. "She told me that she insisted Little Louie go outside when he didn't want to go. She had some business with Mrs. Carroway, and——"

"Well, what if she did? She shouldn't blame herself. Damn it, you can't give every second to these kids." He stared angrily out through the window, and then he said, "You don't mean that Little Louie did this on purpose, do you?"

"Oh, no. Certainly not consciously, anyway, and I doubt even whether he did it subconsciously. The thing is, it *might* all tie up with his fears, and we can't take the chance that it doesn't. We have to get this business cleared up, Mr. Toolum."

"I thought that's what we were paying you for."

"That's right. And we're making good progress. I don't think we really have anything to worry about once we get Little Louie re-established in the family."

"Then you mean he'll get over all this?" Al said hopefully. "Even his stuff about dying?"

"Easier than you might expect. Childhood fears are quite common. I remember when I was a kid lying awake nights thinking about two pioneer cross-Atlantic flyers who'd been lost. I used to spend hours, nightmares, really, picturing them drowning under dozens of different circumstances, each more horrible than the next."

"I had something like that," Al said, "only with me it was starving Armenians."

"And now I can't even remember those flyers' names," the doctor said, "and I fly myself without any fears. Those things don't tend to have lasting effects, *depending* a great deal on the general attitude of the parent."

"What do you mean?"

"Well, for instance—what's your attitude about hopes for the future of the world?"

Al shrugged. "Like everyone else, I've just about given up."

"So did Little Louie, taking his cue from you. But his world is very circumscribed. To him a great goal was his next birthday, and his hopelessness was translated to mean that he'd never reach it."

"So I have to change," Al said. "That's real easy, isn't it?— with the way things are these days."

"No basic change needed. In my talks with Little Louie he tells me that his brothers are always describing **air-raid** drills, relishing the dire results that might occur if they don't perform correctly. Play things like that down. Don't even discuss them, if possible, but if such a subject comes up, make it seem as though this is just one other little step in the whole matter of survival—like eating, or getting enough sleep. Use common sense."

"Are you kidding?" Al demanded.

"Why?"

"I'm supposed to tell him that diving under a desk is the answer to an atom war?"

"Well, not exactly . . ."

"Not exactly is right!"

The doctor seemed nettled. "All right, so life is complicated. No one said this was a simple thing. You have to work when you're a parent."

Al regarded him gloomily. "You know, I'm beginning to wonder about people like you. You say everything depends on how the parents treat their children. When does it start working the other way around for a change?"

Dr. Martin laughed. "I don't know, but I think a start is being made in that direction. I read the other day of a club organized by a man named Hays called the S.P.P.I.C.—the Society for the Protection of Parents against the Inroads of Children. Perhaps this is the counterrevolution."

"Sign me up," Al said.

Emily anticipated his arrival by opening the door and standing on the porch to wait for him. As he bounded up the steps he had a moment when the dreadful moment recurred when he pictured Little Louie in the street. Emily looked so tired—but when they embraced Al felt both had gained a little strength. They said nothing, just smiled at one another.

Herman and Sherman were watching television at the Carroways', and Dr. Martin stayed only a moment, just long enough to say good night and to remind Emily that Little Louie was due at the Child Guidance the next day.

"Shhh," Emily warned, as she and Al entered the living room. "Little Louie's asleep on the couch."

Al stared down at the tiny figure under the light blanket. So small and so angelic in sleep, this was the boy who had given him one of the worst moments of his life. He shook his head sadly as Emily motioned him into the kitchen.

"Would you like some dinner? I've kept something hot for you."

"They had a buffet at Koola Kola, so I'm not hungry. Maybe a cup of coffee, though."

"How did it go? Was *Life* magazine really there?"

"Yeah, and they took lots of pictures. Only thing . . ." His voiced trailed off.

Emily was at the stove. "Only thing what?"

"Well, you know, the Koola Kola people put a lot of money in this new drink—this Kandi Kola. John Bell says maybe a million dollars. And I was the first outsider to taste it—in the whole world. Pretty big deal. All the scientists were there and the big shots from Koola Kola." He paused, shaking his head. "I hope John doesn't lose his job."

Emily stared at him. "What happened, for goodness' sake?"

"Well . . ."

With a crash, the kitchen door opened, and Little Louie appeared. "What's the bangin' around in here?" he demanded sleepily, and then he saw Al. "Hi, Papa, did you just get home?"

Al nodded and waved him over. Then, holding him gingerly, he made an inspection. "Let's see, cut on the cheek—must've put the Band-Aid on yourself, it looks so crooked. Hurt here?" Little Louie winced when Al pressed his arm. "Lucky it's your left arm, won't interfere with hoisting ice cream sodas. Bump on your head back here—*that* won't do any harm with a head that's like a rock. You must've put an awful dent in the car." Little Louie began to giggle as Al folded him in his lap. "Little Louie," he announced, "I pronounce you in A-1 condition."

"Did you bring me a surprise?" Little Louie asked.

"It should be in the mail tomorrow," Al said, thinking of the Hashknife Harry outfits.

"For me? Special?"

"No, there's one for Herman and Sherman too, *but,*" he added, when he saw the look of disappointment cross his son's face, "I have figured out something *real* special—thought about it all the way out on the train."

When Little Louie looked eager, Al said, "You're going to meet Albert Einstein—just you."

"Who's he?" Little Louie asked suspiciously.

"He's the man who invented the atom bomb." He smiled at Emily's startled glance. "You'll see what a nice old man he is."

"Boy," Little Louie exclaimed excitedly, "that sounds great."

"It's being arranged," Al said. "I'll know when soon."

"But now bed," Emily said. "Upstairs, Little Louie."

Al set Little Louie down and took his hand. "Come on, I'll tuck you in."

When he returned to the kitchen, the coffee was ready, and Emily was stirring cream in thoughtfully.

"You're going to have to give me a couple of hours of your valuable time tomorrow," she said, handing him a cup. "I have to have some signs for the Minute Maids, and *you're* the man to paint them."

He groaned. "You still wound up in that rat race? What good does it do?"

"You'll see," she said. "Now, tell me about the Kandi Kola."

"Nothing really to tell. A couple of models in shorts came out with a big glassful, and I tasted it."

"So?"

"So it was too fizzy."

"Too fizzy?"

"Yeah, it hurt my tongue."

"Did you tell them that?"

"Sure I told them. What was I suppose to do—lie?" He paused, thinking back to the afternoon. "I think nine guys are going to commit suicide. Can you imagine taking such a thing so seriously?"

He bent to his coffee and then looked up as Emily started to laugh.

"What are you laughing about?" he demanded.

"Oh, Al," she gasped. "A million dollars. Al, you're the end. Really the end."

"But I tell you, Em, it hurt my tongue."

But she didn't hear him. She was laughing too hard.

Sixteen

John Bell was nervous. This was not the first time he had ever lunched with Paul Welton, but never before had they been alone. And, although he had been telling himself he didn't give a damn one way or the other, deeper reflection forced him to admit he *did* give a damn. It was too, too depressing to think of being without his job at AAC. Essentially, John realized, he was an extremely lazy man, and he hated the thought of searching for less expensive living quarters, of looking for another job and of relinquishing the many extras that being a reasonably wealthy man brought him.

Ever since the Kandi Kola incident, there had been what John interpreted as a conspiracy of silence on the Yankee Doodle proposition.

In the half-hour that they had been sitting over two pre-lunch cocktails—waiting for Al to arrive—Paul Welton had said nothing about Yankee Doodle. Instead, he seemed reflective, probing, his conversation leading down channels indicating that even Paul Welton lived in doubt. John bowed gladly to the role of listener and prompter, while wondering whether Welton were just softening him up for the big blow.

He now whirled the stem of his empty Manhattan glass meditatively as Paul Welton said, "One thing I've learned in all my years in advertising, Bell, is that People Like People."

Without thinking, John corrected, "You mean, some people like some people."

Flatly, "No! I mean People Like People." To close the point, Welton signaled the waiter for another drink, and turned his attention to the other occupants of the room.

Funny, John thought, how little Welton resembled the average man's conception of the big advertising executive—

Damn the average man! another part of his mind told him.

Yet the thought persisted as John realized that, even stranger, Welton knew less about the average man than the average man knew about him. To Welton, Alfred Toolum was a walking, talking graph, an embodiment of a mess of facts and figures with no margin for error. But even Welton had to realize by now that maybe the average man was like the weather : you could get as scientific as hell with him, predict day and night as to his probable actions, but he'd wind up doing as he wanted in the end.

John wondered whether it had ever occurred to Paul Welton that Al Toolum had a soul or could dream beyond the range of the jagged graph lines. Would it ever occur to Welton that Al Toolum tramped through virgin snow as a symbolic gesture or dreamed of himself as a discoverer, such as Balboa? Probably not, he answered himself, because he had learned these things only by accident himself. On the day they had gone to the Koola Kola offices he and Al had been confined in a cab stalled in cross-town traffic, and Al was saying that it was too bad that Emily wasn't along, because it would be nice for her picture to be in *Life* too, and John said he wished Al had asked him, because it could have been arranged.

"She couldn't have made it anyway," Al had said. "She's too busy with some stuff at home. Sadie Carroway got her all involved in one of those women's organizations. You know, one of those harmless things, but the ladies feel real important."

"I wouldn't know," John had said.

Regarding him obliquely, Al had said, "A nice-looking guy like you—not married. I don't get it. Now that Miss McClain, she looks like a good prospect."

"She wouldn't have me. She thinks this business is dishonest."

Al Toolum, man of the world, waved his hand. "Don't let her kid you. Women are always like that—wanting to change a guy. What does she want from you?"

"She thinks I have prospects as a writer."

"What you're doing is better, isn't it?"

"Much better," John answered shortly.

There was a pause. "But if you divided your time, you could write too."

"I'd have to be a schizoid." Al looked puzzled, and John explained, "A dual personality. Everyone is to a certain degree. You *have* to escape to some corner of your mind in this fouled-up world. It's a question of how much, though. When the make-believe takes over, you're sunk."

"Like Jekyll and Hyde?"

"Exactly. What's *your* Mr. Hyde?"

Al looked thoughtful. "Maybe—well, sometimes I lie awake at night and make believe I've invented a machine, one so different that I don't even know what it could be." He grinned self-consciously. "It sounds silly saying it aloud."

"Not so silly."

"I've been working on other people's machines a long time. I'd like to invent one—not for the money I'd make, but because I want to do something no one else has ever done." He paused. "Did you ever walk outside in the morning after a big snow and clop around in it just because it's snow no one else has ever stepped in?"

John looked surprised, and then he admitted, "Yes, I guess I have."

"Me, too, lots of times," Al said. "You get a feeling, maybe, like when people discover something new. I remember a history book when I was a kid with a picture of Balboa discovering the Pacific. There was a look on his face . . ."

"Noble?" John suggested, when Al seemed at a loss. He tried again. "Overawed, maybe?"

"That's it, overawed—and excited. Sometimes I'd like to have that feeling."

John smiled wryly. "Didn't the news of being Yankee Doodle do it for you?"

"It's really not the same thing," Al answered hesitantly, and when he looked at John and saw him smiling, they both broke into laughter.

Before the cab reached its goal they were on a first-name basis, and later, when Al sent the Koola Kola people reeling back to their laboratories, John was more grieved than surprised or shocked. The cab ride had revealed one or two things about Al Toolum he'd never known before. But Welton would never know these things.

"Here comes Toolum," Welton now said, a thrust of his wrist showing him the time. His expression indicated that he was displeased at Al's lateness. "Who's the grim-looking character with him?"

John glanced toward the entrance where the head waiter was indicating their table, and he saw a short, dark woman, whose eyes, magnified by thick lenses mounted in wide, black rims, looked, even from that distance, to be balefully sizing them up. Without obvious effort she seemed to be physically glued to Al.

John's nervousness returned. "That's a reporter from *Manhattanite*. Toolum told me a couple of days ago on the phone that she was shadowing him."

"Not for a Close-Up, I hope," Welton said uneasily.

"No, no. Just a Manhattan Chowder piece."

Visibly, Paul Welton relaxed. "Good. How much trouble can they give us in five hundred words?"

Then Al was at the table introducing the reporter as Miss Gregg.

"Wanda," Miss Gregg said darkly, grasping John's hand in a firm grip. "Pay no attention to me, boys. Just carry on as though I weren't around."

John fought down an urge to let loose with a string of four-letter words just to see whether her expression would change with *that* kind of "carrying on": he was sure it wouldn't.

They settled back comfortably as Paul Welton, ever courteous, asked Wanda Gregg if she cared for a drink.

"A double, on rocks," she said, "and don't call me madam."

Paul Welton looked startled. He hadn't realized he had called her Madam. And as he signaled the waiter, Miss Gregg stared at each one of them in turn, giving the impression that she was poised with pen and notebook, though her hands were folded on her lap.

John attempted to look frightfully unconcerned, while inwardly he squirmed at the thought of how ridiculous Wanda Gregg could make him seem in her piece. He remembered her by-line from a two-part Close-Up on a theatrical producer who had been so totally destroyed by her stinging satire that, it was rumored, he had later attempted suicide.

"How's Little Louie?" John asked, turning to Al.

"All over his accident, with no bad effects," Al said. "Boy, he sure gave us a scare, though."

When the drinks arrived Paul Welton did what John thought was an extremely courageous thing. "Miss Gregg," he said smoothly, "our business with Mr. Toolum this afternoon is purely personal, and I'd hate for it to go further than this table. I'd prefer not to clamp the off-the-record restriction on you, however . . ." he paused significantly.

With a slight shrug, Wanda Gregg stood up. "I'll take my drink to the bar," she said calmly.

"She's spooky," Al whispered fiercely, when she was safely out of earshot.

Paul Welton's eyes narrowed. "What's she been asking you?"

"Nothing. That's what I mean. She just *looks*."

"Don't be worried," John said. "Just don't get sore when you read her piece. It won't be libelous, because they're very careful about that, but they just like to make fun of people."

"Let them make fun," Al shrugged, "if it sells magazines." Then, a little grimly, "I'd like to see her find something funny in my house right now."

"Having trouble, Al?" John asked, with a side glance at Paul Welton.

"Ah-h, it's my wife. She's going off her nut or something. All day yesterday she had me painting signs for some damn thing her organization is going to pull."

"Organization!" Paul Welton said suddenly.

"Beg your pardon?" Al said.

"I said organization. Have you resigned yet?"

"Resigned! What from?"

"From that commie outfit. I've heard from Washington again."

Al's face cleared. "Oh, the League. No, I haven't resigned yet. Was I supposed to?"

"Were you . . ." Welton broke off and leaned across the table. "Look, Toolum, what were we talking about in my office that day?"

"You just said I shouldn't get mixed up with Reds, and I'm not. Mr. Gomez, the head of the League told me——"

"He told you, eh? Well, *I'm* telling you what Washington says. You're a sponsor of this outfit, they say. Toolum, don't you know the facts of life?"

Al was uncomfortably aware he wasn't referring to the birds and bees. "There's nothing wrong with the League," he started to say.

"It's suspect," Welton rejoined flatly, "and I'm *telling* you to resign."

John took a deep breath. "Mr. Welton, don't you think further investigation is in order before we . . ."

His voice dwindled as Paul Welton fixed him with a direct, icy stare, and he avoided Al's bewildered look that asked for help. "I said *resign*," Welton emphasized. Taking Al's silence as affirmation, he passed a menu. "All right, let's order lunch. Oh, a couple of things before we call Miss Bird-Dog back. Bell has you lined up for a full day next Monday——"

"Monday, I . . ." Al began, but Welton paid no attention to him, continuing, "And you're set to meet Einstein on Thursday, a week from today. Can you get your family ready for that?"

Al's face lit up. "That's wonderful," he said, and then he looked worried. "I've been thinking," he hesitated, "would it be all right if I just took my youngest boy, Little Louie?"

"I thought you wanted all your children to meet him," Welton said sharply.

"I did, but Little Louie—well, he wants to do something none of his brothers have done. It's important to him, and I thought this would be the greatest thing I could do for him. He could be proud of it for the rest of his life."

"That visit will mark the beginning of the decline of the Institute of Advanced Studies," John said drily, as Welton looked thoughtful.

"I'll watch him very carefully," Al promised. "As long as there's no valuable equipment around . . ."

"I suppose we can afford the price of a new fiddle for the professor," John said.

Paul Welton grinned slightly. "I think it will be all right, Toolum. Matter of fact, your reason for bringing that little—Little Louie, might make a cute angle for our releases." He waved for Miss Gregg to rejoin them.

During lunch Al saw a side of Mr. Welton he hadn't known existed. Before he had finished his soup, Al found himself laughing at the series of jokes and witty remarks that Paul Welton threw out in rapid fire. The only person who didn't laugh was Miss Gregg who sat in her chair like an owlish automaton, her only moves those necessary to lift her food to her mouth, a mouth, Al thought, that could use some lipstick.

When lunch was over—why he had to come all the way into the city just for the few remarks that *could* have been made over the phone, Al couldn't determine—he tried to peek at the check to determine his share, not wanting to be a piker in front of Miss Gregg. But, as Mr. Welton kept the total hidden, he drew a dollar from his pocket and placed it unobtrusively next to Welton's plate.

"That should cover my end plus tip," he said.

"Please," Welton said, pushing the dollar back, a pained expression on his face, but Al insisted. Turning to Miss Gregg, he said resignedly, "I guess you're coming with me."

She nodded.

Paul Welton watched them leave. "Man has good instincts," he proclaimed. "It goes with my theory that People Like People."

"I suppose you're right," John murmured. "Toolum is full of surprises, but basically he's a fine man."

"He may be full of surprises for other people," Paul Welton said grimly, "but from now on, Bell, you're to see that he doesn't surprise us. Not when we're reaching the crucial point of the campaign."

John briefly shuddered at the passing thought of how Welton would react at the upcoming issue of *Life* magazine. The caption over the Kandi Kola story was sure to be: "Biggest Fizz in History," but he quickly blanked this from his mind. "I just hope that Gregg gal doesn't get too fancy."

"That *woman*," Welton said, his voice turning to steel. "Did you see her deliberately ignore me? What do they inject those *Manhattanite* people with—resin?" He clenched his fist. "Do you know, Bell, it's people like Gregg who could be the ruination of this structure of ours—the whole thing. Phony intellectuals who have built up this veneer of cynicism, a cynicism satisfied only by the destruction of everything fine. Why—why"—for a moment Welton was at a loss for words, and then he burst out—"Why, do you know, she probably doesn't even believe in Advertising. . . ."

The subject of Paul Welton's outburst stood with *her* subject on the sidewalk, and when he exhibited a great deal of indecision, she finally took pity.

"Come on, Mr. Toolum, let's get a cab. It comes off my expense account."

"I wasn't thinking of that at all," Al protested, his voice trailing off. Then, to show that he was a man of real decision, he darted from the curb to intercept an empty cab that had just squeezed through a red light, barely missing a lady with a baby carriage.

Actually, Al *had* been wondering what to do with Miss Gregg. If they took a bus he had decided he would quickly drop two dimes in the box before she could protest. But he had thought maybe she would drop in the dimes before he had a chance, and this would be embarrassing. He was very frightened of Miss Gregg.

"I hate buses," she said, when they settled in the cab.

"So do I," he agreed, happy to find common ground. "I've got feuds with most of the companies."

Miss Gregg blinked at him. "Oh, yes?"

About to tell her, he fell silent, remembering how he had been warned. His bus feuds might seem very silly to *Manhattanite* readers.

As they slid down the ramp into Penn Station, Al wondered desperately how he could get rid of Miss Gregg. He had to meet Emily and Little Louie at the Child Guidance, and Em would be mad if he had the reporter in tow. When the cab stopped, he had his money all ready—sixty cents for the ride, and a dime tip. Miss Gregg didn't argue. Then they stood on the sidewalk, and Al decided to take the offensive.

"Do you really have to come with me?" he asked firmly.

"Why?"

"Well—well, it's kind of a personal matter. My wife . . ."

He was edging toward the stairway, but she matched him, edge for edge.

"I mean, I *don't* think you should come along." He thought wildly of calling a cop and saying this woman was molesting him.

Then, to his surprise, Miss Gregg nodded. "I have all I need," she said.

He sighed with relief. "Sure you have."

"I'll see you to the gate," she said.

He didn't feel safe until they were past the ticket window, and she made no move to buy one for Fernvale. Expressing his gratitude, he found himself confessing that he had to meet Emily at the Child Guidance.

"It's because of Little Louie," he said.

"This I can understand—having met Little Louie."

"Oh, he's much better than he used to be," Al assured her. "He used to bite strangers."

"Did they ever bite him back?"

"No." Al looked surprised. "Say, that wouldn't've been a bad idea. I wonder . . . Well, it's too late now. He doesn't do that any more."

"You can always have another one," Miss Gregg suggested, "and see how the theory works with *it*."

Al shuddered. "No, thanks," he said, extending his hand as the gate opened.

She took it, and then Al backed off through the gate. "What's wrong, Mr. Toolum," Miss Gregg called after him, "don't you like children?"

"It's not that I don't like them," he shouted, "just as long as there aren't too many of them."

He waved, and turned, chuckling to himself at this last sally. It was a good line to leave her with if she wanted something funny.

Sliding into the car next to Little Louie and Emily, he said, "Monday. They want me to come into the city again on Monday."

"But you can't," Emily protested. "That's the day we do Step B."

"I can't help it," he insisted. "You just have to get somebody in. Call Mrs. Begun. This Minute Maid business is driving me nuts. Emergency meeting last night, emergency meeting tonight . . ."

He fell silent in response to Emily's stony glare, or he would have brought up the emergency meeting that involved a session at Armando's, and a fitting for a new dress.

This, Al had announced indignantly, was too much. In the whole history of the labor movement, he had pointed out, there was not a single mention of an organizer who prepared for a demonstration by getting a permanent and a new gown.

"But this is not the labor movement," Emily had said to him. "If the Minute Maids of America are to make a dignified appearance . . ." and on and on and on until Al had been forced to admit that perhaps Armando should be hired on a sustaining basis by all organizations.

"This Plan B," he said now, as he halted at a red light. "Exactly what does it involve?"

"I'm not talking," Emily said. "It's a secret."

"Even from me who helped make the signs? Is it a picket line, Em?" She didn't answer, and he chortled, "Oh, boy, I bet that's it."

"What's funny about a picket line? You went on one once, didn't you?"

"Sure, but we had a tough fight. It *had* to be tough to make me go out against Henry."

"Ours is just as tough. You should know, complaining about bills the way you do."

"Go to it," Al shrugged, "and I hope you get something done." He grinned. "I have an idea. Why don't you wheel Little Louie in a baby carriage"—Little Louie, who had been quietly working on a lollipop, looked up with sudden interest—"that's always good for sympathy."

"Thanks for the good idea," Emily said sarcastically.

"I'll think of others before Monday."

"No, thanks. Do I tell you how to be Yankee Doodle?"

"No."

"Then don't tell me how to go on a picket line."

"Aw, take me," Little Louie demanded.

"No. There *could* be trouble," she said, glancing significantly at Al.

"You'll probably get into a big hassle with the store owner, and he'll call out the Cossacks," Al said.

"Oh, boy," Little Louie said.

"Nothing like that," Emily protested. "We women will show you men how to achieve our ends without violence. There's been too much violence in the world, the way the men have been running it."

"I'm from Missouri," Al said.

"So are too many other people," Emily said.

Arriving home, they found Herman and Sherman in a state of wild excitement, the source of their joy being a huge box that had been dumped in the living room just inside the door.

"It came on a truck," Sherman shouted, as Al inspected the box carefully and suspiciously.

It was a square crate, and stamped on every visible side were the words National Television, and the boys, joined by Little Louie, churned around the box like a pack of dogs loosed around a treed cougar.

"A television set," Al announced, after a great deal of deliberation. "Okay, which one of you kids ordered it?"

A chorus of innocent denials, followed by a short third degree, finally convinced Al that they were indeed innocent. Once before, Herman had called a television dealer for a "free home demonstration," and it had taken Al five days, plus mutual threats of lawsuits, before the set was removed. Herman had suffered so terribly as a result, however, that Al knew he never would do it again.

"A delivery man with two helpers brought it," Herman explained, "and when I asked him about it, he just said he followed orders, and this one came right from the factory."

Al stood trancelike in the middle of the floor, and then he clapped his hand to his head. "The Consultants," he cried, his eyes flying open. "They did this to me."

He rushed to the phone, followed by a wailing refrain—"Don't make them take it back, Papa," but an answering service told him that there was no one at the AAC at this hour. Then Al remembered John had given him his phone number at home in case of an emergency.

John answered the phone just as he was about to enter the shower, and he listened sympathetically to the irate complaint that crackled over the wire.

"Didn't I tell you about that?" John asked, clutching a towel about his middle.

"No, you didn't."

"Well, it's a gift from the manufacturer."

"Who needs it?" Al complained.

John sighed and sat down in a chair. "That's beside the point, Al. Matter of fact, you can consider yourself damn lucky." He plucked a cigarette from a case on the telephone table.

"Why?"

"Mr. Welton wanted the presentation to be made on National's big show this Friday night. I had a hell of a job getting you out of that. This way you'll only be bothered by a photographer sometime next week who'll take some shots for an ad."

"You mean there's nothing I can do about it?" Al asked ominously.

"For my sake, Al," John begged, "don't do anything for a

while. Keep it until things quiet down, and then you can chop it up for firewood."

There was a long pause. "Okay," Al said finally. "I owe you that much."

"Thanks," John said gratefully. "So I'll see you on Monday—one thirty in front of the Brill Building."

"No possibility of putting that off, is there? My wife—well, she has something special on for Monday."

"I'm afraid not. Barbie has our appointments all set up. I'm meeting her for dinner tonight to talk things over."

"Well—all right."

John was about to say good-bye when a further thought occurred to him. "Al, you still there?"

"Yeah. Where else would I be?"

"What I wanted to ask—have you done anything about resigning from that League? You know, the one Welton is so hot about."

"Not yet," Al answered, and then added truthfully, "I haven't given it any thought since we talked about it at lunch."

"Oh."

"Why?"

"Nothing. No special reason. Just—just don't do anything until we can talk it over. I have something to say about that."

"Okay. I just don't want to get in any trouble, that's all."

"You won't. So long, Al."

" 'Bye."

John hung up, doused his cigarette, and, whistling, made his way into the shower.

It was after nine o'clock when he and Barbie left the restaurant on East Fifty-first Street. It was a warm, lovely night, and by mutual, unspoken agreement, they turned east and walked slowly toward the river. On their right stretched Beekman Place, pointing arrowlike at the darkened United Nations building, and where Fifty-first Street ended was a long flight of stone steps which they slowly descended to the narrow concrete-floored playground with its sand pit and benches.

During dinner John had related to Barbie the story of Kandi Kola and he had found that at no point in the tale, even when Barbie laughed the hardest, did he experience the slightest twinge of conscience in the secret blasphemy. If Paul Welton were to hear this recital there would be one super-idea man walking the sidewalks tomorrow; but to his surprise, he also discovered that this thought didn't chill him with icy fear. His bravado, he admitted, was probably traceable to the two predinner Martinis.

Sitting on a bench, their backs to the rushing traffic that poured along the East River Drive, they gazed up at the row of Beekman Place homes above. Other benches were filled with people whose voices could barely be heard over the hiss of the traffic.

"How'd you like to live up there?" he asked Barbie, breaking the silence.

"Which one?" she asked. "The duplex, triplex or quadruplex?"

"The one with the trellis rising over the garden. Could you be happy there?"

"We'd have servant trouble," Barbie said. "Four in help, at least, and you know how difficult it is to maintain a staff these days. It's not like in Mother's day—or Pater's either."

"We?" he queried.

There was a brief pause, and then Barbie answered lightly, "I meant my husband and I. You don't think I'd live there in spinsterish splendor, do you?"

"Your husband," he said, "would have to be making a potful of dough. Maybe sixty-seventy thousand with the way taxes are today. Do you think you could stand a man who made that kind of money?"

"Depends on how he made it," she said.

"Oh, of course it would be clean, honest work. Like . . ." he paused.

"Like what?"

"Funny," he said, "I can't think of any clean, honest work these days."

"Maybe a shoeshine boy," she suggested.

"Or a subway guard, or a baby photographer. You see—how are you going to live up there?"

"Did I say I wanted to?"

"No—I guess you didn't. Maybe it was I who just wanted to."

"Do I hear the use of the past tense, Johnny? Are you changing your mind?"

He shifted uneasily. "I don't know whether I'm changing my mind, or whether Al Toolum is changing it for me. You see, Welton wants him to do something that I don't think Toolum should do, and I have the feeling that Al senses it's wrong too. He joined some outfit as a sponsor that Welton says is commie. I doubt whether it is, but that's not the point. Welton is condemning without investigation. You know how insidious that habit has become in the trade these days. I'm going to advise Al not to quit—for his own sake."

"But that could make a lot of trouble."

"I doubt it. Not for Toolum anyway. AAC has too much invested in him to throw him over just like that. It could mean trouble for me, though." He sighed. "I have the feeling I'm never for Beekman Place. The AAC was my steppingstone to a duplex."

"There's the title for a modern Alger book," she said.

"What is?"

"Sink or Swim, or From Duplicity to a Duplex."

"Duplicity, huh?" he said, with a faint rise in anger. "Still on that?"

"No, you were," she said. "All through dinner. The inside story of Yankee Doodle, or build a new Machine, boys, this one's on the fritz."

"The Machine can't be wrong," he said. "It picked Toolum therefore Toolum's our man."

"I've been giving that great thought," Barbie said, "and I've figured out what's wrong with that argument."

"And what might that be?" he asked in an exaggerated tone.

"You put into the Machine a whole set of standards that presumedly fits the average family head in this country, right?" He nodded, and she continued, "These standards, hundreds and hundreds of them, guaranteed you would get a man who fits AAC's concept of what he should be, right?"

"Right—so?"

"So *I* think you got things reversed. Instead of the standards fitting Toolum, Alfred Toolum just *happened* to fit the standards."

He looked puzzled. "What's the difference?"

"The difference is," she said, "that the first figure is one of cardboard, a dream figure in an ad. He doesn't live, he doesn't breathe, he doesn't think. He just eats, drinks, wears and does everything the average man is supposed to do. The second person, on the other hand, is the real Alfred Toolum. Even though he fits your standards, he goes 'way beyond them. He's a *man,* a real man, with all the complexities of a man. When you come in contact with him, he surprises you by showing that the so-called average standards are a minor part of his make-up."

"Say that again," he said, after a pause.

"What I mean is—" she began, but he interrupted, "Never mind, I think I know what you mean."

"And do you agree with me?"

"If I said I agreed with you, and had any integrity at all, I would be forced to walk into Welton's office tomorrow morning, slap him across the face with a wet flounder, and tell him I quit."

"Well, nothing quite so drastic, but that's the general idea."

"I'll have to sleep on it," he said, "before I tell you whether I agree or not. Why," he added plaintively, "do you constantly hound me to throw away my job and become a Bowery bum?"

"One thing doesn't necessarily lead to the other," she said.

"That doesn't answer my question. And in the second place, I still insist that you're as guilty as I, since you, too, work for AAC."

"I have a very ulterior motive for staying there," she said; "however, it looks as though the time is growing near when that reason will no longer exist."

"Oh, really?" he said, with great interest. "What's the reason?"

"Can't you guess?" she asked, with a show of demureness.

He looked at her blankly. "No, I can't."

She stared at him for a long moment, and then stood up. "I," she said in a hard tone, "am a private eye secretly hired by Mrs. Welton to dig up dirt on her husband." Taking his hand, she urged John up from the bench. "Come on, Lochinvar, tomorrow's another day."

Seventeen

For Al, the weekend was a time of total confusion. Just plain hell, he told Emily on the two or three occasions that he saw her alone. Working late on Friday and putting in a full day on Saturday at the plant, all he wanted, he said, was to come home and relax a little. But when he did come home the house was overflowing with Minute Maids so overcome with revolutionary fervor that the sight of a lone, unprotected male was enough to send them into increased frenzy. To escape banishment to the basement on Sunday he and Ben took the boys to Jones Beach. Ben, a veteran male auxiliary Minute Maid, took the whole thing very philosophically, but he couldn't convince Al that if women expended their fury against high prices, the lot of the husband would become easier. Al just longed for the pristine days of pre-Minute Maids and Yankee Doodle.

On Monday morning the chore of getting the older boys breakfasted and off to school fell on Al. As usual when he made breakfast, Al's scrambled eggs turned out much too liquid. He always put in more milk than necessary under the theory that this was one way of getting that substance into his sons' stomachs. To add to the confusion he had to run from the kitchen to the telephone a half-dozen times and act as a shouting intermediary between Emily, who was dressing upstairs, and the abstracted Minute Maid on the other end of the wire who wanted to make sure of the time and place of mobilization.

"It's Louise Green," he yelled up the stairs, when the phone had rung for the seventh time. "She wants to know is she supposed to bring her car?"

"Tell her yes," Emily called.

"Put butter on the toast while it's hot," he shouted to Sherman. "Not you, Louise—yes, you're supposed to bring the car."

He listened a moment. "She says Fred wants the car to drive to work this morning," he yelled to Emily.

Appearing at the head of the stairs, Emily was removing the bandanna that had acted as protection for her permanent. He looked at the curlers and shuddered.

"Tell her we have to have the car," Emily insisted. "Unless you change your mind and let me use ours."

"*I* have to go to the city," he told her, and then into the phone, "You've got to bring the car." He rolled his eyes, and said to Emily, "She wants to know how is Fred going to get to work?"

"How does he always get to work?"

"How does he always get . . . The *hell* with it," he exploded, dropping the phone. "Talk to her yourself." He darted into the kitchen as Emily, muttering dire threats and dark remarks about the complete lack of co-operation around the house when *she* was trying to do something, stamped down the stairs.

"Get your hand out of the jam jar," he yelled at Little Louie, but Little Louie's hand was stuck in the jam jar, and he couldn't get it out.

"Easy, easy," Al said, tugging at Little Louie's wrist. "It got in, it should come out. Especially when it's more slippery now."

"It hurts," Little Louie cried.

"Don't get panicky," Al said.

"Hey, Papa, the coffee's boiling over," Sherman said.

"Turn it off. Don't just sit there like a jerk."

Herman asked, "Should I get a hammer?"

"No. Little Louie, damn it, loosen up your fist."

"It's still boiling over, Papa."

"Take it *off* the stove, off the stove. The coils are still hot. Little Louie, *will* you stop twisting around?"

Someone knocked sharply on the screen door. "If that's Sadie . . ." Al started threateningly. "Come in," he called.

But it wasn't Sadie. It was Mrs. Begun, the lady who was going to take care of Little Louie for the day and also clean the house and cook supper.

"Oh, hello, Mrs. Begun. My wife said you weren't coming till ten."

"I had nothing else to do this morning," Mrs. Begun said.

"Well, you can sit in the living room, if you want. There's some magazines to look at."

Mrs. Begun watched his struggles for a moment, and then she asked, "What's his hand doing in the jam jar?"

"It's always in the jam jar," Al said. "It's his favorite place for it, isn't it, Little Louie—and it looks like it always will be in the jam jar."

Little Louie began to sob. "It hurts."

"Herman, get the hammer."

Still holding Little Louie with one hand, Al ate a piece of toast with the other. "Nice day, isn't it, Mrs. Begun?"

"On a day like this my husband died."

"Well, I always say there's some dark cloud to mar the sunshine. Oh, thanks, Herman."

Little Louie wailed louder at the sight of the hammer.

"I'm not going to hurt you. Now, just lay the jar on the table—like so. Now——"

"What are you hitting the child with the hammer for?" Emily cried, choosing that moment to enter the kitchen.

Al dropped the hammer. Facing Emily, he said, with extreme dignity, "I am going into the living room where I will remain until one) Herman and Sherman are gone; two) you are completely ready; and three) Little Louie is out of my sight, jam jar and all."

Without waiting for a reply, he stalked out of the kitchen.

It was just over an hour when Al's three conditions were fulfilled. Emily announced her readiness standing in the doorway, fully dressed for outdoors, her pocketbook in hand.

"I don't understand," Al said, getting to his feet. "You spend a fortune getting your hair fixed, and then you cover it with a great big hat. For all anyone could tell, you are completely bald."

"*I* know I'm not, and what if I had to take my hat off someplace?"

"You win the argument," Al said.

They walked through the kitchen. "I see you got rid of Little Louie."

"He's upstairs with Mrs. Begun helping make the beds."

"I trust you got the jam jar off."

"I did, and very easily too. Simply by running cold water over his hand. *You* wouldn't think of that, would you?"

"You'd be surprised at what I think sometimes," Al said.

"*Sadie,*" Emily called, when they were outside, and then to Al, "Get the signs out of the garage, will you? Sadie's are in there too."

"Where's Ben. Why isn't he here to help?"

"He had to go to work, as you perfectly well know."

"Coward," Al muttered as he went into the garage. It took him a couple of minutes to load the signs into the back of the car while both Emily and Sadie urged him to hurry.

The mobilization point at the corner of Fifth and Main was already crowded with a number of women, all of whom Al knew, but whose faces wore unfamiliar expressions of rugged determination. When Al drove up, the women cried, "Here's Madam Captain;" "Hooray for our leader;" "Let's give it to 'em, girls;" and Al, the only male present, hurriedly unloaded the signs and climbed back into the car, telling Emily he'd better be going.

Emily didn't hear him. Her face was flushed in a way he'd never seen before, and, although she wasn't really doing anything, she seemed to be busy organizing.

"Emily," he called from the car window, "I'll see you later. You want me to phone you this afternoon?"

"What? Oh, no, that won't be necessary. But in case of trouble, where can I call you?"

"Trouble? What trouble?"

"We're dealing with very unscrupulous people, Al, and——"

"Oh, yeah, that. Well, here, I'll write it down for you." He pulled pen and paper out of his inside pocket. The paper was his schedule for the day, and tearing it in half, he wrote busily. "I'll be at the Floy-doy Music Publishers from two until three thirty, and from four until six I'll be at the National Broadcasting Company, studio——" Emily wasn't paying attention, so meekly he finished his note-making and handed her the paper.

"Good-bye, Em," he said, sliding behind the wheel. "And remember Joe Hill."

"Who's Joe Hill?" Emily asked, puzzled.

"Never mind," Al said, shifting into gear, and as he drove away he wondered whether the martyred Wobbly were whirling in his grave at the depths to which mass action had sunk. His last glimpse of Emily was as she burst into the center of the growing babel of voices, crying, "Now, ladies, if you'll just pay attention . . ."

Arriving in the city an hour and a half before his appointment, Al found space in a parking lot on Eighth Avenue, and then, to kill time, he walked up and down Broadway looking at the flashing marquees, pausing now and then to peer at the stills in front of the theaters, but soon this palled, and he began to think of the Little Louie problem.

"You're a hell of a father, Toolum," he accused himself, "letting your kid go through a thing like that."

He'd work on it, he promised himself—really work on it. He'd become pals with Little Louie.

But how do you get to be pals with a little monster like that? a small voice asked him.

He ran into a newsreel theater.

At one thirty he was standing in front of the Brill Building, and not more than two or three minutes later John and Barbie arrived.

"What is this crazy place?" he asked John. "People keep running in and out, and all of them are singing."

"The Brill Building? Why, it's the song-publishing headquarters of the world. When you talk about Tin Pan Alley, this is it."

"What am I supposed to do in there?" Al asked, suddenly suspicious.

"Didn't you tell him, Johnny?" Barbie asked.

"Not exactly."

"Let's have a hot dog," Barbie said. "We've still a few minutes."

Over frankfurters and orangeade at a corner stand, John explained that Al was to be used in an experiment with some popular songs.

"Do you remember I told you that, as the average man, your reactions to certain things would carry lots of weight?"

"Like Kandi Kola?" Al asked.

John grinned. "I hope not. Anyway, you'll listen to some songs, and if you like them the publisher will know they're good—I mean," he amended, "they have mass appeal and might be hits."

"There *is* a difference," Barbie said. "I checked your report, Mr. Toolum, and you said you liked Irving Berlin."

"Who? Oh, yeah, the man who wrote 'Alexander's Ragtime Band.' Well, I didn't have much choice."

"Al," John took his arm gently, "you won't louse me up today, will you?"

"No, of course not. If I like the song I'll tell them. But if I don't like it——"

"You'll tell them that too," Barbie said.

"Right."

"Okay," John said. "That's all I can ask. After this we're going over to a television audition. A big show is being rehearsed for sale to a national sponsor, and they want the average man's response to it. They have a machine——"

"Which should make everything scientific," Barbie broke in.

John ignored her. "It simply tells what parts you think are good and which you think are dull. You push buttons."

"Don't wear out the dull button," Barbie said.

An elevator took them to the ninth floor of the Brill Building, and at the end of the marble hallway was a frosted door, reading FLOY-DOY MUSIC PUBLISHERS. From a half-dozen other doors came the sound of pianos and phonographs.

Two men, both short, stout and bald, burst from the offices of the Floy-Doy Music Publishers, and one was saying to the other, "So I got this creep moaner on the fattest payola of his life, and wad-does he do but plug a real dog right across the board on his half-hour seg."

The second fat man shook his head, as Al, Barbie and John passed, and said, "I'd'a cut his stinkin' heart out."

Al stood transfixed, watching the two men get into the elevator. Then he turned to John. *"What* did that first guy say?"

John said, grinning, "He was telling his friend that he was pay-ing a singer under the table to sing Floy-Doy songs, but the singer double-crossed him by using someone else's tune every day on his half-hour radio program."

"Oh," Al said, as John opened the door.

A blonde girl behind a long counter said, "Help ya?"

"I'm John Bell of the American Advertising Consultants."

"Oh, yeah, I'll call Mr. Floyd."

A moment later a third little fat man, who looked just like the two who had gone out, entered from an inner office. Between his teeth he clenched a long, unlighted cigar.

Thrusting a hand toward John, he said, "Bell, glad to meetcha. Talked to ya onna phone, dint I?"

"That's right, Mr. Floyd. This is Miss McClain, and——"

"Hi ya, baby. For a mint I thought ya was Peggy Lee. Great chirper, that Lee. Hear her on are latest? 'I Gotcha Where I Wancha an' Now I'll Lock the Door.'"

"No, I haven't, Mr. Floyd."

"Great number. Sell a million. And you"—turning to Al —"mus' be Yankee Doodle. Bum-bum-bum-bum-*bum*-bum-bum . . ." He hummed "Yankee Doodle," accompanying it with a soft-shoe shuffle.

"Usta be a hoofa when I was younger," he explained at the end of the refrain. "But no more. Heart," he said, clutching his side. "Got pains alla time. Croaker says I can't even smoke." He waved the unlighted cigar.

Al murmured that that was a shame, and then Mr. Floyd grasped his arm. "Come on inside—alla ya—got some great numbers ya wanna hear." Urging them toward the back of the office, he opened a door leading to a narrow corridor, and called, "Harry. Hey, Harry, c'mere."

A dark, lean man wearing a battered hat on the back of his head poked his head from a booth, one of the many that lined the corridor.

"You want me, Mr. Floyd?"

"Yeah, ya ready?" The dark man nodded, and Mr. Floyd explained, "We'll go to the big audition studio," and they walked down the corridor.

The "big audition studio" was a room about fifteen feet square with an old upright piano in one corner. Once white, the piano was dirty and scarred from hundreds of cigaretttes that had been allowed to burn to an ash on its surface. The rest of the room was filled with wooden folding chairs, and on one was a portable phonograph, chipped and topless. The floor was littered with cigarette butts and bottle tops. A half-open window faced Broadway.

"Harry," Mr. Floyd said, as the thin man entered carrying a stack of records, "this is that Yankee Doodle man who's gonna give us the go-ahead on the tunes."

"Meetcha," Harry said, putting the records down on a chair.

Mr. Floyd whipped some sheets of paper from a pocket. "Now, we're gonna do this real scientific," he announced, handing a sheet to Al and pressing a short chewed-up pencil along with it, "just like the polls. I don't wancha to make any comment on any tune until we're all through—no matter how great you think it is," he warned. "Jus' mark down what you think where you're supposed to."

John peered over Al's shoulder at the sheet which had, typewritten down the side, three categories: SENSATIONAL, WONDERFUL and JUST OKAY—and across the top were numbers, and below these were boxes where Al was to make check marks.

"What did you mean," Al asked nervously, "when you said I was going to give you the go-ahead on the tunes?"

"Oh, that. Well, ya see, we got what we call plug tunes, which are the ones we think got a chance ta make a splash. We put a lotta dough in 'em," he added solemnly, "spreading 'em around amongst the right bandleaders, singers and disk jocks. That's how ya get a hit—make the right people plug ya tune." A faraway look came into his eyes. "If oney we could find somebody with the common ear—a guy who could listen to a tune an', right away, tell is it gonna be a hit, this guy could make a million. Maybe you're him, huh?" he cried.

"I don't know," Al said doubtfully. "I'm not much up on these things."

"Ya don't hafta be," Floyd said. "Jus' tell us if ya *like* it. Ready, Harry?"

"Check." Harry sat on the piano stool, and the others sat on the wooden chairs.

"Harry'll play an' sing this first one. It's a rhythm novelty, an' I'd hate ta tell ya who wrote it. Ya'd be staggered, so I won't influence ya. Oney thing"—he leaned forward confidentially—"this guy steals from Berlin, an' in my opinion, he's *better*."

"What"—Al hesitated—"what's a rhythm novelty?"

"Ya'll hear inna mint," Mr. Floyd cried. "This here is the greatest since 'Three Little Fishies Inna Itty-bitty Poo.' Okay, Harry . . ."

Striking the keys with a flourish, Harry played a short introduction, and then, turning to his audience, he sang, in a thin, cracked voice:

> "Igga digga digga
> My heart is like a trigga
> That goes click for you.
>
> "Igga digga digga
> It keeps on gettin' bigga
> 'Cause I love you true.
>
> "Toujours l'amour, toujours l'amour
> Ya got me talkin' French.
> How I'd love ta translate
> Out on an old park bench.

"Igga digga digga
Igga digga digga
Igga digga digga doo."

The lyrics completed, Harry bent to the piano, and started pounding out another chorus.

"Sings jus' like Waller Huston usta," Mr. Floyd cried, over the piano. He was bouncing up and down in his chair, both feet tapping on the floor. "Now dig this great melody without the words."

His eyes slightly glazed, Al "dug" the melody. Watching John for some reaction that might help him, Al saw that John was leaning forward in what seemed to be intense concentration, his face buried in his hands; and Barbie, who had left her chair, was standing at the window, her shoulders shaking in time to the music.

Once more Harry sung the words, and when the number was ended with a flourish and an oompah, oompah, boom-boom, Mr. Floyd leaped to his feet. "Great, Harry, really great. Well, whatta ya think, Yankee Doodle?" and quickly he raised his hand. "No, don't tell me. I don't wanna influence ya. Jus' mark it down."

Al stared at the sheet of paper in his hand and chewed the end of the pencil. The song, to his way of thinking, had been the most horrible thing he'd ever heard. No, that wasn't quite fair: he had heard much worse—everyday on the radio. Thus comforted, he checked WONDERFUL, and experienced a twinge of terrible guilt that he was selling his soul. But he felt so much out of his depth—and, after all, Mr. Floyd *did* keep saying it was great. He made the check mark heavier.

Removing a record from the top of the stack that Harry had brought in, Mr. Floyd turned on the phonograph, and while it was warming up, said, "Now this here is somethin' ya'll be able ta tell ya grandchildren about. 'Member a coupla wears ago Mike Todd, the producer, got some tunes from the King a' Siam? Well"—his voice fell—"I won' say it was a phony, but"—his face broadened in a smile —"the tunes were strickly dogs. Now this here"—he tapped the record—"is—should I tell 'em, Harry?"

"Yeah, why not? How long can we keep it a secret?"

"Not much longer," Mr. Loyd said solemnly. "We promised

Winchell the first break, an' if Waller hears we bin playin' this aroun' . . ." He whistled.

"Please," Barbie begged, "tell us what it is, Mr. Floyd."

Mr. Floyd held up his right hand. "If ya'll all swear . . . Okay! *This here tune was written by the Grand Lama of Tibet.*" His eyes closed in a brief reverie, as he appreciated the stunned silence that had fallen around him.

"I won't say any more," he stated humbly, "except, the State Department would give a million to know how we got this tune." Carefully, he placed the test record on the phonograph and held up the tone arm. "Ya ready?"

"The title, Mr. Floyd," Harry cried. "Give 'em the title."

"Oh, yeah, the title." His hand paused briefly, and, reverently, he said, 'Lhasa Lullaby,' by the Grand Lama of Tibet . . ."

The tone arm fell.

It would have surprised Al to know that, at that exact moment, but some forty-five minutes from Broadway, another song was being presented for the first time, but this one was written by a composer whom he knew well. Militantly marching in good order up and down in front of the Great Goose Supermarket (Home-Owned and Home-Operated) were the Minute Maids of America, and their voices were lifted to the "Battle Hymn of Price Control," words by Sister Sadie Carroway, music by the composer of an earlier, more well-known "Battle Hymn."

> "We won't buy meat in here until the price comes down.
> Have a heart, Mr. Grocer, for all the folks in town.
> You've got the food, but we haven't got the dough,
> So listen to our tale of woe.
>
> Go easy on the family bu-u-get,
> Go easy on the family bu-u-get,
> Go easy on the family bu-u-get,
> Oh, bring those prices down."

they sang, as Emily, from her vantage point on the flank of the picket line, exhorted the ladies to wave their signs as they sang and marched.

"Louder, girls, louder! And swing those signs. Let them see 'em!"

Two more choruses satisfied Emily, who then cried, "Slogan Number Four. Give it to them good. One, two . . ."

"This grocery owner has no feeling
His prices have gone right through the ceiling"

the ladies chanted over and over again as Emily, seeing that the growing crowd of onlookers seemed impressed, called for the slogan to be repeated. Thank goodness for the emergency meeting for songs and slogans, Emily said to herself.

"Sadie, what time is it?" she asked, when the chant started to weaken.

"Almost exactly two thirty," Sadie answered, her sign bobbing up and down as she glanced at her watch.

"Squad A, fall out," Emily ordered, in a military manner. "Leader of Squad B, take charge." Half the ladies from the line stepped smartly to the side, and Sister Edna Corning, Leader of Squad B, took Emily's place.

"Half-hour, girls," Emily reminded those who had fallen out, "and take care of your signs," she admonished needlessly.

The emergency meeting dealing with Formation of the Picket Line had decided that equally divided squads would march a half-hour each with a third half-hour at full strength. Now they were starting the second round.

As Squad A dispersed, the remaining marchers took up the chant:

"Don't buy—too high"

and the scattered members of Squad A, off in search of a cup of coffee, cheered each other with morale-boosting statements, such as; "We've got a big crowd, girls, let's keep it up." . . . "Did you see that newspaperman taking pictures? What did he ask you, Emily?" . . . "*Four* policemen, my goodness." . . . "Only three customers since we started."

This last came from Sadie Carroway, leader of Squad A, who

had fallen in step with Emily, as they pushed through a group of young men dressed in T-shirts who leaned against a corner lamp-post.

"G'wan back where you came from, you old bags," one of the youths cried.

Stony-faced, Emily and Sadie passed without diverting their gaze.

"Why doesn't the policeman ask them to go away?" Emily whispered, when they were safely past.

"Those cops," Sadie said scornfully, "they wouldn't save their mothers from being killed by robbers."

They had to walk two blocks before finding a coffee shop that wasn't crowded with Minute Maids.

"I don't want no trouble," the proprietor cried, as they entered.

"You be quiet!" A stout lady, obviously his wife, emerged from the rear kitchen. "Come on in, ladies. Make yourselves comfortable."

"Thank you," Emily said, sitting at a small table. "I hate to admit it, Sadie, but my feet hurt."

"Mine too," Sadie confessed. They ordered two coffees from the stout lady.

In the distance Emily listened to the rising chant of Squad B, and she felt a warm glow. "Isn't it wonderful, Sadie!" she marveled. "They can't ignore us now."

But even more wonderful, Emily told herself secretly, was the way she had done most of the organization for Step B. When Sadie had first proposed they do something drastic about high prices, Emily, as well as everyone else, had been highly in favor of action. Nevertheless, her enthusiasm for the project had dampened when she had found herself voted the head of the committee. It was only when Al kidded her about the Minute Maids that she became resolved that this was a job she would do—and do well.

"They certainly can't ignore us," Sadie said. "And that worm of a store owner, coming out and shouting at us to go away."

"I feel a *little* sorry for him," Emily admitted. "After all, prices really aren't his fault."

"Never mind feeling sorry for him. He's responsible for those mean boys. I saw him talking to them when they first came around."

When the coffee arrived, Emily made a big effort to relax. The build-up to Step B had been a time of such tension that now, when it was successfully underway, she felt a strong, nervous reaction.

They were drinking their second cup when the door opened and Sister Ruth Berg, Squad B's runner, puffed into the shop.

"Emily, Emily," Sister Berg cried, "Edna says you're to hurry back."

"What's wrong?" Emily asked, alarmed.

"It's those boys. There must be twenty of them now, and they keep calling us names, trying to shout us down."

"Oh, dear." Emily rose quickly. "Let's go, Sadie. Ruth, sound the call for all Squad A members. We're cutting this rest period short."

The jeering hecklers almost drowned out the Minute Maids who, despite their reduced numbers, were doing yeoman service in their vocal output. There were *six* policemen on duty now, Emily noticed, as she and Sadie reached the line. From all directions came Squad A members in answer to the call, and quickly Emily reorganized them.

At full strength once more, the Minute Maids successfully topped the efforts of their detractors. We have a lot of people on our side, too, Emily consoled herself, for in the crowd were many friendly faces, men as well as women.

"We're in the right, and that's what counts," Emily told herself firmly.

Later, when questioned, Emily could truthfully say that she had absolutely no idea where the rock came from, except that she was morally certain no Minute Maid threw it. All she remembered was the sense of horror she had felt when, a split second after the sound of the crash, she saw the splintered glass of the big window-front of the Great Goose smashing to the sidewalk.

Then everything took on the feeling of a slow-motion nightmare. From inside the store rushed the screaming owner, his red face expressing hysterical anger. The chant was cut off with startling abruptness, and the march slowed momentarily to a bewildered shuffle as the ladies stared at the broken glass.

Emily heard her own voice crying, "March, girls, march," as though someone else gave the order, and mechanically the line took up the march again.

Then the policemen moved forward, and Emily saw the smiling face of a rather nice, young officer, who was saying, "All right, lady, time to break it up now." He held out his hand as a sympathetic gesture, and all down the line his fellow officers moved into position.

Glad that the decision was now out of her hands, Emily was more than anxious to comply with the word of the law. Turning to give the necessary orders so that, at least, the Minute Maids could withdraw with dignity and honor, Emily caught sight of Sadie Carroway tramping toward the policeman, a determined look on her face.

What's she doing? Emily asked herself, puzzled, and then Sadie's purpose became all too clear.

"*No,*" Emily implored. "No, Sadie, put down that sign. *Don't hit that policeman.* Oh-h-h . . ."

"How was that one?" Mr. Floyd exclaimed, as the music, after a shrieking crescendo of trumpets and bongos, wailed to an end.

"What was the name of it again?" Al asked weakly.

" 'Tea For Three,' " Harry said.

Mr. Floyd had explained before playing the record that "Tea For Three" was a sequel to "Tea For Two," after the people involved had got married and had a baby. "It's a switcheroo on the revival of old hits," he had further explained.

Al, staring at the sheet of paper, added another WONDERFUL to the lengthy list of WONDERFUL's. He had long given up the idea of checking a SENSATIONAL or a JUST OKAY, preferring the middle road as the safest course.

"Now," Mr. Floyd said, carefully placing his cigar down and drawing himself up with a gesture that showed he had something of great import. "Now, we come to the best. It's a country tune—one that'll make the 'Tennessee Waltz' sound like a hunka schmaltz. And even though it was penned right aroun' the corner in a delicatessen, ya couldn't tell the difference between this and, say, the *best* of authenticity."

He drew himself erect even further. "Authenticity," he repeated, his eyes misting, his voice becoming lyrical. "You imagine the willows in the bayous, the happy peasants singing inna cotton fields, the old mule travelin' down the dusty road. Oney thing is," he said in his normal voice, "we can't decide onna title, an' maybe you can make the decision for us, Yankee Doodle."

"I'll try," Al said. At this point he was willing to try anything.

"We can't decide between 'The Louisiana Lament' or 'The Doomed Lovers.' "

"I think——" Al started to say, but Mr. Floyd cut him off imperiously. "Stop. Wait'll you hear the number. Ready, Harry?"

Harry was apparently more than ready. For this he had removed his hat. "Ready, Mr. Floyd," he said, and cleared his throat.

But at that moment the door opened, and the blonde girl poked her head in. Looking directly at Al, she said, "You Mr. Toolum?" and when Al nodded, she said, "Telephone."

"Hurry back," Mr. Floyd called, as Al left the studio.

It was with a feeling of disquiet that he picked up the receiver, and this feeling was more than justified when, after he said, "Hello," Ben Carroway's voice shouted. "Al! Al! all *hell's* broken loose."

Al closed his eyes. "The kids?" he asked quakingly, his mind a jumble of careening trucks, exploding stoves and open second-story windows with crumpled bodies on the ground below.

He almost sank to the floor in relief when Ben said, "No, no, nothing like that. The kids are okay."

"My wife?" Al demanded.

"Your wife, my wife, everybody's wife," Ben shouted. "They're all in jail."

Al felt an uncontrollable desire to laugh. What a funny thing for someone to be saying to him over the telephone.

"Al, you listening? Al!"

"Sure, I'm listening. You say in jail. Where?"

"Mineola."

"Mineola. *In jail?*" he screamed. *"What are they doing in jail?"*

"Oh, Al," Ben groaned, "I can't tell you the whole thing over the telephone. It's too awful. Can you come right away—county courthouse?"

"Sure, sure, I'll leave this minute. In jail. Murder. The kids. Wait a minute, the kids. Ben, do me a favor."

"Anything, Al, only hurry."

"Call my house. Tell Mrs. Begun we'll be late for dinner. Tell her—oh, tell her anything."

"I'll call as soon as we hang up."

"Now!" Al slammed down the receiver.

"All set, Yankee Doodle?" Mr. Floyd demanded, when Al ran into the studio.

Al grabbed John by the lapels, paying no attention to Mr. Floyd. "John, I have to go right away. My wife—my wife . . . Oh," he moaned.

Immediate concern rushed over Barbie's and John's faces. "What's wrong, Al?" John demanded.

"I can't tell you, I can't tell you. I just have to get to Mineola right away."

"You want me to drive you?" John asked quickly. "You don't look in any shape to drive a car."

They herded the completely demoralized Al into the corridor as Mr. Floyd followed, tugging at Al's sleeve. "You gotta hear this just once," he said. "You gotta."

"Please," John said, "can't you see Mr. Toolum's gotten bad news?"

"It'll kill ya," Mr. Floyd said. "A *double* SENSATIONAL if there ever was one."

"Let's go," John said. "Got your hat, Barbie?"

"Didn't wear one."

"One chorus," Mr. Floyd pleaded. "I'll do it myself."

Opening the door, John said, "Sorry, Mr. Floyd, I'll call you tomorrow," but the president of the Floy-Doy Music Publishing Company was in another world.

"She was such a happy dancer," he crooned in a lamenting voice, "But deep inside had cancer . . ."

The door slammed!

Eighteen

It was ten after four when they careened to a stop in front of the county courthouse in Mineola. Knowing that this could not be kept a secret in any case, Al had repeated Ben's words over the telephone to Barbie and John, but if he had expected recriminations, he was wrong. Barbie expressed immediate concern and sympathy, and John, saying nothing, had only tightened his lips and stepped harder on the gas pedal.

On the steps leading to the police station section was a crowd of men. Scanning their faces in the hope that one of them was Ben, Al ran up the steps; and one of the men shouted, "That's him!" the cry being followed by the popping of a half-dozen flashbulbs. John's mouth tightened all the more as he pushed Al through the crowd, saying, "No questions, fellows."

Inside, Al gulped and wiped his brow. "Where's Ben?" he croaked, and just then Ben Carroway burst from a door that led from the main corridor, shouting, "Al, I saw you out the window. Come in here, quick."

"Tell me, Ben—tell me what happened."

Grouped in the small anteroom where Ben led him were a dozen husbands of the incarcerated Minute Maids who, upon seeing Al, set up a furious clamor.

"Wait a minute," Al begged, "wait a minute, please. Ben, tell me what happened."

Dramatically, with a great display of arm waving, Ben told an approximation of what had happened in front of the Great Goose, up to and including the throwing of the stone.

"But why drag them off to jail?" Al asked in a bewildered voice when Ben, red-faced and indignant, had finished his tale.

"Why? Ha!" It was Nat Berg who thrust his face in front of Al. "Go on, Ben, tell him. Tell him, I dare you."

Ben's face grew long with sorrow as Al prompted, "Well?"

"When the cops wanted to break it up," Ben said, finally, "somebody hit one of them with a sign."

Al closed his eyes, feeling a sudden numbness. "Who's somebody?" he whispered.

"Sadie," Ben said painfully.

His eyes flew open, and he almost giggled, the relief was so great. "Sadie," he repeated. "Oh, brother." His face took on a grim expression. "That's really great."

"But that just started it off," Ben said. "There was kind of a little riot—which didn't last very long. And nobody got hurt," he emphasized.

Al looked around the room, meeting Frank Corning's accusing glance. "You've got to do something, Toolum," Corning stated. He was an accountant, and Al could see where having his wife in jail was going to throw the neat little books in his mind far off for this quarter. "After all, your wife got Edna into this whole mess."

"Oh, yeah?" Al snapped. "If you didn't want your wife getting into this, why didn't you assert yourself?" This was an unfair question, Al knew as he asked it, because Edna Corning outweighed her husband by a good thirty pounds.

"What's going to happen now?" he asked, turning to Ben.

"They've called a judge to come for a hearing. The only one they could find was playing golf. He'll be here any minute."

Barbie opened the door and tugged Al's sleeve. "Would you like to see your wife, Mr. Toolum? I fixed it with the sergeant."

He was led to another room, small and bare, and there was Emily sitting on a worn wooden chair. Bareheaded, she was staring out the window to the street, her face a mask, and her lips tightly compressed. Only her hands, nervously clutching her purse, showed that beneath the calm exterior boiled inner tension.

"Emily," he said woefully, when the door closed behind him, "Emily, I never thought I'd see you behind bars."

Her hands jumped slightly, but there was no change in her facial expression. "I don't see any bars," she said.

"A figure of speech." He sighed and sat down. "We'll have to bring you orange juice during visiting hours," he said thoughtfully. "Keep up your vitamins."

Her head swiveled. "Now, quit that," she snapped, and then her voice broke. "How are the boys?"

"How could they be—with their mother in jail?" The flash that shot into her eyes warned him to stop the nonsense, and quickly he said, "I had Ben call Mrs. Begun. The boys are being taken care of."

She turned away again. "You want to tell me about it?" he asked.

She shook her head.

"Why not?"

"Because I'm mad," she said. "Mad right from top to bottom. Oh, Al," she cried, "I wanted Step B to be a success so bad."

He nodded his head understandingly. "Maybe it was. Lot of newspaper guys outside. You'll get plenty of publicity, and that's what you wanted."

"But not *that* kind of publicity. People will laugh at us." Taking a handkerchief from her purse, she wiped her eyes. "Just a couple of months ago I was thinking what a rut we were in. *Now* look at us."

"We're doing fine, Em."

"No, we're not. How can you say that? I wish we were back where we started from."

"Like the man says, Em, you can't go back."

"It's all your fault," she said suddenly.

"My fault?" he said indignantly. "How does that figure?"

"If—if you hadn't gotten to be Yankee Doodle I wouldn't have wanted to get *my* picture in the paper——"

"Wait a minute"—he shook his finger at her—"*who* talked me into being Yankee Doodle?"

She began to sniffle. "That's beside the point."

"Oh-h," he scuffed the floor angrily, but as Emily's sniffles grew louder, he took his handkerchief from his pocket and handed it to her.

The door opened a crack, and Ben called, "Al, come on, the judge is here."

Taking Emily's arm, he helped her up. "Where's your hat?" he asked.

She made a gesture toward her hair, as though realizing for the first time that the hat was missing. "I don't know. I—I guess it got lost."

"Anyway, I'm glad you got a permanent," he said, opening the door. "It'll impress the judge."

Judge Tremont, however, was impressed, and disagreeably so, only by the fact that his golf game had been interrupted. Tall and gaunt, his loud, angry voice directed the sergeant in the business of herding everyone into the small courtroom. Still clad in plus fours, with a colorful sweater drawn over a white golfing shirt, he kept calling, "Come on, come on. Let's go there."

Finally, everyone was arranged. The accused Minute Maids were grouped together on one side of the room between the bench and gate, and behind the gate were the husbands, members of the press and several uniformed policemen.

"Let's get this over with," the judge snapped.

A police sergeant stepped forward and whispered lengthily into the judge's ear. When he was finished, Judge Tremont grumbled, "Okay, read off the names of the women involved."

As the names were read, all the husbands stared mournfully at the wives, while none of the wives looked at the husbands.

"Where's this Mrs. Alfred Toolum?" the judge asked, when the clerk ended his reading.

Hesitantly, Emily drew forward. "Come on, come on," Judge Tremont urged. "Toolum," he said thoughtfully. "Isn't your husband somebody? I mean, don't I know him from somewhere?"

"In the newspapers, maybe, your Honor," Emily said. "He's Yankee Doodle Fifty-two."

"He's *what?* Oh—oh, yes. Is he in the courtroom?"

"Yes, sir."

"Well, just don't sit there, Toolum," the judge called. "Move up here."

Dry-lipped, Al left the safety of his fellow husbands, passed through the little gate and shuffled up to the bench. "Stand over there," the judge directed, as Al, becoming panic-stricken, was wondering whether the laws allowed a husband to be punished for his wife's sins. He moved to the side opposite the Minute Maids. "Now, let's get on with this. What happened?"

A policeman came forward, and in an arid monotone told the story of the picket line. "And then, sir," he ended, pointing to Sadie, "that lady hit me with a sign."

"Where's the sign?" the judge wanted to know. "An important piece of evidence."

The sign was produced. To add to Al's shock he saw it was one he had painted.

" 'Fight For Price Control,' " the judge read. "Aren't you taking that too literally, madame?" he asked Sadie coldly, and without awaiting an answer, snapped, "Next complaint."

The owner of the Great Goose was next, but his hysterical story was cut short by an impatient wave of Judge Tremont's hand. "All right, all right—so your window was smashed, and your business ruined. Did you see one of these women throw the stone?"

"No. No, sir, your Honor."

"You covered by insurance? Civil riot comes under a comprehensive, you know."

"I—I guess so, your Honor."

"All right, step down."

There was a long silence while the judge rocked back and forth slowly, the only sounds in the courtroom being the creak of his chair and an occasional dry, nervous cough.

Then Judge Tremont said, "Mrs. Toolum, you seem to be the leader of this little revolution"—Emily's hands fluttered as she wanted to explain that she headed just one small committee. "Can you give me your word that no one from the picket line threw that stone?"

"Oh, yes, sir, I give my word. No one would do anything like that."

"Uh-huh." He seemed lost in thought. "By all rights, I suppose," he said in a barely discernible voice, "I should lock you all up for about ten days." There was a concerted gasp. "Hmmm," the judge said, "I imagine most of you have children at home, don't you?"

An answering wail rose and fell.

"Mr. Toolum," the judge said gravely, "step up here."

"Yes—yes, sir."

"You're a responsible citizen, Toolum," Judge Tremont said, fixing Al with a sharp glare. "I might say a prominent citizen. As the most average man in the country, your actions are the business of everyone in the community, because they reflect the community, do you understand?"

"Yes, sir. I mean, I think so."

"And, by the same token, your family comes under the same scrutiny. Now, Toolum, do you think you can keep your wife under wraps for a while?"

"I . . ."

"Do you?"

"Yes, sir."

"All right—I'm making you responsible not only for your wife, but every other woman here. They're on six months' probation. I understand," he said, as Al was about to protest, "you can't dictate to other women, but you *can* show the other husbands by example.

You're to carry out the wishes of this court." He arose. "Now get out of here, all of you," he shouted, "and don't let me see any of you again."

For a moment, until the judge darted from the bench and back into his chambers, Al stood immobilized, and then slowly he turned toward the ladies, the shepherd looking to his flock.

"Tremont," Sadie cried, thanking the policeman from whom she had got the information. "Edward Tremont. I knew that judge looked familiar. You know who he is, Emily?"

"No, who?" Emily asked in a disinterested voice as they passed, in a body, out the door and onto the steps.

"His wife is Jennifer Tremont, present Molly Pitcher of our Mineola chapter. Oho," she crowed, "I'd like to have seen him do anything to us."

"Shut up, Sadie," Ben said.

"*What!* Why, Ben Carroway, you——"

"I said shut up. Al"—turning to the newly appointed leader—"what's the word on these females?" The group paused, and Al found himself the center of the anxious gazes of the assembled husbands.

"Word? I don't know."

"You're responsible," Nat Berg said, and he was echoed by a chorus of, "Yeah . . . yeah . . . you've got to tell us what to do."

"I don't think we do anything," Al said. "It's just like before."

"Oh, no," Frank Corning groaned.

"I think we can trust them not to do anything wrong," Al said, looking at Emily.

"But they didn't do anything wrong this time," Ben protested, "and look what happened."

"You have to take that chance," Al said slowly. He saw John smiling crookedly at him. "In this crazy world things happen when you least expect them to. Some things are good, and some bad, but you can't crawl into a hole just to avoid the bad things. Can you?" No one said anything. "Only thing, Ben, just keep an eye on Sadie, will you? Get her a color television set, or something, to keep her home awhile."

"Well!" Sadie gasped.

John linked his arm through Al's. "If you'll drive Barbie and me to the station, we can catch a train to town."

"Swell, John. Come on, Em."

When he was settled behind the wheel, Emily leaned over to him, and whispered, "Thanks, Al. I'm proud of you."

"Hold on to that for six months," Al said, "and then we'll see if we thank each other."

Nineteen

Al was the first out of bed the next morning. Unable to sleep all night, he had been painfully aware that Emily hadn't got much rest either. When she had fallen into a deep sleep about five, however, he had continued to toss fitfully until seven, when he gave up.

Along with the four bottles of milk on the back steps, he found a pile of newspapers, and looking more closely, he saw that someone had written in heavy black pencil on the front pages. "See Page 3," one message read; "Pictures in middle section," another said, and with a sinking feeling, Al took the papers into the kitchen.

"Good old Charlie Simpson," he muttered, staring at the pile of papers that Charlie, obviously, had brought personally. "Like a vulture. Who needs him?"

He'd better have a cup of coffee before he looked at anything, he decided, and fixed the percolator.

Fifteen minutes later he opened the papers, looking first at the middle section with the pictures.

"Oh, murder," he moaned, clutching his head.

the heading over the first picture, of Emily leading the picket line, read. Number two was captioned:

. . . AND THEN TO THE CLINK

and there was Emily being firmly led up the steps of the Mineola police station. As his eyes blurred, Al peeked just briefly at the third, saw that the heading said . . . AND HERE COMES YD TO THE RESCUE, and he pushed the paper aside as though it carried some fearful germ.

When the boys tumbled down the stairs, Al hid the papers, but he couldn't avoid their questions.

"What did you send us upstairs for so quick last night when you got home?" Sherman demanded.

"Never mind," Al said.

"Is it 'cause Mama was in jail?" Herman wanted to know.

"Did Mrs. Begun tell you that?" Al cried, threateningly.

"Nah, we listened at the head of the stairs," Sherman said.

"Oh, you did, huh?" Hearing Emily's footsteps, he lowered his voice. "Now, listen, not one word of this, do you hear? One guy cracks wise, and I'll— I'll— Oh, good morning, Emily," he sang. "Boys, say good morning to your mother."

"Good morning, Mama," the boys chorused.

"Hey, Mama," Little Louie said, "how does it feel to be sprung?"

Emily looked sadly at Little Louie. "I have an awful headache."

Little Louie yelped as Al held a chunk of the boy's posterior between his thumb knuckle and index finger. "Nice little boy," he said. "How about if I cream you one?"

"Try it," Little Louie said belligerently. "Dr. Martin says I don't hafta take anything from you I don't want to."

"I've got a surprise for both you and Dr. Martin," Al said, raising his hand.

"Please," Emily implored wearily, her hand to her forehead.

The phone jangled, and Al rushed out of the kitchen to answer it.

"Hello," he said.

"Mr. Toolum?"

"Yes."

"This is Miss Lilley of the American Advertising Consultants." The voice was cold, impersonal.

"You get up awful early," Al said.

"What? Oh. Now, Mr. Toolum, Mr. Welton would like to see you in his office at ten o'clock."

"I'm working today," Al said. "I *have* to work, or I'll be out——"

"Ten o'clock," Miss Lilley said. "You'll be there, please." There was a click.

He walked slowly back into the kitchen. "Who was it?" Emily asked.

"The Consultants. I have to be there at ten o'clock." He looked into her eyes and saw the fear that he felt. "It'll be all right, Em."

He turned to Herman and Sherman. "Maybe you boys better skip school today to take care of your brother, since your mother doesn't feel too hot."

"We can't," Sherman said. "Today's the last day of school, and we're having a picnic this afternoon."

"The last day of school!" Al looked up in surprise. "Boy, did I lose track of time. Em, can you get someone to take care of Little Louie? No, wait a minute," he said, looking at his youngest son. "I'll take him into the city with me. I have a feeling, anyway, this meeting won't last too long."

He looked up at the sign that said TRUTH *ADVERTISING* HONOR, and he paused for a moment, remembering the time, the early April day, when he and Sherman had stood in this very spot. All the crazy things that had happened to him since then—it was like one of those funny dreams, and it would take years until the jumble in his mind would become straightened out. And then he might be able to think back on this and be able to sort out all the good things, weigh them and decide whether it was all worth it.

"Come on, Papa," Little Louie said, tugging his hand. "I wanta ride that elevator."

Upstairs, he didn't have long to wait. As soon as the girl at the desk saw him, she made a call to an inner office, and a moment later John Bell came out, his face solemn.

"Hi, Al." They shook hands.

"Bad?" Al asked.

John shrugged. "Depends on how you look at it. Come on in."

"Wait here, Little Louie, and, please," he begged, "don't do anything."

Little Louie nodded.

John led him into the room where he had gotten his scroll as Yankee Doodle '52, and where he had first appeared before the television cameras. The memory was still strong enough to cause a chill to come over him.

There was a difference in the room, however; a long gleaming table stood in the center with high-backed chairs around it, and at the end of the table, his face averted, was Paul Welton. He was alone. The early morning sunlight beamed through the window and stabbed at him like a giant arrow.

It almost looks like a church in here, Al thought.

Silently, another door opened, and Barbie entered. Holding a notebook in her hand, she sat next to Mr. Welton, and when John led Al to the table and indicated that he should sit down, Paul Welton turned slowly.

"Good morning," he said. From his appearance, no one could have told that he, too, had spent a sleepless night.

Al nodded. His eyes were glued on the pile of newspapers and magazines fanned out on the table in front of Welton, and when the head of AAC spoke, it was obvious he was wasting no time.

"Mr. Toolum, I'm a fair man. Would you agree that I'm a fair man?" His voice was pitched low with almost an hypnotic quality about it.

Again Al nodded, but this time without much conviction. This was worse than he had thought.

"My business," Welton said, "is predicated on the fact that we can assure people of our integrity. Do you know what that means?" he asked, with the first hint of sharpness.

Al looked toward John for help, but John was staring over his head at the wall, his hands clasped behind his back. "It—it means you're honest," Al said.

Paul Welton picked up a thin magazine. "This is an advance copy of the *Manhattanite* that comes out tomorrow. I think it will surprise you."

Al's heart dropped another notch. Here came trouble from an unexpected quarter.

"Let me read from it," Mr. Welton said softly, turning to a place he had well-marked.

"Learning that the nation's most average man lived but a stone's throw from our fair city [he began] *we recently made the trek to Fernvale . . ."*

"We'll skip that," Welton interrupted himself. "The writer spends a column and a half describing your household as a sort of bourgeois sideshow. To go to the end . . ."

Al opened his mouth to protest, but Welton was reading again:

". . . 'What are you going to do?' Toolum said as we stood waiting for his train. 'You bring your kids up the best way you know how, doing what you think is right, and the first thing you know some guy with a PhD is telling you the kid hates you, wants to kill you, even. And then you find yourself taking him to a Child Guidance a couple of times a week, and you learn there that everything you thought you were doing right turns out to be all wrong.' His train was called then, and we shook hands. 'Don't you like children any more?' we called, wanting to know how Yankee Doodle felt on this subject, but as he turned, his words were lost in a whistle blast from a near-by train. Then, shoulders drooping, America's most common man went on his way to meet his youngest son at the Child Guidance."

Paul Welton stopped reading, and Al waited expectantly. "Isn't there more?" he wanted to know.

"No more," Paul Welton said.

"But that isn't fair," Al cried. "I said something funny at the end. Why didn't they print what was funny?"

"That," Mr. Welton said, "is beside the point." He closed his eyes. "Child Guidance . . . Neurotics. Mr. Toolum," he said in a strained voice, "what kind of average man are you?"

Al stared at him. "When this gets out about your son, we'll be the laughingstock of the country," Paul Welton continued. He shook his head. "The average family——"

"So I have trouble," Al interrupted. "Everybody has trouble. Maybe that makes me even more average."

"But not your kind of trouble. What kind of nation would this be if every family had neurotic children in it?"

John Bell turned around. "What kind of nation are we?"

"You be quiet," Paul Welton snapped, and then, with obvious effort, he regained his composure. "And then these." He smeared the morning papers across the table. "I suppose you've seen these."

Al nodded.

"I had a lot to say about these," Welton said grimly, "but I see I'd be just beating a dead dog." He drew himself up. "I'm a man who doesn't waste time. I don't procrastinate, or, to put it into terms you might understand, I don't horse around."

"I know what procrastinate means," Al said. "Even though I'm not as educ——"

"Never mind! I've reached my present position by being able to make decisions. No matter how tough the decision, no matter what the consequences, I'm able to survey, weigh and decide."

He tapped a pencil on the table. "Mr. Toolum, you're through. I'm through. I'm through with *you*. As of right now. Miss McClain, are you taking notes?"

"Yes, sir," Barbie said in a low voice.

Al shrank into his seat. "Do you have anything to say?" Paul Welton demanded.

Slowly, numbly, Al shook his head.

"All right. We'll come to a gentleman's agreement. The AAC

will meet every obligation made to this point, *if* you promise to cause us no more trouble. Just get off our backs, Toolum."

Al thought of Little Louie in the outer room. "How about Albert Einstein?" he asked.

"Einstein is out, canceled. No more. Lord knows, it'll be hard enough to get out of this as it is. The money we tied up, the————"

"Not so hard," Al interrupted, and then, surprised, he wondered, What made me say that?

"What did you say?" Welton demanded.

Al cleared his throat, sensing a truth creeping up on him. "I mean, I don't think anybody'll give a damn." He found himself standing up, and to the astonished face that peered at him, he said, "I bet nobody outside of you people here will even know about it. To the few people who know me, and a few other people who see my face in ads, maybe it'll matter—but only if they wonder for a second whatever happened to that guy who was Yankee Doodle Fifty-two. But if you think anybody's going to commit suicide—you're nuts!"

"What? That's just *your* opinion," Welton snarled.

"That makes it the average man's opinion, doesn't it?" Al asked. He wondered why Barbie was looking at him as though she might faint, and he worried about her not taking notes. She might get fired.

"I guess that's all, then," he said, wanting to leave as quickly as possible.

"That's all!" Paul Welton's palm exploded against the table.

Al turned and walked slowly out of the room.

Downstairs, he and Little Louie stood on the curb, but as the light changed in their favor, he held Little Louie back, saying, "I've got something to tell you."

Little Louie looked solemn. "They can you?"

"Yeah—how'd you know?"

"Nobody in there gave me a lollipop. I figured the heat was on."

"Full blast," Al said grimly. "But the worst thing—don't get sore at me—they aren't going to let us see Einstein."

Little Louie sighed mournfully. "I figured something would happen to louse that up."

"But we'll do something else, Little Louie, I promise."

"Let's do it now," Little Louie said eagerly. "Right now, Papa. Here we are, you and me."

"But what?"

"I don't know. Something. You think of it. Please, Papa."

Al closed his eyes in deep concentration for almost a minute, and then they flew open. "Say, I've got it—something Sherman and Herman have never done. Something *I've* never done."

Little Louie's eyes sparkled. "What's that, Papa?"

"A ferryboat ride to Staten Island."

"Hey," Little Louie shouted excitedly, "that's a great idea. That's a better idea even than Einstein. Let's go, Papa."

Better than Einstein, Al thought, as Little Louie tugged him toward a bus stop. Someday you'll know you were wrong. But not now, he thought happily. Right now a ferryboat ride looks better, and that's what counts.

"Not the bus," he said firmly. "We take the subway."

"That's the Statue of Liberty," he said, from their position against the rail. "Maybe next week we can go there. That's something I've never done either." He was marveling at how easy it was to make Little Louie happy. Sometimes you felt like a con man, it was so simple.

"Just you and me, Papa?" Little Louie asked, looking up from his Koola Kola bottle.

"Well—maybe we'd better take Herman and Sherman. But that's up to you. I think, though, we shouldn't keep them from the finer things in life, either."

Little Louie gave the question judicious thought. "Maybe," he said. "We'll see."

"You want another hot dog?"

"No." Little Louie looked up at him. "Papa, you sad about gettin' canned?"

"Sad?" Automatically, Al shook his head vigorously, and then he retracted, "Well, maybe a little."

Yeah, he admitted to himself, just a little. For a while you were a big guy, and now you're a nobody again. For a while people looked up at you, bought you fancy meals, took your picture—thought you were important, and now you're back in the same old grind.

But not quite the same, he told himself slowly. There's a difference. Something happened to you that'll never wear off. All the things I learned, he thought. Get around, meet people, and you find that among the ones you thought were such hot-shots, the ones you always used to envy, there are just as many heels and no-goods as among anybody else. You learn that, and maybe you aren't so envious any more.

And look at the way Judge Tremont treated me, he thought. A responsible, prominent citizen. Well—no longer prominent, but what did that have to do with being responsible? All the men, he remembered with growing pride, had turned to him yesterday, because he was *somebody*—not just a title—but *somebody*.

He'd have to keep on trying to be a somebody, he promised himself. Maybe it wasn't so tough—about as easy, maybe, as being pals with your kid. Once you tried, you saw how easy it was.

Reaching down, he put his arm around Little Louie's shoulder, and when he did, the boy came just a little bit closer. Not much closer, but close enough.

Twenty

Emily was just putting a bowlful of gelatin into the refrigerator to chill when there was a hesitant knock on the screen door. Peering out, Emily saw that it was Sadie.

"Come in, Sadie—and since when have you waited for me to say that?"

"Since just now," Sadie said, entering doubtfully. "Since the morning papers came out."

"Oh, those. Pretty dreadful, weren't they?"

"I didn't want to meet Al here. I saw the car in the drive-way——"

"Oh, he and Little Louie took the train into the city," Emily said.

Sadie looked relieved. "Anyway, I wouldn't have come over at all if I didn't have good news. I thought you'd be very angry at me."

"No reason for me to be angry. That's a good picture of you hitting the policeman."

Sadie flushed, and looked slightly ill.

"What's the news?" Emily asked. "It better be *very* good, because Al phoned me about an hour ago——"

"Something wrong, Emily?"

"No more Yankee Doodle," Emily said flatly. "The Consultants had enough."

"Oh! Oh, dear." For a moment Sadie seemed about to burst into tears. "It's all my fault. At breakfast, Ben said——"

"Never mind what Ben said. Al told me he had a feeling it was all up anyway. These pictures weren't all by a long shot. There was a lot more. And you know what?"

"What?"

"Al called just after he and Little Louie got off a ferry from Staten Island—that's how they spent the afternoon—and he said he never felt better in his life."

The two women stared at each other, and Sadie said, "How about you, Emily?"

"I?" She paused. "I haven't really thought about it," she said slowly, and turned to the sink where a pan of potatoes awaited her attention.

That wasn't quite true, because Emily had been giving it a lot of thought. After Al had called, and the full meaning of his news had sunk in, she had felt a deep, aching disappointment. It was almost as though she were a child again, remembering her first ride on a merry-go-round and how she felt when the music stopped and the merry-go-round no longer moved. Hearing about Al gave her that same feeling of emptiness.

Then she had thought, But it's not me who should be disappointed — it's Al. He's the one to lose out on all the exciting things. Yet Emily was honest enough to admit that she, too, had found an excitement in the activities in which she had been a part. And even when Al was alone, on radio and television shows, or having his picture taken, she had felt a part of it, and now they were back where they had started.

But not *quite* where we were, she had decided. Things had changed a little. It was hard to say exactly how they had changed, but she could see in Al a difference. He was more sure of himself these days, as though the experience of being taken out of the crowd and being spotlighted meant that he would never go back into the crowd again, to be lost as before.

"Emily, look here," Sadie said, braking the silence and holding out a piece of yellow paper for Emily so see. "This will make you feel a lot better."

"What is it?" Emily asked, wiping her hands.

"A telegram that came just a while ago." Her eyes mirrored a growing excitement, and she lowered her voice to almost a whisper. "It's from the Grand Chapter. They're giving us a citation."

"A citation?"

"Yes—and you're named in it."

"Let me see," Emily said, taking the telegram. It read:

Fernvale Chapter No six hundred and thirty-three Minute Maids of America is to be congratulated for its direct action taken on June twenty-ninth against the insidious inroads of high prices that are destroying the economic structure of our Nation Stop The chapter and committee chairman Sister Emily Toolum will receive a special citation for meritorious service at a meeting in Fernvale on July fourth Stop Your action in keeping with the traditions of the Minute Maids of America was far above and beyond the normal call of duty
                                                          Sister Lettie Hogan
                                                          Grand Molly Pitcher

"Oh," Emily gasped, when the contents of the wire had been digested, "this—this is like getting a medal from the President of the United States."

"Better," Sadie said. "Very few women ever got the special Minute Maids citation. Emily, you'll be in a wonderful position next election for the job of Molly Pitcher."

"But I couldn't," Emily protested. "I haven't been active nearly enough."

"This makes up for it," Sadie said. "*I* will manage your campaign. And then, who knows . . ." Her eyes looked into the future and saw glory.

"As long as the election is more than six months from now . . ."

"It is," Sadie assured her. "Which reminds me, if Al is due home I'd better skip. He's liable to be less forgiving than you and beat me."

She darted out the door, leaving the telegram in Emily's trembling hands.

Leaving the Fernvale station, Al and Little Louie, hand in hand, crossed the Sunrise Highway and started walking down Main Street. They hadn't gone more than a few steps when Little Louie said, "Papa, look, there's Herman and Sherman."

The two older Toolum boys had just come out of Orbin's Sweet Shop, and when they saw their father and Little Louie, they stopped.

"Where you kids going?" Al asked.

"Down to the park," Herman said.

Looking across the street at Warren's barbershop, Al felt a vague longing. "How about taking over Little Louie for a while. I might drop into Warren's for a little bit."

Herman and Sherman nodded, and telling them to be home in time for dinner, Al hurried across the street, feeling singularly free from any care or pressure. It was funny the way Herman and Sherman had seemed to change in their habits toward Little Louie ever since the accident. Almost as though they liked him a little bit. They were also a little in awe of the fact that Little Louie was going to the Child Guidance.

"What happened in the city?" Herman asked Little Louie.

"The Consultants don't want Papa any more. They fired him."

Herman and Sherman looked at each other—and then they shrugged.

"So what?" Herman said.

"Yeah, it was getting to be a pain in the neck any way," Sherman said.

"We went on the Staten Island ferry," Little Louie said, "and next week Papa's taking me to the Statue of Liberty." He thought he detected envy in the way Herman and Sherman looked at him. "You guys can come along *oney* if I say it's okay. Papa and I are gonna do lots of things from now on," he bragged.

His brothers looked thoughtful. Then Herman said. "Let's go to the park," and he and Sherman started walking. To his surprise, Little Louie found that, instead of having to tag along several paces behind, he was permitted to walk between them. Even more than that, Sherman solicitously held his arm.

"You wanna ice cream cone?" Herman asked, before they had gone very far.

Little Louie practiced the taste of an ice cream cone to see how it felt.

"Nope," he said.

"Candy?" Sherman asked.

"Uh-uh."

They walked along silently for a few moments. "Hey," Sherman said brightly, "how about us playing a game where you and Herman are heroes, and you blow *me* up."

"That's a good . . ." Little Louie started to say, and then he shook his head. "Nah, 'cause you guys wanna play baseball."

Another few moments passed, and then, casually, Herman asked, "How's the tooth, Little Louie?"

A protective hand automatically flew to his mouth, and he muttered, "Fine."

"Oh, don't worry," Herman said hastily. "I wouldn't touch it.

You know, I remember my first tooth I lost years ago." A distant expression came into his eyes as he recalled back through time. "I wouldn't let *anybody* touch it. A guy's tooth is his tooth, is what I always say. Right, Sherman?"

"You bet. Nobody should bother with a guy's tooth except the guy himself. It's—it's personal."

He lowered his hand. "It's kind of loose," Little Louie said happily. "Maybe any day now."

Herman's eyes expressed brief longing. "We could help . . ." He broke off at the quick look of mistrust that came over Little Louie's face. "What I mean is, a guy's tooth is his own."

When they reached the park, the ball field was already crowded with boys. All action halted, however, with the arrival of Herman, who was acknowledged captain and leader, and the boys gathered around for the choosing up.

"You'll be on my side," Herman said to Little Louie.

Little Louie gave an astonished gasp.

"You can play right field," Herman said, as though completing a painful duty.

"What are you doing, Herm?" a boy demanded, who had overheard. "You know the rule we got about kid brothers lousing up the game."

"This one won't louse up anything," Herman said fiercely. "Didn't you see his picture inna paper with Leo Durocher?"

"Yeah, but——"

"But nothin'! Durocher doesn't make a move without first askin' Little Louie. Right, Little Louie?"

"Wait a minute, Herman . . ."

"We can borrow you a glove. Okay, let's choose up. I got Little Louie."

A desperate struggle was going through Little Louie's mind. How many hundreds of times he had dreamed of this moment when Herman would ask him to play! Usually, in his dream, he was called upon to bat in the late innings when Herman's team was losing, and the bases were loaded, and —beefo, boffo—over the fence went the ball.

"Herman," he whispered, tugging at his brother's sleeve. "Hey, Herman."

"I got Jerry," Herman said, ending the side-choosing. "What's'a matter, Little Louie?"

"I was thinkin'," Little Louie said. "I haven't been playin' much lately, an' I ain't really warmed up. Maybe—maybe today I oughta just be bat boy."

"Bat boy!" Herman eyed him calculatingly. "You *really* wanna be bat boy?"

The opposing team was taking the field, and Sherman walked up to the plate as first hitter.

"Yeah," Little Louie said. "Maybe—maybe next year I'll really be warmed up. You an' Sherman an' me can practice in our back yard this summer, huh?"

"Sure," Herman said, handing him the bat. "Next year you'll just about be ready."

Taking the bat, Little Louie ran to the plate and handed it to Sherman. Then he backed away and clapped his hands just as Herman did when he was cheering a batter on.

"C'mon, Sherman," he yelled, kneeling on the grass. "Give it a real ride." He plucked a green blade from the ground, chewed on it for a moment and then spat it out fiercely. Herman, he noticed, was kneeling right next to him, and their two voices made a loud, shrill chorus.

Next year, Little Louie told himself. Next year I'll really belt that old ball all over the place. Biffo, beefo, boffo—all over the lot. . . .

There was a man sitting on the curb in front of the house, as Al came down Bigelow Street, and when Al, trying to make out who it was, drew abreast, the man stood up.

"Hi," John Bell said. "I've been waiting for you."

"For cryin' out loud," Al said, "what are you doing here?"

"I wanted to talk to you. I chased after you this morning, but when I got downstairs you were gone. I decided to come out late this afternoon."

"What the heck you sitting out here for? Why didn't you go into the house?"

"I was afraid Mrs. Toolum would brain me," John said wryly.

"Don't be silly. Come on." They started up the walk.

Inside, Al called, "Emily, I'm home," and the kitchen door burst open as Emily ran to him. They embraced for a long moment and then parted, their faces showing embarrassment.

Then Emily said, "Why, Mr. Bell, it was nice of you to come with Al. Are you going to stay for dinner?"

"I . . ." John turned to Al.

"Sure, he'll stay."

"Maybe I'd better. I have to start saving my money from now on."

"He fired you, huh?" Al asked in a low voice.

"Let's say we came to the same decision at the same moment."

"Where's Little Louie?" Emily asked.

Al told her the boys were in the park. "What are you going to do?" he asked John.

"I'm investigating an opening for a pots-and-pans salesman in the Idaho-Montana territory." He grinned. "Don't look so grim, Al. I never felt better in my life."

"That's funny. Al said the same thing on the phone before," Emily said, and then the conversation was interrupted by a loud clatter from the kitchen. "The boys are home. I'll keep them in there for a while and give you men a chance to talk." She left quickly.

"Do you really mean that?" Al asked, when they were alone.

"About the pots-and-pans opening?"

"No, about feeling so good."

"That's right. But I was worried about you, Al. After all, I'm the guy who did this to you."

"I feel fine," Al said. "Just fine. It was coming, anyway. You see"—he paused—"I'd made up my mind not to resign from that League outfit."

John brightened. "I'm glad to hear that, Al."

"Not that they'll want me for a sponsor any more," he said slowly. "I'm nothing to them when I'm not Yankee Doodle. But I figured I'd tell Mr. Gomez I'd like to stay even just as a member. Maybe I could write a letter every now and then like he said."

"How do you know they won't want you as a sponsor? Everybody isn't like the AAC, you know. The important thing, though, is you didn't get scared. You didn't let them scare you."

"How can you get scared? You have to do *something*, don't you? You can't just give up, can you?"

"No," John said, "you can't."

The phone rang, and Al went to answer it.

"Hello," he said, and then he turned to John. "It's Miss McClain, and she wants to talk to you." Emily came out of the kitchen to see who was on the telephone, and she looked expectantly at John.

"Tell her"—John shrank deep in a chair—"tell her I don't want to talk to her."

"He doesn't want to talk to you," Al repeated. "She says, okay, she doesn't want to talk to you either, only as two—what was that you said?—two ex-employees of the AAC she thinks you ought to celebrate together." He listened a moment more. "She says she has two tickets for the stadium concert, and you don't have to talk—just listen."

"*Ex*-employee?" John said in a vastly puzzled voice.

"She says now both of you have to save money if you are going to be a writer and starve in a Bronx walk-up."

"What does she mean, *ex*-employee?" John demanded.

"He wants to know what you mean by ex-employee?" Al asked over the phone, and then, after a moment, repeated to John, "She says now that you're not there any more, she hasn't any reason to be there either. She resigned."

John stood up suddenly. "Tell her I'll meet her at the information booth on the Long Island level of Penn Station in"—he glanced at his watch—"about an hour."

After repeating the message, Al said, "She says she's twenty feet away from that spot right now, and if you weren't coming in, she'd be coming out, and you'd better hurry up."

"Tell her good-bye," John said.

"Good-bye," Al lowered the phone.

"Does that dinner invitation hold for some other time?" John asked, as he approached the front door.

Emily nodded. "For two."

"I'll walk you to the station," Al said.

"Walk, hell," John cried, opening the door. "I'm running. See you." The door slammed behind him.

"Well," Emily said, a slow smile creeping over her mouth. "Just like an ending in *Family Friend* magazine."

Al put his arm around her shoulder. "Em, would you be sore if we canceled our subscription to *Family Friend?* Sherman's liable to get more ideas from it."

"Not me," Sherman's voice said, and the door opened to show the three boys crowded in the doorway. "I'm not a poet any more. I'm gonna be an actor."

"Only thing I'm sorry about," Emily said. "We never got to go on Mr. Schlepp's yacht."

"All you have to do is call him up, Em, and mention goulash. I bet we go out on that boat yet. That is"—he raised his eyes—"if Miss Wilcox comes along. I see she got elected Miss Schlepp, and I have to have *something* to do while you and Mr. Schlepp are in the galley eating goulash."

"I think we'll stay home," Emily said. "I can do without yachts."

"And I can do without Miss Wilcox," Al said, "but it's a sacrifice."

They grinned at each other.

"Look at 'em," Little Louie said in disgust. "Any minute they're gonna kiss."

Sherman pulled at Al's jacket. "Hey, Papa," he said, "if I'm gonna be an actor I have to study stuff—like television. How about it?"

"How about what?" Al asked.

"The television set," Sherman said pointing to the large box that had been moved into a corner.

"Oh, *that* one." Al paused and looked down into three pairs of pleading eyes. "I suppose"—he hesitated—"the least we should do is open it."

"I'll get the hammer," Herman shouted

". . . and me the screwdriver," Sherman cried.

". . . and me the saw," Little Louie squeaked.

In a moment they were back again with the tools, and Al said, "Well, let's look the situation over."

Emily stood in the doorway to the kitchen watching them as a furious sound of hammering and the squeal of protesting nails being drawn from wood filled the room.

"Boy, it's a red one," Herman yipped.

"Little Louie," Al yelled, "get your head out of there before I tear it off."

"Wow!" the boys chorused. "Wow! Look at that."

Crowded back onto his haunches, Al looked up at Emily and shrugged in resignation. "Well," he said, "at least out of all this we got a television set."

"Yes," she said, smiling at him. "At least we got that."